THE CRYING OF
ROSS 128

Book 1 in the Ross 128 First Contact Trilogy

DAVID ALLAN HAMILTON

DeeBee

THE CRYING OF ROSS 128
Copyright © 2018 by David Allan Hamilton.

All rights reserved. Printed in the United States of America. No part of this book may be used or reproduced in any manner whatsoever without written permission except in the case of brief quotations embodied in critical articles or reviews.

This book is a work of fiction. Names, characters, businesses, organizations, places, events and incidents either are the product of the author's imagination or are used fictitiously. Any resemblance to actual persons, living or dead, events, or locales is entirely coincidental.

For information contact :
davidallanhamilton00@gmail.com
http://www.davidallanhamilton.com

ISBN: 9781896794433

First Edition: May, 2018

10 9 8 7 6 5 4 3 2 1

For my Dad

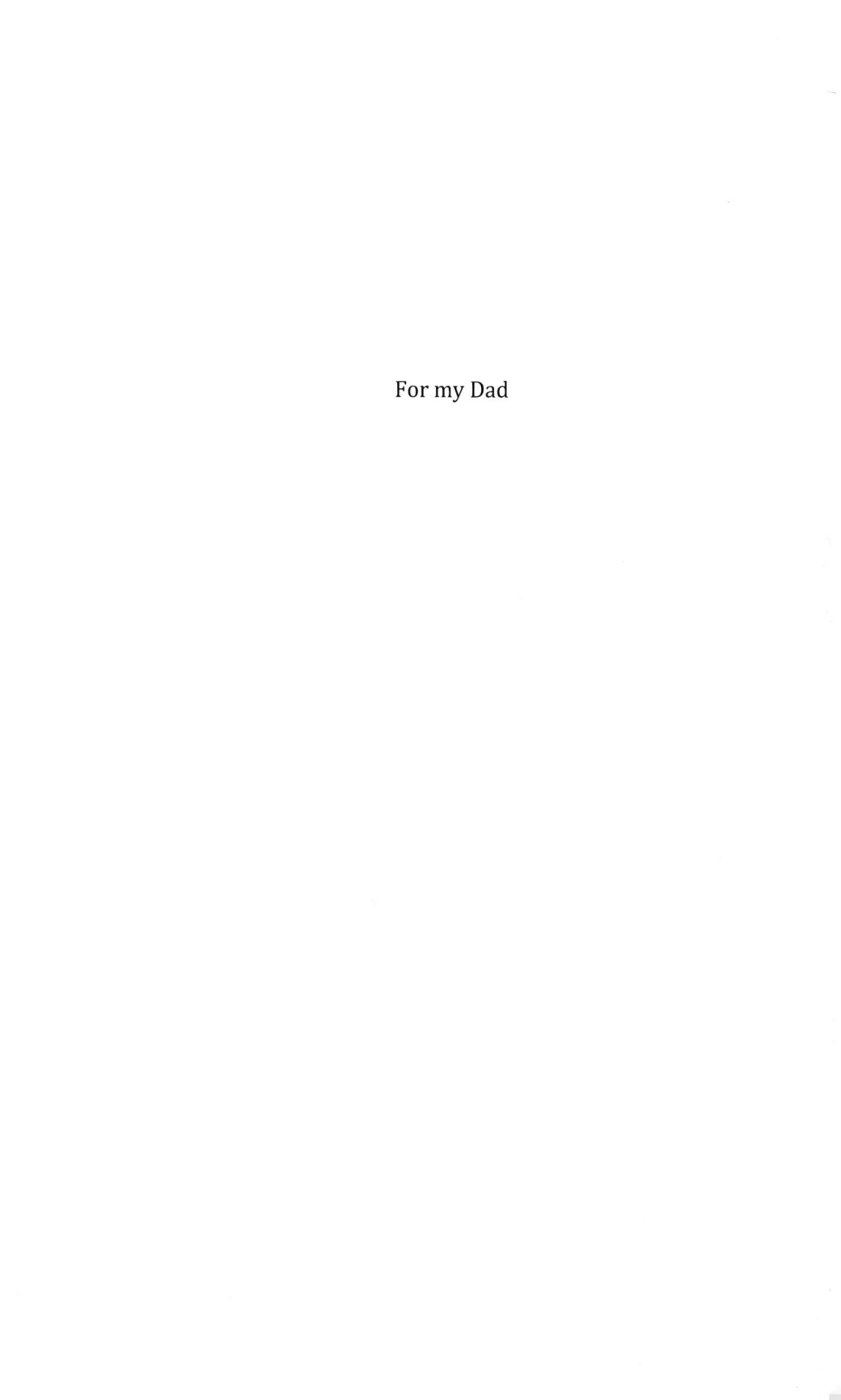

"Those who try to lead the people can only do so by following the mob. It is through the voice of one crying in the wilderness that the ways of the gods must be prepared."
    Oscar Wilde

"All warfare is based on deception. Hence, when we are able to attack, we must seem unable; when using our forces, we must appear inactive; when we are near, we must make the enemy believe we are far away; when far away, we must make him believe we are near."
    Sun Tzu, *The Art of War*

ONE

Tuesday, September 25, 2085
San Francisco, California Congressional Republic

Atteberry

JIM ATTEBERRY RAKED THROUGH A PATCH OF SUBSPACE STATIC, hunting for distant radio signals, wondering as he always did if tonight the course of human history would change forever. It was a bit like fishing in unknown waters, he mused: never quite sure what you might snag. But with the new iterative filter, he could penetrate the noise field of the ELF electromagnetic spectrum further than anyone, go deep into the cosmic mud, and poke around the birth pains of the universe. Most amateur radio astronomers looking for signs of intelligent alien life searched for coherent signal patterns *above* the noise, but he wanted to know what the softer, buried voices had to say, the dim murmurs overwhelmed by a shouting crowd.

Hollow echoing bursts and crashes filled his earphones, like he was listening to garbled rumblings under water. He varied the filter's cut-off frequencies using Kate Braddock's processing algorithm to analyze the modulation data for sequences, and swept across the amateur radio subspace band. But after several minutes of static and hissing nothing unusual presented itself, not that he found that surprising. Most civilian astronomers surveyed the skies as a harmless hobby, without truly expecting to hear any strange sounds. On the off chance someone detected an anomaly, well, they'd follow the accepted protocol and notify the professional geeks in the Terran Science Academy.

But that seldom happened. And when it did, inevitably those events were identified as human origin.

Kate's new filter design could find patterns in noise, no matter how intricate, she said, but Atteberry remained skeptical. After listening tonight, there was nothing to report other than the same old noisy static crashes and echoes of ancient exploding stars.

Atteberry tidied up the bench and logged his radio time, but just before he set the receiver to automation, a small red LED flashed on the screen. The filter, indeed, had detected an unknown pattern.

He hesitated. Probably a weak quasar vibration or pulsar. Or... The automated VFO stabilized on the signal's frequency and the computer's internal recorder chimed that it was working. Data began streaming across the screen as the radio station sprang to life. He put the headphones on again.

What he heard made Jim Atteberry's eyes widen. He fell into his chair, scrambling to grab a pencil and notepad on the bench. A faint, distant signal pattern appeared unlike anything he'd ever identified. It sounded like a series of scratches on sandpaper or static discharges, meshed against a backdrop of eerie, hypnotic white noise. Several minutes passed as he watched the graphic sequence repeat itself over and over.

Chicka.

Chicka.

Chicka Chicka Chicka Chicka Chicka Chicka Chicka Chicka.

Each scratch timed out at the same duration, unlike any known Terran code or satellite transponder beacon. And, Atteberry observed, they were too slow and *intentional* for any known pulsar. His mind raced, fingers trembling as he tweaked the filter to isolate the signal.

Atteberry sketched on his notepad, counting out the sounds. *One... two... three-four-five-six-seven-eight-nine-ten.* Repeat. *What did it mean, this clunky ten-digit code? Where did it come from?*

The pattern ended abruptly a few minutes later, and the red alert light blinked out. With a muted click, the scanner resumed its methodical sweep across the band and the automated recording ceased.

Atteberry removed his headphones and scratched his beard. The signal and relevant frequency information had been captured, but no origin had appeared to indicate it was a known source. He punched up the locator algorithm and analyzed the data—a process that would take ten minutes or so, he guessed. He left the basement and ran upstairs to tuck Mary in.

She was reading, slumped against her pink pillows, with *Pride and Prejudice* lying awkwardly in her fingers. A love of literature was a trait she'd inherited from him. She glanced up with warm, heavy eyes. "Hey, Dad."

"Hi, kiddo. Looks like your day is over."

"Yeah, I was trying to finish this book tonight, but I'm just too exhausted." She marked her place then studied her father. "Dad, what's wrong?"

Atteberry marveled at how bright and sensitive she was for a ten-year-old going on 20. She got her brains from Janet, but her curiosity about the world came from him.

Janet... how long has it been since she left us? Twenty-nine months, 18 days. Not that anyone's counting.

"Dad, you're doing it again."

"Sorry, just thinking about stuff." Then he suddenly asked, "Mares, if you needed to talk with someone who spoke a language you didn't know, and you couldn't see them, so pointing and arm-waving wasn't an option, how would you do it?"

The wheels spun in the little scientist's head as she worked out the problem. Finally, Mary scrunched up her face and mouth and said, "I'd have to think of other sounds, wouldn't I? Like your Morse code."

"Well, yes, that's how ancient tribes talked over long distances—drumming, singing, tapping in codes. But do you see a problem with this if you tried to talk with someone in another country who didn't speak English?"

Mary closed her eyes. "You'd use math, or something that doesn't need words, I suppose. Why all these questions, Dad?"

Atteberry sat on the bed beside her. "The funniest thing, Mares. The radio picked up a weak signal I've never heard before, a simple sequence, but I have no clue what the pattern could be."

"What does it sound like?"

"It's a series of taps that goes like this: *one... two... three-four-five-six-seven-eight-nine-ten* and then it repeats itself."

Mary cocked her head. "So... a tap code."

Atteberry looked at her closely, amused, "That's right, each one is a single scratch. Then the same sound again, then another eight times for a total of ten scratches." He took her hand and tapped it with his thumb. "Like a musical beat."

Mary smiled. "But it's not like you're counting *different* things in a row, is it, Dad? It's more like the same one note over and over, you know: an apple, another apple, then eight apples. Not an apple, banana, and a bunch of other fruit. More like a drum beat keeping time." She yawned. "I gotta get to sleep."

Atteberry kissed her on the head and pulled the covers around her. "Goodnight, Mary. I love you." He turned off the light, closed her door, and shuffled into the kitchen.

How would I talk to an alien? If I was thirsty, how would I ask an unseen non-English speaking creature for water using non-alphabetical math, physics or chemistry, music or art? He took a glass from the cupboard and poured himself a drink from the cooler.

I'd like some water, he thought, and took a sip.

Water.

A liquid.

H_2O.

Would chemical symbols work? No, not quite, because you'd need a common alphabet and a similar understanding of molecules. Nevertheless, there was something vaguely familiar about the two hydrogen atoms. He recalled his high school chemistry days, but couldn't remember much other than unpleasant memories of leaky pipettes and weird smells best left buried in the past. He trod downstairs again to his workbench and searched the Calnet for information.

Hydrogen... the most abundant chemical substance in existence... atomic number one...

One apple?

A periodic table appeared next. Whatever intelligence might be out there, and however they understood science in *their* language, he thought, the laws of nature presumably operated the same across the entire universe.

Atteberry found what he was looking for in the table and swallowed hard; the element with atomic number eight. He scribbled nervously on his notepad.

One-One-Eight equals the *pattern*.

H-H-O equals the atomic numbers corresponding to the above pattern.

Two Hs and an O.

A cry for water in the deep dark.

TWO

Atteberry

THE WAITING WAS THE WORST PART. Time elasticity seemed to punish him inversely to his desire for results; the faster he wanted something, the slower it took. Every single time. Atteberry paced around the dim basement wondering what to do as the locator algorithm kept processing data long after it should have completed its computations, defying his wishes.

If the signal originated on Earth, or anywhere else in the solar system, then its location would be known by now. Why is it taking so long?

He breathed in deeply, exhaled, and then sat in front of the computer screen. "Call Kate Braddock."

The monitor snapped to a picture of an ancient telephone. Kate's number scrolled across the screen and the image shifted to a live view of her apartment as the link was established. She sat in silhouette against a backdrop of random white lights.

"Hey Jim, you're up late. What's going on?"

"Kate, you won't believe this, but I believe I heard a bona fide alien signal on the radio bands tonight." He sounded much calmer than he'd imagined he would.

"Hang on a second." She killed a powerful light behind her and her face came into view, hard lines in the contrasting shadows. "There, tell me more, professor!"
The sweater she wore on campus was now a sleeveless tee shirt showing the full artistry of the tattoos up and down her arms. She didn't show them at the college.

Atteberry recounted his evening of scanning the radio bands and then hearing this odd pattern in the noise that, at least to him, appeared to be tapping out the atomic numbers for the water molecule.

"That's as far as I got, Kate," he said, "but I needed to tell you right away."

"Totally fascinating! Really, it is." Kate lay down on the floor in front of the screen. "But you know I've got a million questions, right?"

"That's why I called."

"Ha! Well, okay, here's one for starters: Where in space does the signal come from, or is it another one of those satellite echoes?"

Jim studied the analyzer window at the bottom of the screen. "It's been processing over 20 minutes and the source remains a mystery."

"That's odd, isn't it?"

"Sure is. Any source in our solar system is usually identified in a few minutes."

"Okay, so what did the signal sound like?"

"I'll show you." Jim opened another window and isolated the ticks in the data recording. "Have a listen."

Kate reached off-screen and brought back headphones. She put them over her short-cropped hair and studied the signal. "Weird," she said, removing the headphones. "I can see where you get the one-one-eight. It's a simple pattern, isn't it? But if you're right about the correlation with H_2O, and it *is* alien—why water?"

Atteberry regarded her with a puzzled look. "Yeah, great question, Kate. Of all the signals you could send into the universe, why *water*? Shouldn't you fire off coordinates or some binary code or one of a million other things?"

Kate kept fidgeting and looking off-screen. "I'm a programmer, Jim, and I prefer keeping things simple. The answer to your question may not be complicated at all."

"What do you think?"

"Perhaps this alien—if that's who sent the signal—was thirsty."

Atteberry scratched his beard. "I thought so too, but don't you find that strange?"

"Not at all. Suppose you're out in the desert dying from the heat and a million miles from the nearest town. What do you want more than anything else?"

"Water."

"Exactly, so maybe that's what the sender is doing too. This cosmic cry may be someone begging for the most basic foundation of life as we understand it." She smiled and Atteberry noticed her male features coming through in the shadows. Kate's former life as a Spacer corrupted her sexuality, but she seemed to have landed on the feminine side.

"So maybe the alien is dying and needs help," he said.

"Perhaps. Or maybe it's more like cheese."

Atteberry laughed. "Cheese? What are you talking about?"

"You know, cheese in a mousetrap, a ruse, an underhanded trick." She looked off-screen again, distracted by something. "Listen, Jim, I gotta go, but let's talk more. Can we meet up at the cafeteria tomorrow before I teach?"

"Sure thing, yes. Maybe I'll have the signal origin by then."

"Great, goodnight." She ended the link, and the screen shot reverted to the antique telephone.

Atteberry's mind raced. In his gut, he felt the signal truly was alien, but Kate raised an important consideration, one that underlined the schism in the Astronomical Society between those who would contact aliens and those who would not.

If the signal was a cry for help, he felt it his responsibility, as a human being, to take action. But if it was a hostile trap, then the rules change. Suppose we sent a ship out there to investigate—even an old space tug—and it turned out to be a ploy, would we jeopardize the entire human race?

The source locator window popped up on the monitor.

Analysis Complete, press MORE for details.

"More," he said.

A slick report snapped on-screen where the key results appeared showing data related to the signal itself: duration, strength relative to the background noise, frequency, amplitude, subspace parameters.

Atteberry glossed over these and went straight to the origin findings.

Right Ascension: 11hr 47m 44.3964s

THE CRYING OF ROSS 128

Declination: +00deg 48' 16"
Constellation: Virgo
Origin: Ross 128

He licked his lips with a dry tongue.

"Basic data surrounding the star Ross 128," he said.

The screen switched over to the Calnet and an image of a red dwarf star appeared along with reams of relevant information. Atteberry noted the distance to this star—10.8 light years—and how small and faint it appeared compared to our own sun!

"How long does it take a subspace signal to travel from Ross 128 to Earth?" he asked.

The machine responded verbally. *"Twenty-two minutes, 13.4 seconds with current subspace technology."*

Atteberry recorded the time on his notepad, then looked at the screen. "Is there any history of alien signals coming from Ross 128?"

"Negative. Although in 2017, unknown signals from that system were received at the University of Puerto Rico at Arecibo. They were later dismissed as Terran satellites."

Ghost signals. That happened sometimes due to the multitude of satellites orbiting Earth back then, and now around the moon and Mars. Signals would bounce and echo off them all the time, like ripples in a pond bouncing off rocks and plants.

"Speculate as to the origin of this signal if it's a ghost."

"Processing..."

Atteberry calmed down as he dove deeper into the source. The initial thrill of a potential new discovery gave way to the rational collection of information, a systematic process, including speculation of alternatives.

"Ready."

"Proceed."

"If the signal is a ghost, it is most likely an artifact of the Second American Civil War circa 2070. The Northern Democratic

States and the Confederate States often used ghost signals as decoys to confuse enemy communications."

"The civil war ended 10 years ago. How do these ghosts still exist?"

"The most likely scenario is they have echoed off distant objects in line with Ross 128, and bounced back."

So that's it, Atteberry thought, he's been chasing old civil war ghosts. If subterfuge was the goal, then it made sense, and *water* was such an important, common necessity. Atteberry sank in his chair and snorted. So much for the great alien discovery! Yet the question of subspace remained, and, as far as he knew, neither side in the civil war used the emerging FTL technology. It wasn't sufficiently developed until after the new republics separated.

"What is the likelihood that these Ross 128 signals are satellite ghosts?"

"0.02 percent."

"What's the probability the true source is the Ross 128 system itself?"

"74.8 percent."

Atteberry leaned forward on his workbench and realized the results were inconclusive. "What's the probability that these signals are naturally occurring... a pulsar or a quasar for example?"

"Zero percent. The signals are artificially produced with slight variations in pattern frequency, suggesting unknown transmission methodology."

"Human?"

"Improbable. There are no known humans in the Ross 128 space."

Atteberry feared asking the next question; he swallowed hard. "Alien?"

"99.8 percent probable."

THE CRYING OF ROSS 128

Tears filled Atteberry's eyes and his body shook, his mind racing at the magnitude of this apparent discovery. He remembered the excitement humans felt the day microscopic life on Mars was confirmed. When delicate worm-like creatures appeared on Ganymede, we really wondered about our role and purpose in the galaxy. But this was different. These signals were clearly alien and he knew the next thing to do was return a message and let them know they'd been received.

He considered planning an impromptu meeting with the amateur astronomers to share his findings and see if anyone else with a subspace receiver picked up the signals. Grabbing his notepad, he scratched out his main speaking points, signal data and graphics. Then he stopped writing, closed his eyes, and cast a vision of the Earth's future and human potential as one of many cosmic races.

Atteberry already knew he wouldn't sleep tonight. How could he when we were no longer alone?

The next morning, after Atteberry dropped Mary off at school, he met Kate in the sunlit City College cafeteria. She grinned as he joined her, a cup of coffee in his hand.

"Good morning, Jim."

"Hey, Kate."

"I see you haven't been abducted yet."

"Too funny." His fingers shook as he fumbled with the coffee lid.

"Let me guess, you didn't sleep at all last night?" She took a bite of her protein bar. "So, tell me more about your mystery signal."

Atteberry brought his notepad out from his jacket pocket. "You won't believe this, Kate."

"Try me."

He reviewed his new findings and discussed how the signal was artificial and most likely came from Ross 128. She studied his face carefully as he spoke.

"You mean to tell me it's real?"

"Yes."

They sat together in silence for several minutes before Kate said, "I'm not quite there yet, Jim, but let's suppose for a second you have detected a real alien signal, and a coherent one at that. Isn't there a protocol to follow for these events?"

"Sure there is. When we find something of unknown origin, we first vet it through the astronomy group so others in the community can comment." He sipped his coffee and continued. "That's where we usually find out that a signal came from a Terran satellite, or some random military test... maybe a distorted star burst—that sort of thing."

"So are you going to share your findings with this group?"

"That's the plan. I sent an e-comm to them all early this morning and we're video linking in a few hours."

He watched her brush the crumbs off the table in front of her. She wore a long-sleeved blouse and leather vest; mannish today.

"That's good," she said, "but did anyone else hear the signal?"

Atteberry looked down at his coffee and notepad. "Not that I see. The comm boards are quiet, which leads me to speculate I'm the only one going deep into the static."

"So this finding is just yours?"

"Yup, so far."

"And I thought I was the only badass teacher in this place!"

Atteberry laughed. He liked her male side.

"Listen, I need to set up the computer lab in a few minutes, but I gotta ask you something."

"What is it?"

"If the signal turns out to be naturally occurring, or a hoax, then that's the end of it, right?"

"Yes. If the evidence says it's not alien, then we can't argue with that."

Kate grabbed her bag and stood up to leave.

"But if the signal turns out to be real," she lowered her voice, "what will you do next?"

"I feel a human obligation to contact whoever sent that message, so I must find a subspace transmitter, I suppose. The TSA's got the only one in the world I know of, so they'd have to do it."

Kate stared at him closely, then hustled off to the lab.

The rest of the morning dragged by. Atteberry completed his second-year lecture on 21st century graphic novels, met with a couple of students from his first-year class, and survived an hour-long departmental meeting on some proposed new *"Why am I here?"* academic regulations. At two o'clock, he checked in with Mary through the schoolnet's continuous monitoring channel and then reviewed his presentation notes again. He hung a *"Meeting in progress"* sign on his office door.

When he logged on to the designated Calnet channel at 2:25 p.m., most of the society members were already linked in. He watched nervously as their faces and accompanying names scrolled down the left-hand side of the screen. While he hadn't said explicitly what he was presenting, these types of meetings were always popular just in case something amazing appeared; Terran satellite echoes were particularly popular. He recognized a few names from overseas.

At the precise start time, Atteberry clicked his microphone on and welcomed everybody. He thanked them for being able to attend, especially on such short notice, and then got down to business.

"Last night, I tested the new static filter I told you about at our last meeting. For those who missed it, this is an intelligent audio filter I co-designed with Kate Braddock at the City College Ocean Campus, and it's specifically used for detecting signals *within* the noise spectrum—not above it."

Some new attendees pinged on to the channel and joined the bottom of the list. There were over 67 on now. Atteberry paused.

"Well, I was listening in on the subspace C-band last night when I put the new filter on, and that's when I detected something completely new." Two more attendees pinged, including the new director of the SETI program over at the TSA, Dr. Esther Tyrone. Cool.

"Here's the signal." Atteberry hit the key and the one-one-eight pattern played over the channel. Written questions poured into the on-screen dialogue box.

"Thank you for the questions, colleagues, I'll try to get to them shortly, but before I do, I'll answer Patty Lebrowski's first. Patty wants to know if I have determined the signal's origin; the answer to that is *yes*," he paused for a moment, then announced, "It comes from the Ross 128 system."

The channel exploded in a chaotic tangle of questions and comments scrolling by in the dialogue box. Some attendees left altogether, and a few called him directly on his indie-comm; he didn't answer them.

Finally, the society president asked Atteberry for the floor. It was the custom to yield the floor to the president whenever he or she wanted it, so he muted his mic, clicked on Dr. Jerome Taylor's, and established his video feed.

"Thank you, Jim, for sharing this with us. It's intriguing, of course, and encouraging for those of us who've been searching a long time." Taylor paused, working his mouth as if chewing on his words. "But I do have several questions for you."

This was always the toughest part for presenters who thought they'd really heard a true extra-terrestrial, intelligent signal: The vetting was about to begin.

"First, did anyone else copy anything anomalous on the C-band last night? Please answer in the dialogue box." A handful of attendees responded, and they were all negative. But a half dozen others reported they'd been monitoring the same C-band at the same time as Atteberry, and they detected nothing suggesting an intelligent signal.

"Is there any reason you were the only one hearing this pattern, Jim?"

Atteberry turned on his mic. "The only difference I can point to is the new filter I'm using. It's not designed to detect signals above the noise, but instead goes right into the static and looks for patterns there—in the noise itself."

More dialogue chatter scrolled by and he read a few messages before the burn of humiliation smacked him.

"This is a hoax!"

"Nice try, bud."

"Pretty convenient to use a noise filter no one else has access to."

"A signal in the noise is by definition noise, right?"

Many of the attendees logged off at this point, and Atteberry realized it was over. But he wouldn't give up, his resolve growing with each passing comment.

"I know it sounds strange and, believe me, I'm just as skeptical as you. But there's more." He took a deep breath. "Do you hear that one-one-eight pattern? I think whoever is sending the signal is using atomic numbers to communicate. *One* is for hydrogen, and *eight* is the number for oxygen."

Taylor shifted uncomfortably in his chair, making notes. Atteberry continued. "The messenger is looking for H_2O. Water."

More nasty, mocking comments flew by on the screen.

Dr. Taylor looked up from his notes, "Jim, there are obviously questions surrounding your findings and, of course, that's a healthy and necessary reaction. What I'd suggest to the group is the following: For the next few days, perhaps a week, let's all train our receivers on the Ross 128 coordinates and have a listen, both normal and subspace. Use whatever filtering configurations you can. If someone else hears that pattern, we'll take another closer look." Then he spoke again, this time to Jim specifically. "The signal is still there, isn't it, Jim?"

Atteberry knew he would regret answering this. "Dr. Taylor, I only received it for a few minutes and then it disappeared. My station's set up to monitor the frequency continuously, but unfortunately, no alerts have come since that first one last night."

"I see." Taylor put his pen down carefully, precisely. "That changes things, doesn't it?"

Atteberry didn't know what to say, so he remained silent while the comments continued to pour in. He could see Taylor reading some of them.

Finally, the retired physicist said, "Folks, let's not jump to any conclusions either way. It behooves us as scientists, professional or civilian, to approach this signal as we would any other one. Let's monitor the Ross 128 frequency for the rest of the week and reconvene in seven days time."

After this pronouncement, most of the remaining attendees left the channel.

It wasn't supposed to unfold this way. The group loved to ask tough questions and prided itself on its healthy skepticism; Atteberry knew his colleagues were thorough when considering intelligent life in the universe, but he hadn't been prepared for this attack. Unlike many of the astronomy society members, he was not a trained scientist, and several of them reminded him of this whenever it convenienced them. Still, he worked hard to learn as much as he could, to ask probing questions and contribute to the knowledge base. But this time, the group had become dirty in a hurry—they had him in their sights.

Atteberry took a deep breath and sighed. Perhaps a glitch in the new filter existed? It was quite sophisticated after all. He had designed the mechanical aspects of it—that was the easy part—but it was Kate who had coded the filtering algorithm. He'd asked her if she could design a more lateral-thinking, intuitive program to detect patterns in cosmic noise and she had given him code to beta test last week. He knew he should understand her work better so he could trust the results, and he hadn't taken the time to prepare properly.

Ten people remained logged on. Some of them were chatting together, but not about his findings. He noticed, however, that Dr. Esther Tyrone was still on too. She'd joined the TSA only a few months ago from somewhere in the Northern Democratic Union, but he'd never met her and she hadn't attended any of the society meetings before.

Her on-screen avatar was a photo of Titan, and he watched it over the next few minutes as he mentally licked his wounds. Then it silently winked out.

THREE

Atteberry

"Hi, Dad, I'm home now!" Mary's face filled Atteberry's indie-comm screen. He was still in the office, pushing papers into his already-stuffed briefcase when she called.

"Okay, honey, I'm just about to leave. How was school today?"

"Boring, mostly. Nothing to be done, but Godot might come tomorrow!" She giggled.

"True, you never know who might show up at your door one day, hm? I'll see you soon."

Since his presentation to the society a couple of hours ago, Atteberry's office phone had pinged incessantly. He was still sore and recovering from the verbal barrage he'd received and in no mood to speak with anyone, so he'd ignored the machine. He softened now after chatting with Mary.

Atteberry yanked the strap closed on his bag, turned off his computer and reconnected his office phone. He turned out his office light and opened the door to leave when that office phone pinged again. His shoulders slouched, and he sighed. *Let the VR pick it up.* It pinged again and his curiosity rose; he glanced around to see if he recognized the caller. The phone screen shone "*Dr. E. Tyrone, Terran Science Academy*" in light blue letters.

Intrigued, Atteberry tossed his bag on the chair and picked up the receiver.

"Hello, Jim Atteberry speaking."

A friendly voice replied, "Hello, Dr. Atteberry, it's Esther Tyrone calling from the Terran Science Academy."

"Yes?"

"I hope I'm not bothering you but I just wanted to say that I attended your presentation this afternoon and—"

"Ah, and you want to tell me how foolish I am?" Atteberry's patience was already worn thin.

"Not at all. We haven't met, but I'm the director of the SETI program here, so any finding related to the search for intelligent life is important to me, no matter how incredible it appears."

Atteberry leaned against his desk. "Sorry, Doctor, I'm not usually that snarky. You can imagine it's been a trying afternoon for me."

"Indeed I can. We seekers are always being told how off-base we are, aren't we?" Atteberry could almost see her smile in her voice.

"How can I help you?"

"I'll get right to the point: I'd like to understand your filter algorithm better."

"Oh?"

"If it works, it's something we—I—could really use in my own research. Would it be possible to come in tomorrow morning to discuss it more?"

Atteberry jumped up and said, "Yes, of course! I teach until 10:30 but I could meet you after that." He surprised himself with how quickly his mood could change.

"Great! I'll see you then."

"Oh, one more thing, 'Doctor.'"

"Yes?"

"It's just *Mister* Atteberry, not Doctor."

They said their goodbyes and ended the call. Letting out a sigh and picking up his briefcase, Atteberry said to no one in particular, "Well, how about that?"

His older model hovercar waited in the standing area outside Batmale Hall on Cloud Circle. He climbed into the vehicle and said, "Home." The car chimed, lifted a foot and a half off the asphalt, and pulled ahead, easing into the traffic on Phelan Avenue, heading east.

Finally, someone who doesn't think I'm a complete idiot. Well, not yet at any rate. He realized he'd have to undertake a detailed study of the filter, on the mechanical side and especially on the programming side. When he asked Kate to come up with an intelligent algorithm for detecting patterns in the noise, he trusted her thoroughness completely, and still did. But if he was meeting the new bigwig at the TSA, he needed to be sure it worked flawlessly. By convincing her that what he heard was real, others could come on board as well.

"Call Kate."

The car chimed and in a moment, Kate's voice filled the quiet space. "I was wondering how it went this afternoon," she said.

"Not great, no one believed me at all."

"You haven't let that stop you before, Jim."

"True, but it still stings. Anyway, I just got off the phone with a Dr. Tyrone at the TSA. She heads up the SETI program there and wants to know more about the filter's pattern recognition algorithm." The car slowed at an intersection, calculating the trajectories of the other vehicles on the road, and smartly threaded through.

"You've forgotten how it works already? I'm disappointed," she laughed.

"Yes, well, I was wondering if you were free tonight to come by and walk me through it. I really need to understand how it works and whether it's reliable with real data."

Silence.

Then Kate answered, "Sorry, Jim, I really can't tonight. I'm totally swamped with shit this week."

Atteberry frowned. "Okay, I'll see what I can do on my own." He leaned back in the seat and stared out the side window at the passing scenery. He'd just have to do his best and focus on testing it against known pulsars, extrapolate from there. The key for tomorrow's meeting will be on the signal and what it means. *Is it a cry for help in the wilderness, or something else?*

That's when Janet popped into his head like a burst of light. She could probably help him, but he had no idea where she was. She'd taken off in the middle of the night and never came back. The only thing he got from her was an old-school letter from Canada on Mary's eighth birthday. *"Don't try finding me"* was all it said. It wasn't signed or anything, but he knew it was from her.

He and Mary had both struggled with the loss, but lately they'd found a new rhythm, a happier pace, and a return to normal.

Speaking with Esther Tyrone had reduced his bitterness. He replayed their conversation in his mind, trying to detect any sign of malevolence, but the only thing he continually noticed was the warmth in her voice, and how professional and friendly she seemed.

The car stopped in front of Atteberry's home and settled on the ground in one continuous motion. He hauled himself out of the vehicle, and it rose and floated away for recharging at the filling lot half a block away. Mary met him at the door and gave him a hug. She had his old boots on and made clopping noises as she walked.

"Godot!" she chirped, "You made it!"

They laughed and bounced into the kitchen to get supper ready. Atteberry cherished this time with Mary, preparing food, setting the table. She told him about her day (it wasn't nearly as boring as she'd joked earlier) and he told her of his disastrous meeting with the astronomy society. She wasn't concerned at all.

"What'll you do now?" she asked as she pulled a couple plates from the cupboard.

Atteberry stopped cutting up the vegetables and scraped them into a salad bowl. "I'm going to take a really close look at my new filter and make sure it works properly."

"Can I help?"

"You bet, as soon as your homework's done." He grinned at her and she gave him the look right back, the one that said *"Okay, but we both know that hunting alien signals is way more interesting than memorizing European capitals."*

Atteberry took their meal to the table, and they ate quickly.

As they finished up, he remembered his phone call with Dr. Tyrone. "Oh, Mary, I almost forgot. One of the scientists at the Academy called me right after I spoke to you when you got home."

"Who was it?"

"Dr. Esther Tyrone. She's in charge of the search for alien life program."

"Wow, Dad, what did she want?"

Atteberry stood up from the table and collected the remains of the meal. "She wants to meet with me in the morning to talk about what I heard on the radio."

Mary swallowed her last bite of salad and stared at him. "That's good news, isn't it?"

"I think it's fantastic news, and I feel much better. She sounded really friendly on the phone, too." They cleaned up their dishes in the kitchen.

"Well, you better get down to the workbench and figure out your filter thing."

"Yup, as soon as I do the dishes."

Mary pushed him away from the sink. "Dad, you go. I'll clean up here."

Jim Atteberry woke up earlier than usual the next morning. He and Mary had spent a couple of hours in the basement the night before, reviewing his filter circuit and Kate's algorithm, and parts of her code were coming back to him, but he was still having trouble following her work. He wished Kate could have joined them, but at least he felt confident about discussing the filtering concept with Dr. Tyrone.

After Mary went to bed, Atteberry had listened to the subspace bands for the mysterious Ross 128 signal; he heard nothing but static. *If it was real, where could it have gone?*

He taught two morning classes on Thursdays and the time sailed by. Although he loved his profession—and could put on a good show, as they say—he always felt drained afterwards. So as the hovercar flew him to the TSA, he closed his eyes for a quick nap.

The Terran Science Academy was the only tenant in a five-year-old building facing John F. Kennedy Drive on the western side of Golden Gate Park, right along the edge of the Pacific Ocean. It was all glass, several storeys high with curvilinear structures reminiscent of Frank Lloyd Wright's designs, green lawns, palm and walnut trees.

Atteberry admired the place from the front entrance. Small groups of men and women—some in lab coats—walked by, and other groups of students sat around laughing, flipping through books. It reminded him of being on his own campus at City College, except this one had more money behind it.

The main lobby was massive with a huge vaulted ceiling and murals of the solar system along the deep grey walls and marble floors. Inlaid stone in the marble hinted at the asteroid belt. His footsteps echoed as he approached the reception desk where a small woman in a white uniform greeted him.

"Good morning, sir, is there something I can help you with today?"

"I have an appointment with Dr. Esther Tyrone. My name's Jim Atteberry."

She checked the screen in front of her and smiled. "Yes, Mr. Atteberry, she is expecting you." She put the bio-screen in front of him. "Please look at the yellow dot."

The screen chimed and a moment later, she handed him a security card. "Be sure to wear this everywhere you go and sign out when you're finished. You'll find Dr. Tyrone waiting for you on the third floor." She waved the direction to the escalator with her arm.

Atteberry thanked her and clipped the security badge to his jacket pocket. Then he marched to the escalator and rode it to the third floor.

Esther Tyrone was waiting for him at the top as he stepped off.

"You must be Jim Atteberry," she said, extending her hand out to greet him.

Atteberry admired her no-nonsense, practical greeting and all-business, shoulder-length hair. She wore a dark blue jacket and skirt, and carried an indie-comm in her hand. Short finger nails, no polish. Easy smile.

"Dr. Tyrone, I presume?" He shook her hand, firm grip.

"Please come this way." She guided him down the hall and past open office space, small meeting rooms, terrariums and computer facilities. At the end of the hall, she invited him into her office. It had a spectacular view of the ocean and coastline, and Atteberry stood agape for several seconds.

"It's beautiful... the first thing I loved when I arrived here a few months ago," she said, "but nothing compared to the sky at night with a full moon over the water."

He studied the rest of the office and his gaze stopped on a poster of Titan hanging on the wall along with several degrees and photos of her and others. Then Atteberry noticed a small, much-loved hobbyist's telescope set up behind her desk.

She saw him looking at it and said, "Yes, that old thing... it's not much, I grant you that, but I've had that telescope since I was a kid growing up in Vermont. I enjoy just looking at the sky occasionally, not for work, you understand. Just pleasure."

She motioned him to the couch. "Please have a seat."

They sat together and he studied her face as she leafed through a notebook and tablet. Friendly, plain. More crow's feet than him.

"Dr. Tyrone," he began, "first let me thank you again for this meeting. I was thinking no one took me seriously after my presentation yesterday. You know I'm not a scientist, don't you?"

"I know you're an amateur radio astronomer and that you teach at City College, but that's it."

"Yes, I'm an English literature teacher."

"Really? You teach English and search for aliens in your spare time. That's not a common pairing."

"I suppose it isn't, but then again, does it surprise you?"

"No, no it doesn't. The civil war changed a lot of things including what we used to think of as 'normal' activity." She gazed out the big window as a flock of seagulls flew by. Atteberry fidgeted with his tie.

"Mr. Atteberry—"

"Please, call me Jim."

"Okay, Jim—I'm fascinated by what you heard the other night and just as interested in what you used to hear it. And you can call me Esther."

Atteberry leaned back on the couch, raising his arms in a hallelujah moment. "Finally, someone believes me!"

"I didn't say that. I don't know enough yet to draw a conclusion. That's why I'd like to learn more about what you did."

"Oh." He couldn't hide his disappointment but Dr. Tyrone's facial expression and tone of voice hadn't changed at all.

"Can you tell me what you were doing on Tuesday night when you detected the anomaly?"

"Sure." Atteberry recounted everything he did: how he scanned the subspace bands with the new filter, noodling around with the settings, and how the alert sounded when the algorithm detected a pattern.

"That's what we heard yesterday at the presentation, wasn't it?"

"Exactly," he said, "but the exciting part about it was the message itself."

"Right. You think the taps you heard represented atomic numbers for hydrogen and oxygen."

Atteberry looked her straight in her grey eyes. "I do. I'm certain it's a cry for help, like if you were in real trouble, you'd think about nothing other than what you need most."

"Water."

Dr. Tyrone stared back at him, as if she was studying his face or trying to read his mind. Atteberry felt light-headed again. The same feeling he had when they'd talked on the phone yesterday.

"Jim, can we set aside the water interpretation for now, and focus on *how* you detected a signal from cosmic noise? Can you tell me more about the technical aspects of it?"

He knew this was his weak spot. Although he enjoyed tinkering with electronics and could build things from schematics, he wasn't a scientist, engineer or programmer. He looked at the coffee table in front of him.

"The mechanical filter is a straightforward design. I built it from plans on the Calnet using spare coils and capacitors to vary the bandwidth, like any other audio frequency filter."

"Same thing we use here, it sounds like."

"Most likely. They help distinguish between competing signals on or around the same frequency, but the real magic is in the computational algorithm."

"What does it do?"

"Conceptually, it's a lateral-thinking, iterative subroutine."

"AI?"

"Yes. It compares individual signals with one another and then reconfigures them into coherent patterns using probability theory. The key is generating all the possible signal combinations while sampling different frequencies. Normally, you'd need quantum computing power, but this one doesn't."

Dr. Tyrone leaned forward, eyeing him carefully. "And this AI process gave you the water signal?"

Atteberry noticed her smile had disappeared.

"This method is highly speculative at first glance. Is it possible the algorithm gave you what you *wanted* to see?"

Atteberry felt defensive again, like yesterday when the comment board blew up during his talk.

"I—I don't know, I mean, I don't think so."

"Did you write the program yourself?"

"No, my colleague from City College did. She's a programming expert, Kate Braddock."

"I see." Dr. Tyrone stood up and strolled to her desk where she picked up a few business cards and sat down on the couch again. "Jim, I'd like to give these to you. Keep one for yourself and if don't mind, please give the other to your colleague and ask her to call me when she has a moment."

"Okay, what's this other one?"

"It's one of my colleague's cards." She handed it to him and Atteberry studied it. *Dr. Marshall Whitt, Director, Space Operations.* He'd heard of him. Ex-military. "Marshall is the fellow in charge of things like satellite tracking, cargo operations—anything to do with scientific equipment in space. He's a fine scientist, too." Her hand brushed against his arm and he shivered. "I will ask him to meet with you to learn more about your filter and algorithm. He'll be able to get into the technical details with you."

Atteberry knew this meeting was over and anxiety crept over him, rustling the hairs on the back of his neck. Did he say too much, or not enough? He stood and walked to the door. "Dr. Tyrone, before I go, may I ask you something?"

"Sure, I love questions."

"Do you believe what I heard was real?"

She paused and thought for a moment. "I think you definitely heard something, but I can't say if it was a real alien signal. Not yet. It's too early and there are many questions to consider."

Atteberry couldn't hide his disappointment. He tried putting on a brave face, but he knew his eyes betrayed him.

"Jim, you realize that if your signal checks out and it really is from an alien world, it will change everything. Everything."

Atteberry considered the state of the dying Earth, the continuing conflicts, the millions of people dying of starvation, the runaway climate change, Janet's disappearance.

"That's what I'm hoping."

FOUR

Esther

ESTHER TYRONE PEERED OUT HER OFFICE WINDOW at the lush courtyard in front of the Academy building. She'd escorted Jim Atteberry to the main doors a while ago, yet there he sat outside, reading on a bench in the shade of a walnut tree. *I suppose, as an academic, he has a few more liberties with his day than the rest of us.* A twinge of envy and regret entered her mind.

She pulled a small mirror from her desk drawer and checked her hair. He was an interesting man, that Atteberry fellow, and met several of her most-desired features in the opposite sex:

taller than her own five feet eight inches, bearded (like her father), easy on the eyes, pleasant to talk to, and a reader. The men she'd dated since college did not know Dickens, Shelley, or even the emerging impressionists from South America. They were odd science types or dropouts. No middle ground.

And there he was, sitting on a bench, reading. She shook her head, well, he must be ten years younger. And married, if that ring on his finger still meant anything. She accepted the age difference but marriage meant a full stop. Still, this curious signal would at least give her a chance to see if he was the type of fellow she might want to settle down with. Now that she had attained the position she wanted in her career, perhaps the time to find a suitable partner and have a couple of kids had arrived. Or not.

She sat at her desk and opened the internal computer network. "Find Marshall Whitt."

"Dr. Marshall Whitt is in the Space Communications Lab, Level B-3."

"Ping him."

A few seconds later, Marshall Whitt appeared on her computer screen, unkempt beard and white hair. "Hi Esther, what's up?"

"I met with the fellow from the college—you know, the one who heard a signal."

Marshall wiped his hands on a cloth and cleared his throat. "Ah yes, the cosmic diviner. Moranski briefed me on his presentation. It's an unfortunate part of your job that you have to follow up on these cranks who hear voices in the stars, eh?"

"Oh I don't mind. Most of the crazy ones get filtered out before they ever reach me." It was true, her responsibilities included thorough checks on every anomalous cosmic signal, but few ended up in her office. The astronomy society networks around the world routinely challenged each other's observations, and most unsolved signal mysteries died there.

However, two things differentiated Atteberry's findings from others: First, the intelligent filter system he used would revolutionize the art of signal processing. Second, if his signal was proven to be real, it meant we were not the only intelligent lifeforms in the universe; that alone would open a million other lines of enquiry. Why Ross 128, for example? What's there? And why the cry for water?

"But Marshall, I recommend going over this fellow's findings."

"Why's that? My real work here is piling up, so couldn't Farley or Sneddon take it?"

Esther smiled patiently. "They could, I'm sure, but this business is more up your alley. Mr. Atteberry and a colleague of his have designed an intelligent, iterative noise filter that he claims can detect coherent signals weaker than the ambient noise levels."

Whitt stopped fidgeting and stared at her through the computer link. "Really? We've been experimenting on more robust filters without success. Are they using a quantum computer?"

"No, just a regular everyday one."

"Interesting. I need to study his findings."

Whitt threw the cloth off screen and pulled his indie-comm from his pocket. "Can you send me his coordinates, Esther? I'll try to give him a shout this afternoon."

Esther tapped a key on her screen. "Keep me updated." Then she added one more thing. "He's not a trained physicist, Marshall, but don't let that fool you. He has a sharp mind."

"Noted, thanks."

Whitt ended the link, and Esther stood up and stared out her window again. Atteberry had gone, the silence crept around her office, and her mother's voice filled her head. Her own negative self-talk crushed her spirit.

No one could love you.

Marshall had come on to her the first week after she'd arrived at the Academy, but she'd brushed him off even though she enjoyed the attention in an odd, perverted way. The next time he asked her out, more politely, she agreed to meet him for a drink. He never showed up at the hotel bar and they hadn't talked about that evening since. She'd taken several days to digest the humiliation.

Don't be too smart. Try to look pretty for once.

She played with the pendant on her necklace. "When's my next appointment?"

"Inter-call at 12:30 with the International Geophysical Union Planning Committee."

She picked up her tablet and settled on the couch to prepare for the inter-call. The soft white sunlight danced across her grey carpet. "Open a Calnet connection."

The tablet chimed. She paused a moment and gazed over the ocean again at the muted sun behind wisps of cirrus clouds, and another idea came to her.

"Query Jim Atteberry, English teacher, City College of San Francisco." Esther scanned the public archives material and other mentions of Atteberry, then felt the heaviness of guilt and straightened her back. "Clear that request," she said. "Download the documents for the IGU Planning Committee meeting."

Atteberry

LATER THAT EVENING, ATTEBERRY AND MARY CHATTED together in the kitchen. He spooned their supper out into bowls, a spicy concoction of various meats and leftovers, and Mary wrote a journal entry on her tablet.

"Let's eat!"

Mary dumped her work into her schoolbag and hopped to the dining table. He sat at the end, facing no one. Mary sat in the middle.

"So tell me about your favorite part of school today."

Mary's excitement rivaled that of the first day of school when the new term began. A couple of older boys from the collegiate had come to talk about their new science project. "And get this, Dad. They specifically asked me to join them! Ms. Bender had to give me permission, but whatever. We're looking at extending the life of indie-comm power sources by tying them to a network of routers. It's a boss idea and it's real science!"

"Really? Tell me more about these boys." *Crazy kid. Is it possible she's getting interested in the opposite sex already? What happened to my little girl?*

When a break appeared in their conversation, Atteberry, buttering a dinner roll, said, "Mary, what would you think if I started dating?"

She threw him a suspicious, quizzical glance. "What do you mean, like going out on a date with Kate?"

"Well, sort of, but not Kate. No, I'm talking like, oh I don't know, someone I meet at the grocery store or the library."

Now her eyes narrowed, reflecting a combination of fear and anger. "What about Mom?"

Atteberry wasn't prepared for that reaction, but this was as good a time as any to talk. "Your mother—Mom—has disappeared, honey. She left us two-and-a-half years ago. I don't think she's coming back."

"But what if she does and you're having sex with a librarian?"

"Mary, it's not like—"

"Not like what, Dad? You can't just pretend she's gone forever!"

Atteberry realized this wouldn't end well. Awkward didn't even begin to describe the sudden shift in mood. "Okay, I understand. I won't date. We'll keep waiting for Mom, just you and me, okay?"

Mary pushed her half-finished bowl back and drummed her fingers on the table top. "I've got a lot of homework to do. May I be excused?" But she didn't wait for a response, instead, she ran down the hall, forgetting her schoolbag in the kitchen.

The house became eerily quiet. The love and laughter at the start of the meal was all gone now, replaced with the ache of tense silence. A few minutes later, while Atteberry slowly finished his meal, the muffled sound of soft crying drifted out from her room.

Whitt

"Sunrise 7:03 a.m.
Temperature 15 degrees Celsius.
Dew point 11 degrees Celsius.
Humidity 64 percent.
Wind west-north-west at 19 kilometers per hour.
Visibility 16 kilometers.
Sea level pressure 101 —"
"Off."

The sun wouldn't rise for another half hour but the sky was already waking up.

Dr. Marshall Whitt floated to an automatic stop in his new black hovercar at the TSA employee entrance. The Chang thrusters in this model were a real treat compared to the old first-generation engines, and he marveled at how quickly the anti-grav technology had found its way into passenger vehicles. He put the papers he'd been reading away in a thick satchel and stepped onto the concrete porch. The hovercar lifted immediately and purred off to park itself at the recharging station. Today will be another busy one, Whitt thought, and he wanted to get an early start.

Whitt flashed his bio-card in front of the reader and the heavy doors swung open. Rather than stop at his office on the third floor, he rode the elevator straight to the Space Operations Lab on the third underground level. Two of the overnight techs were working on a prototype satellite propulsion system. Ignoring them, he marched directly to the heavy computations workstation. He waved his bio-card at the computer screen and the equipment jumped to life.

"Agenda."

The monitor blinked and Whitt's daily calendar appeared. Most of his day was booked off in blue blocks—lab time—and two meetings this morning outlined in green. Other non-scheduled tasks filled the right side of the screen, and the first of those was a reminder to call Jim Atteberry, the increasingly popular space enthusiast.

Whitt remembered the half dozen phone calls he'd received on voice comms yesterday afternoon from colleagues both in the Congressional Republic and across the divided states. Apparently, the word about his presentation findings was out and piquing curiosity.

An autoserver rolled by his workstation and Whitt poured himself a fresh coffee and took a couple of protein bars from its dispenser. He nodded at its eye, and the autoserver whirred out of sight.

Yes, it's unfortunate about this one being picked up by the media, but understandable. A supposed cry for water from deep space wasn't an every day occurrence. His colleagues pestered him, wondering what he honestly thought about all the fuss; and the truth was, he lacked sufficient information to conclude anything, but he'd learned to keep an open mind about such things.

Whitt checked the time: 6:39 a.m.—early afternoon in London. He would contact Foster Kimani at the British Astronomical Association. Kimani was on the Astronomical Society call the other day and could give him more information about it.

Whitt commanded the computer to ping Kimani and in a moment, the happiest astrophysicist on the planet appeared. Nothing could faze this man, he was the eternal optimist. Whitt braced himself for a long-winded, one-sided conversation.

"Dr. Whitt, how lovely to see you again! I was wondering about you right there in the middle of this alien signal business. That fellow's presentation, by the way, blew my mind, just blew it all over the lab! What an intriguing revelation! Of course, without any details, assessing its viability is impossible but that conclusion of his, the water thing, well that's a new one isn't it? I mean, we've always assumed if there's intelligent life out there then they'd look like us and think like us, and who knows, drink water like us, too?"

"Foster, I—"

"Yes, yes, you want to know my impressions, don't you? Well, what can I say, if it's a hoax, it's brilliant."

"How so?"

"Ross 128, of course! It makes no sense to pin the origin of an alien signal in Ross 128 unless it really came from there, you see?"

Whitt had given this some thought earlier. The tricksters usually picked a region in space with Goldilocks planets, following the questionable logic that life out there must be like us. It made one wish they'd try to be more sophisticated; idiot time-wasters.

"Foster, you actually attended the society presentation, yes?"

"Oh yes, I wouldn't—"

"Great, so maybe you can give me your unfiltered impressions about it. The recording was fine but didn't give me a real sense of the discussion. I have a meeting with this fellow Atteberry, so I'd like to understand what really happened."

When Foster Kimani got excited, his distant Kenyan accent revealed itself. "I am so jealous, my friend, so jealous! My, how I wish I could be there to meet Mr. Jim with you!"

"Let me link you in." Whitt knew he would refuse, and he did before launching into his impressions of Jim Atteberry's presentation to the society.

Kimani did not dismiss the findings outright. Even though he was encouraging and optimistic about the search for non-Terran life, he was no fool when it came to claims of hearing aliens.

"The thing is," he said, "with the amount of subterfuge undertaken not only during your own civil war but also by others around the world, separating the real from the false is increasingly difficult. You understand that well, don't you?"

Whitt recalled his work with the Confederate military immediately after the war. His specialty was intercepting NDU communications and piggybacking viruses and other disruptive algorithms on them. "Director of Cold War Shenanigans" his team leader had labeled him.

"When you meet with Mr. Jim, if it were me, I'd be asking about borrowing his equipment. I can't recall exactly what he used, but it sounded like a garden variety mechanical audio filter in tandem with an AI-processing algorithm."

"Yes, that's my understanding of it. Esther confirms that, too."

"Well, anyone can build an audio filter—hell, the ones you have at the TSA are probably the most sophisticated in the world."

"They should be. I designed them."

Kimani ignored the quip but Whitt knew he'd got him. He tried to hide a smile.

"Whatever, you should focus on getting a copy of that algorithm and putting it through some rigorous tests. It's the key, you understand, there's no point debating the meaning of the signal until you can verify the accuracy and reliability of the processing algorithm itself."

"Thank you, Foster, that's exactly what I'll do."

"Keep me posted. We're all watching."

Whitt terminated the link and snapped one of the protein bars apart. He needed to convince Mr. Jim Atteberry to show him this algorithm, or better yet, give him the code so he could thoroughly review it. If it checked out, and he wasn't convinced of that yet, then the space sciences would undergo a quantum leap in knowledge. However, the military's interest and power trumped all scientific endeavors, and he wasn't prepared to share it with them. Not yet.

Whitt planned his next actions carefully. His meeting with Atteberry would be low-key and focus on testing the algorithm. If the filter turned out to be flawed, then everyone could return to regular business—nothing more to see at this crash site. But if it worked and could uncover intelligent signals buried in the noise, then hiding it from the military was paramount or they'd certainly lose the SETI program.

So he'd have to get the algorithm, validate it completely, and keep the results to himself unless they were bogus. Publicly, he would dismiss them anyway, and Atteberry too, until Whitt had conducted his own extra-terrestrial search with the program.

Whitt sent a voice comm to Atteberry's post at the college, requesting a private meeting in the TSA's Space Operations Lab, and to bring his filtering equipment, the algorithm and any notes he'd made about that Ross 128 signal.

Today would be a great day.

Atteberry

"It's not too late to change your mind, Kate. I could swing by your office in half an hour and we can meet Dr. Whitt together."

Atteberry paused from entering his grades in the departmental database. It'd been a weekend of wall-to-wall essay marking. Many others in the department had switched long ago to the automated marking programs, but a few holdouts like Atteberry still preferred the old-fashioned way of reading students' papers, no matter how ugly they could get in this post-writing world.

Kate's face filled the televiewer on his computer screen. "I want nothing to do with them, Jim. If it was anyone else, maybe, but not the TSA."

Her experience as a Spacer had been brutal: Ripped from her family at Mary's age, sterilized, womb removed, breast buds hacked away, then brainwashed, isolated and trained to work in radioactive and toxic space environments. She blamed scientists—many of whom now worked at the Academy—for stealing her childhood and her identity; even though she mostly settled on being a woman now. The civil conflict changed everyone.

"Things are different now, Kate, but I do understand. When I see how Mary thinks, I..." Mary hadn't said much to him since the messy dating conversation last Thursday. They'd spent much of the weekend tiptoeing around each other with the occasional smile—he needed to fix that.

"Listen, you go have a good meeting this afternoon with the Academy. You'll do fine," Kate assured him. "But remember, I wrote the code for you, not anyone else, okay? Don't let them see it. Are you still good with the algorithm?"

"Yes, thanks again. The outline you sent over was great."

"All right, knock 'em dead. And let me know how it goes."

"I'll give you a call tonight."

Atteberry spent the rest of his Monday morning finishing up his grade entries and planning his lessons for the week. He was fortunate that Helen was able to cover his afternoon class so he could meet Dr. Whitt and a couple of the techs at the Lab. He looked forward to demonstrating exactly how his system worked, and he wanted to see their equipment up close and personal. Still, he wondered why Dr. Tyrone wasn't able to join them; Whitt gave no reason.

One o'clock chimed on his indie-comm and he signaled for his hovercar to meet him at the building entrance. Then he sent a voice comm to Mary.

"Hi Mary, it's your dad. Listen, I know we haven't said much to each other the past few days, but I wanted you to know how much I love you and how proud I am of you. Not for anything you've done—for being who you are. Let's talk later, okay?"

When Atteberry arrived at the TSA reception desk, the security woman smiled at him warmly and welcomed him back. She ran his bio-card again and asked him to wait until an escort could take him to the lab. He smiled nervously, feeling a bit jittery, especially since according to their weekend reports, the mysterious signal had remained undetected by the society members. But he knew what he'd heard and recorded last Tuesday night and confidently awaited this opportunity to show his findings to the scientists and prove himself. The sooner he could do that, the sooner he could convince them to establish contact.

A young, clean-shaven man in a powder blue lab coat met him in the lobby, introduced himself as Mark or something, and led him to the bank of elevators.

Atteberry searched the third floor at the top of the escalator he rode the other day, but she wasn't there. Mark turned out to be some poor grad student who led him down to the Space Operations Lab and scanned the door open for him.

Atteberry took a couple of steps inside then stopped, his mouth agape as he surveyed the cavernous room. The ceilings must have been 30 feet high, more so in some places, and there were dozens of workstations, benches, canisters of carbon dioxide and massive crates stored along one side. Every thing was white except for the blue lab coats that some technicians and scientists wore, and the multi-colored, glowing computer screens.

Marshall Whitt strolled up from an enclosed room near the entrance and greeted him sternly, professionally. He snapped at the techs to carry Atteberry's small equipment case, then led him to a bank of radio astronomy micro-stations near the lab's center.

"Dr. Whitt, I don't know what to say. This place is truly impressive!"

"I take it you haven't been down here before."

"No. We had a fellow from USF give a talk once at the Astronomical Society. He showed us some pictures of this lab, but they are nothing like seeing it in person."

Whitt flashed his bio-card at the computer screen and a large power supply hummed to life below the station bench. Atteberry marveled at the gear. All state-of-the-art radio astronomy equipment—much more powerful and sensitive than his own—covering all radio frequencies including the subspace and dark bands. But the one piece he was hoping to see was missing.

"Where's the subspace band transmitter?"

Whitt eyed him carefully. "Oh we don't keep it here on the floor. You can understand why, I'm sure."

Subspace receivers were available from specialty electronics shops, but many radio enthusiasts like Jim Atteberry preferred to build their own from plans. They were simple enough to construct, no different than normal space-time receivers, except they had dedicated circuitry to handle the frequency multipliers for translating compressed space-time signals.
Transmitters, however, were a different matter. It was one thing to *listen* to cosmic signals, but no Terran government dared risk allowing some basement-dwelling hobbyist to make first contact with aliens.

"Everything goes through the Oxford Orbiting Antenna Array, doesn't it? Even transmitted signals?"

"Oh yes. That's the only way to manage subspace signals." Whitt looked perplexed. "Why do you ask?"

"I ask because I think we—I mean, the Earth—should contact whoever sent the Ross 128 transmission." Atteberry removed his filter and cables from his suitcase and set them on the bench.

"Some feel that we have no business contacting alien worlds at all, Mr. Atteberry, that we're inviting an invasion or a plague."

"Well sir, I'm not one of them. If alien creatures are going to invade the Earth, they would have done it by now, don't you think?"

Whitt smiled knowingly. "And you're certain of this?"

"With due respect, Dr. Whitt, I don't think we're here to open this debate again. The UN established that the Earth wouldn't go transmitting our whereabouts to anyone out there. But I disagree with that decision." Atteberry closed his suitcase and gave it to one of the technicians.

"You're right. Let's see your equipment." He studied Atteberry's filter. "Can you walk me through what we have here?"

Atteberry's mood lightened quickly as he removed the filter's cover and showed him the main circuit coils, reactive networks and frequency drivers. One of the techs recorded the discussion on his indie-comm while another took notes on a small pad. Whitt, his hands behind his back, inspected the device with military precision, his thickly-bearded face only centimeters from the filter's circuits.

"Excellent workmanship, Mr. Atteberry. You must have a well-equipped workshop at the college."

"Oh, I don't do this at the college. I have my own shop in the basement. Strictly a hobby of mine."

"Indeed. Shall we hook it up?"

Atteberry showed the technicians where to connect the equipment to the receiver's input. They clearly had used this kind of external filter before, judging by their level of comfort with installing it in their radio network. The grad student asked whether one of the filter's chips contained the programming code.

"Part of it is, the material in the public domain, but I keep the primary code separate. My colleague, Kate Braddock, from the college actually wrote it based on several discussions we had. Unfortunately, she wasn't able to join us today but I'll do my best to guide you through it." He pulled the data stick out of his jacket pocket and pushed it into a mag slot on the filter. "You need to link this app to your computer."

One of the techs sat down at the station and punched the keyboard. Instantly, the screen showed a link with the data stick, the filter and the receiver. Dr. Whitt studied the on-screen graphic. "Does this switch to turn it on?"

"Not exactly. It's a passive filter. You can either use it manually or else the algorithm will drive it. You turn the program on here," he pointed to the *ENGAGE* button on-screen, "then to look for deeper, weaker signals, you initiate that subroutine here." He indicated another button called *DEEP FILTER*.

"Is that what you used to hear your signal?"

"Yes, Dr. Whitt. I was in the deep filter mode with an auto-sweep across the subspace bands. When it picked up the signal, the sweep stopped, and the data were all recorded."

Dr. Whitt studied the computer screen. "This is fascinating. What kind of testing did you do for its accuracy?"

"Well, I admit not much yet. That's what I was hoping you'd be able to help me with. Kate tells me the code is clean and flawless, and I believe her, but if there's any residual bias built into it that we've overlooked, we need to find it."

Whitt peered up from the station. "Well, I think we may be able to help you with that. As you can see," he motioned with his hand to the entire lab, "we are not without resources here."

"Great! When do we start?"

"Soon, Mr. Atteberry. I should caution you that we've dealt with these sorts of mysterious signals before. Dr. Tyrone's predecessor used to ask us to check into the technical parameters of so-called alien signals all the time."

Atteberry's face blushed for some reason at the mention of her name. Whitt raised an eyebrow almost imperceptibly.

"No signal we've ever analyzed has confirmed intelligent alien life, so don't get your hopes up."

"Sure, I understand, but I have a strong feeling about this. I know what I heard."

Whitt's voice softened slightly. "You heard *something*, Mr. Atteberry. There is little doubt about that. But," he added quickly, "we need objective facts and thorough testing first."

Atteberry pursed his lips, checking his rising frustration with this scientist and his cold, methodological approach. "Yes, of course, but I heard what I heard. It was definitely real, and the message was a cry for water."

"Perhaps, but it is curious that no one else picked up your signal and there's been nothing but static since."

"I know what it looks like, but I'm telling you—"

Whitt put his hand on Atteberry's shoulder. "Don't worry, Mr. Atteberry, we'll have the answers shortly. And either way, the truth shall set us free, yes?" The hum of heat sink fans and underground generators filled the space between them as Whitt paused and grinned, bordering on aloofness. "Let's see how it works."

He adjusted the frequency to that of Atteberry's signal and pressed the *DEEP FILTER* button on the computer screen.

Atteberry and Whitt grabbed separate headphones and listened to the deep, hollow, pulsing cosmic hiss. On the screen, the background noise amplitudes varied in shades of orange and red across the subspace band.

A COUPLE OF HOURS LATER, Whitt turned the equipment off and turned to Atteberry who wore a stern, disappointed look on his face. "The fish aren't biting today, it would seem."

"Yeah, I don't understand what happened to them. Maybe it was some natural occurrence after all."

Whitt stood and stretched his arms. "I tell you what. Would you be able to leave your equipment with me for the rest of the week? My associates can put it through all our regular testing protocols to make sure it's performing properly."

Atteberry had a strange gnawing feeling in his stomach about leaving his gear, and Kate's code, there. He had no reason to distrust Dr. Whitt or anyone else at the Academy, yet he remembered Kate's experience and what some of these scientists were capable of doing.

"I don't know if I should."

"We'd have it only for a few days. You can come back Friday and we'll review the results together."

Atteberry sighed. He needed to verify the legitimacy of his signal and that meant validating the algorithm and filter first. Who better to test the equipment than the experts?

"Alright, but please don't share it with anyone. I trust you folks, but I also promised my colleague I wouldn't give her code away. For proprietary reasons, right? If some of those jackals in the society get hold of it... who knows what they'll do."

FIVE

Esther

EARLY THURSDAY EVENING, ESTHER TYRONE LOOKED UP from the computer in her office and noticed how still the world had become. The endless chatter and phone calls of the day had given way to the silent hum of the office air recyclers, the whirr of overnight servers, and an echo of footsteps drifting up from the lobby. People all had places to go, families to live and laugh with, but Esther never felt that kind of eagerness to leave her work.

The evening silence reminded her of those rare times in graduate school when she'd lock herself in the optics lab, where no one could disturb her, and read. There'd be more time to indulge in her books once she graduated and found work, but that didn't happen. Esther glanced over at her bookshelf, the one Jim Atteberry admired so much the other day when he was in here, and told herself tonight was a reading night, a book night, a night to disappear in another world completely.

She stood up from her desk and stretched. The sun glided low in the sky and she reflected on the past couple of days. Inevitably, the media would latch on to the signal story. It was impossible to keep news of this significance under wraps for long, no matter how often the official TSA messaging focused on: *We're studying the anomaly, but caution against reading too much into it.*

The first call from New York hit her at 7:30 Tuesday morning from one of those geeky tech channels. Then other outlets picked up the story, so by the time lunch ended, the calls on her screen numbered 25. Finally, she gave Jasmine in media relations a quote to use: "...the signal is being reviewed by our best scientists, but we have found nothing conclusive. We investigate signals like this frequently and they have all ended up negative." That allowed her to work on other priorities, which these days seemed a lot like planning and managing and discussing other people's projects rather than doing the actual work of searching for alien life.

Jim Atteberry and other amateur enthusiasts got the fun stuff.

Esther remembered watching the videos when astronauts confirmed evidence of past life on Mars. Even though the world fully expected to hear that, the reality of life existing on another planet was the news story of the century. Then, when a later generation of explorers identified sea-worms under Ganymede's frozen oceans, a similar interest broke out, but without the same overwhelming discussion and coverage. The previous fascination with microbes and sea-worms waned, but the new possibility of discovering intelligent life fired the world up again. This was much different, more thought-provoking. For some, more dangerous.

"Is Dr. Whitt still in the building?"

"*Dr. Whitt is in the Space Operations Lab.*"

He didn't answer her comm right away. Must be in the middle of something… so she left a message to call her when he had a minute. Esther picked up the tablet, settled into the couch, and kicked off her shoes.

The propagation forecast on the Calnet showed band conditions worsening as the solar activity increased through its cycle. Her dad was a ham radio operator and although she never followed him into that hobby, she'd picked up a lot of knowledge just from keeping him company as he talked to others around the world. He liked to bounce radio signals off the moon's surface.

Her tablet pinged and Marshall appeared on her viewer.

"It seems, Esther, that you and I are always the ones working late."

She smiled. "Yeah, I was thinking how quiet it gets around here, how most people are able to separate work from their private lives. I could never do that."

"The pursuit of knowledge is not an eight to five job, is it? Now, what's on your mind?"

Esther pulled up another tab on her screen with notes she'd made earlier in the day. "Marshall, have you finished verifying Jim Atteberry's algorithm yet? Usually your team does its testing in hours, not days."

Whitt sat down at one of the radio astronomy benches. A couple of techs worked in the background.

"You're right, Esther, but this one is tricky," he said. "I can tell you it works in the sense that it hunts for patterns in random noise. We've given it known signal sources, buried them in static, and the filter finds them. However," he looked straight at her, "we haven't been able to access the code itself."

"So you can't determine whether there's bias in it."

"Not just that, we don't even know *how* the algorithm works. The code's encrypted like nothing I've seen before, although parts of it are familiar. It seems to work on known sources, but until we solve the encryption, pull the code apart and really understand the pattern recognition protocols, we can't test its reliability on unknown signals like Ross 128."

Esther pulled up another tab, one showing Kate Braddock's face and where she worked at City College. "Were you able to speak with this Kate Braddock person?"

"Not yet, none of my calls have been returned. How about you?"

"No, she's ignoring mine, too. I've looked her background up on the Calnet but she's got high-level privacy blockers engaged all over the place, the kind usually reserved for VIPs. Quite the mystery."

"Good to know. I won't waste any time looking there. Still," he paused, "Braddock is the programmer, and that makes her very important. We need to speak with her and get her to open this code for us."

"I agree." Then Esther had a brilliant thought. "Let me talk with Atteberry and I'll see if he can introduce us. He seems approachable and eager to help."

"Just a second, please." Whitt scribbled down notes, oblivious to everything. Esther respected that need to complete a thought or capture an idea when it hits, irrespective of an ongoing conversation. She did it herself.

"That's a good idea, Esther. While you're at it, perhaps you could invite him in tomorrow to discuss the findings with me. He can bring his colleague with him." She agreed and Whitt closed the link.

Esther scanned the Calnet for Jim Atteberry's information. Unlike Braddock's, his background was there—where he worked, where he went to school, a list of publications, some photos of him at conferences. Personal information remained hidden, a normal occurrence. Curiously, his involvement with the Astronomical Society appeared nowhere.

She called his office number on a slim hope he might still be there. No answer. She focused again on the Calnet and this time followed threads of his publications, leading to different discussion boards related to literary research and such. Nothing that gave her any additional insights into the man.

Esther expanded the search parameters to include what others may have posted about him. That led her to a series of essays and opinions he authored, many of them posted by a Janet

Chamberlain. At once guilt rose in her around this kind of legal voyeurism. Because of this unfettered access to information, the Congressional Republic enacted the stricter Calnet privacy laws at the end of the civil war. Notwithstanding her hesitation, she continued with her research.

Within these articles, she found an old essay of his that Chamberlain posted on a political discussion board about the need for institutions to be more open and accessible, including a piece written just before the American conflict really flared up. Out-dated material now, of course, but at the time the debate centered on whether nations and individuals ought to be fully open or secretive. He argued for openness in this paper, which explained his current desire to contact the Ross 128 aliens if there were such things. Doing the math, Esther realized he would have been in graduate school or perhaps just starting out in the working world when this was posted.

She read through more of the discussion threads but his name didn't appear again. Esther remembered her own idealism as a young scientist wanting to change the world when the civil war broke out and smiled out loud.

She pulled herself up from the couch and wandered over to her books, unsure of what she'd like to read tonight; nothing too long, nothing too heavy. She poked around the shelves, fingering anthologies, Dickens, even some of that crazy new wave science fiction. Finally, she settled on Forster's *The Machine Stops*. Maybe it was that thought about the sea-worms on Ganymede that led her to choose that one.

She pulled the book of short stories from the shelf and ordered a tea from the service cart. Within seconds, the autoserver rolled into her office and dispensed the drink, then disappeared.

Before turning off her tech for the evening, Esther wanted to leave a message with Jim Atteberry to have him call her first thing in the morning. She pinged his number at the college again, but this time, he answered, audio only.

"Dr. Tyrone, I'm glad it's you."

Atteberry

THE CRYING OF ROSS 128

JIM ATTEBERRY SAT AT HIS CLUTTERED RADIO ASTRONOMY BENCH, clearing a spot for his notebook, the comm link on speaker. Mary sprawled out in his huge recliner, working on her languages project, on the other side of the warmly-lit basement. She looked like a doll in the oversized chair.

The conversation they needed to have had taken place, and they'd agreed it was okay for him to have women friends, but nothing serious unless another discussion happened. Now, the previous tension in the house had disappeared completely.

"Hello, Mr. Atteberry, I didn't expect to get hold of you, but this is a pleasant surprise. Are you still on campus?"

"No, I forwarded my calls home so I can screen them. It's been crazy with people wanting to discuss the alien signal."

"Same here, I can assure you." Esther sounded tired. "Potentially intelligent life has grabbed the entire world's attention." Papers shuffled in the background. "Listen, the reason I'm calling is to learn more about the algorithm you used."

"Oh, that's Kate Braddock's thing. She's the coding genius, not me." He chuckled, then added, "Say, Dr. Whitt just asked me about her too."

"Really, when was that?" The tone in her voice changed ever so slightly.

"A few minutes ago, right before you called. He pinged my campus line same as you and told me what they've been testing in the lab. That's what I wanted to talk to you about."

The comm was silent for a moment.

"Dr. Tyrone, are you still there?"

"Yes, I'm still here. Just a little confused, I guess, but nothing you need to worry about. Tell me more about your conversation with Dr. Whitt."

Atteberry relayed the main points of the discussion he'd had, how the testing protocols were positive but still inconclusive, and whether he could stop by the lab in the morning. Dr. Tyrone remained silent.

"And that's when he asked me about Kate." He heard Dr. Tyrone breathing lightly on the other end of the link. "So I'll tell you what I told him: Kate wants nothing to do with sharing her code with anyone. In fact, she's a little embarrassed by all the attention."

"Why do you say that?"

"She gets really nervous whenever I ask her to join me, whether that's for the Astronomical Society presentation or meeting you people at the TSA." Mary came tumbling over, sat on Atteberry's knee and leaned into him.

"Curious. I wonder if she'd speak with me about that? I'd love to meet you and Kate and open up the algorithm itself, see how you came to analyze this signal. It's important, Jim. We need to understand her code and its significance."

"Well, I'm game, but not Kate. She likes to keep her work her own private business. But tell me," he said, "what's so difficult about understanding her code?"

"The encryption is challenging, Jim, so basically we can't test it to make sure it's free from programmer bias."

"But Dr. Whitt said it works."

"Yes, it *functions*, but I'm sure you understand the importance of a line-by-line analysis to ensure that what you heard is real in every sense of the word. It doesn't take much for a small error to propagate through a system and cause havoc."

Atteberry reflected on the number of calls he'd fielded since his ugly presentation at the society. Each person wanted to know whether the signal was real; whether we remained alone in the universe or not.

"Yes, I get it that no one officially wants to state we're not the only intelligent creatures around. That said, there's one way to prove the signal is true without knowing Kate's code."

"What's that?"

"Send a signal back to Ross 128 and see what happens."

Dr. Tyrone said nothing. Instead, Atteberry listened to her gentle breathing and papers rustling on the other end. Mary tried suppressing a giggle and smiled at him.

"Well, that's not a position we can abide officially. I take it you support full and transparent first contact with alien species?"

Mary nodded and, before he could speak, she blurted out, "He sure does!"

"Sorry, Dr. Tyrone, that's my daughter, Mary, who *ought to do her homework now, right*?" He gave her a mock-frown.

"Oh, hello Mary. My name's Esther."

"I figured," she said, "Dad talks about you all the time. Bye!" She slipped off Atteberry's knee and returned to the recliner.

"Well, so much for formal introductions."

"She sounds delightful. I'd love to meet her someday." A pause. "Look, I'm afraid I have to run, but we'll talk again soon."

"Sure, I'll ask Kate about joining us but can't promise anything."

"I'd appreciate it if you could try, Mr. Atteberry."

"Please, call me Jim."

"Okay, call me Esther."

"Haven't we done this before?" Her voice smiled, and yet, something in the way she spoke revealed an odd, distant quality. Mary's interruption? Maybe Kate's wish to stay out of it?

Atteberry cut the link, crossed the room, and kissed Mary on top of her head. She looked at him and said, "She sounds nice, Dad. Is she?"

"I think she's one of the more fascinating scientists I've met."

"How come?"

"Well, she has this awesome old telescope in her office, and she studies the stars with it over the Pacific. There's a massive wall of books there, too. Not just science stuff either, but real books. The kind we read."

"Science is real, Dad. We've had this conversation."

"Just kidding! No, but really, she's an interesting woman."

Mary pushed the recliner back and found her tablet down the side of the chair. "Well I like the way she talks. But she sounds sad, too, doesn't she, Dad?"

He brushed a few long strands of hair from Mary's face. "It's hard to understand what people have gone through in their lives, kiddo. You can't be sure about what they've lost or experienced. Just like us."

He returned to the radio bench and called Kate. In a second, she appeared on the televiewer wearing a loose-fitting denim shirt and sweat pants.

"Hi Jim, hey Mary!"

Mary waved from across the room.

"Have you news from the lab rats?"

"I have, Kate. I guess it's still not conclusive yet, but so far they tell me there's no reason to believe the signal is fake."

She flopped on her couch, grinning. "Well how about that," she said dryly, "I'm in the presence of a space hero."

Atteberry chuckled and brought her up to date with everything Esther and Dr. Whitt said to him.

"So, real alien life, eh?"

"Yes, but the TSA won't confirm the findings and may never. You can imagine how skittish they are about first contact."

"Sure can, they're a no-risk organization. But I can tell you as a friend, Jim, I don't trust them at all. Hidden agendas are everywhere, and motivations exist that you may never have considered."

"Okay, but like what, some internal politics? That's routine crap at the college."

Kate's smile disappeared. "It's more dangerous than that, Jim. I mean, look what they did to me and the others like me. We were no older than Mary when…" Atteberry turned around but Mary was fully engaged with her tablet, ear buds in, foot tapping in the air. "Sorry, I wasn't paying attention."

Atteberry lowered his voice and said, "It's okay, I remember those times too. That war brought out some of our most evil human traits." He pictured soldiers in the streets, doublespeak, neighbor against neighbor, then shook himself back to the subject. "They really want to understand your code, by the way. They both asked about it."

"Ha! I don't doubt that, but I enjoyed putting one wicked encryption on it. They'll never crack it."

"I know, so here's the problem: They're confident the algorithm works fine for pulling coherent signals out of the noise, but they can't verify whether there's bias in it unless they see the code. It's one thing to detect a pattern, but it's another to analyze it fully so that what I recorded was the actual transmitted signal and not some Heisenberg anomaly."

"That won't happen."

"I figured, and I won't press the point, but I wonder if you'd be at least interested in meeting Esther Tyrone and talking with her about stuff."

"Not gonna happen, Jim."

"I'll be there too. We'll just chat about things. Esther—Dr. Tyrone—just wants to meet you."

"No can do." She sat up on the couch and looked at him sharply. "Wait a sec, how did they know about the encryption? What did you show them?"

Atteberry looked around nervously. "All I did was spend a couple of hours there. We hooked the filter box and the algorithm up to their equipment and listened to the subspace bands. I showed them how to drive it. That's all."

"Really?"

Atteberry felt a hot pain in his stomach. It rose in his face. "No. I'm sorry, Kate. I left it all with them. Obviously, they poked around—"

"—and that's how they discovered the encrypted code." She paused. "Jim, I trusted you to keep my program away from those bastards."

"I'm sorry, but what harm is it? And it's critical to know the truth about Ross 128."

"You'd make Machiavelli proud, my friend."

Atteberry scrambled to lighten the mood. "Well, at least they didn't get past your encryption so they couldn't steal your work."

"Jim, seriously, do you think this is about intellectual property? You don't understand! I used a top secret war-time encryption routine on the code, one that is highly effective but one I agreed not to use when I left the program."

Atteberry's heart sank as the full weight of her message hit him.

"We used encryption codes like that in the war all the time. The Spacers, I mean. And when we could finally leave, they made us agree never to use any of the things we developed for our own personal or commercial use, blah blah blah."

"Kate, I never realized this. Do you think anyone suspects?"

"Oh, I'm sure Whitt does. Did he tell you what he did during the war?"

"No."

"Look into it some time. He may not remember me, but I remember him. Now, I don't know this Tyrone woman, the name's not familiar from my time in the Service, so she was probably a civilian all her career."

Atteberry squirmed in his chair and doodled on his notepad. "Kate, I really am sorry and I'd hate myself if this ruined our friendship. I need you to keep me straight, focused, so how can I make it right?"

"Let me think about it and we can talk again tomorrow." She hesitated before adding, "I shouldn't have written that program in the first place, so that's on me, but please get everything back, especially the code. Yeah, especially the code."

"I will. Anything else?"

Her voice darkened. "Do you know the penalty for breaking this international agreement with the Service?"

Atteberry was familiar with the nasty rumors surrounding rogue Spacers, but they were nothing more than stories, urban myths.

"The best I could hope for is losing my career."

"If that's the best, what's the worst?"

"The penalty for a treaty breach like this is death, Jim."

SIX

Whitt

"Good morning, Esther, you're in bright and early today." Marshall Whitt hovered over her at the long blue row of soft leather chairs in the Pi Pit. She looked like she had slept little. That made her vulnerable, of course. Yet, he found her plain looks attractive, alluring, the cropped, shoulder-length hair and full breasts under a dark green sweater vest.

"Truthfully, Marshall, I was up reading last night and before I knew it, it was early morning." Whitt sat down beside her, and she crossed her legs, holding a mug of coffee. "Marshall, there's something bothering me about our call yesterday evening."

"Oh? What's that?" He only half paid attention as a couple of young female grad students entered the rest area, laughing.

"Yesterday, I said I would call Jim Atteberry and ask him about meeting with his programmer. Then, when I was speaking with him, he mentioned you'd already talked to him about the code and the meeting."

"Yes, so?"

Her gaze locked on him and Whitt saw more of that focused resilience and inner strength that had solidified her reputation as a tenacious researcher. She could latch on to an idea like a pit bull and not drop it.

"Marshall, let's be clear. I don't know what your Nietzschean game is here and frankly, I don't care."

Whitt felt his cheeks flush.

"But if you continue to undermine my authority and responsibility for Ross 128, I'll come after you, no holds barred."

Whitt's smile faded, and he spoke quickly. "Esther, please, what are you talking about? If I put you in an awkward position somehow, I apologize. I'm not in the habit of playing politics with colleagues or anyone else."

Her steady gaze remained fixed on him and her breathing was quick and shallow. She was in a fighting mood and he needed to diffuse the situation.

"That discussion with Atteberry, I swear, just hit me randomly. I was studying his work, and I'd forgotten about asking you to call him. I was distracted and just absentmindedly picked up the comms. Really, I didn't intentionally go behind your back."

Esther finally broke eye contact, and Whitt relaxed his shoulders and sipped his coffee. Her light perfume tickled his nose, and he closed his eyes.

"Anyway," he said, "we've more important matters to discuss. Can you join me in the lab?"

They left the rest area and walked to the elevator bank, Whitt leading the way. Once in the lab, he took her to the workstation where Atteberry's equipment sat, uncovered. He rolled a chair over for her and they sat down.

Whitt flipped through his notes from the previous day's testing. "Esther, how much do you remember about the Spacer Program?"

She looked at him quizzically. "Spacer Program? Pre-civil war era indoctrination of gifted kids, wasn't it?"

Whitt picked up his coffee and leaned toward her in a plotting pose. "Yes, but it was so much more. They recruited these kids, spayed and neutered them like animals, trained them up in various disciplines, and sent them to work in dangerous radioactive space environments."

"Sure, I met a few at a bar in Paris just after the conflict ended." She sipped her coffee. "Strange that the warmongers used human beings instead of robots for that work."

Whitt eyed her closely with a hint of suspicion. What was she doing in Paris, post-war? Everything had a reason behind it, including her recent appearance in the TSA—an outsider. "Well, robots performed many functions, but the Spacers were a special group. Young adults did things robots could not. During the war, muddled leadership of the program caused all kinds of problems. Some units fell under the Northern Dems and others went with the Confederates. Some kids were abandoned on the lunar scientific lab, not sure who they belonged to anymore. It was a complete disaster management-wise." He put his notes down on the desk. "But that's not important. The program's covert field operations on Earth included chemical and bio-warfare, radioactive bio-mass experiments on live humans..." He thought for a moment, then continued. "Also programming and encryption of strategic comms."

Esther raised her full eyebrows. "And you think Kate Braddock's encrypted code is like this?"

"Spacer encryption code has a certain... distinguishable odor. I recognized something in it immediately, but couldn't place it right away. I can now."

"Hm." Esther stood up and leaned over Atteberry's filter hooked up in series with the radio astronomy receiving apparatus. She did not seem impressed or interested in what he'd just told her.

"Esther, I sense you don't appreciate how troubling this is for me. If Kate Braddock used Spacer encryptions to hide her algorithm, what else has she been doing? Do you understand that when the war ended, these freaks were sworn to secrecy? We couldn't afford falling into live conflict so soon after signing the truce."

She turned. "*We*, Marshall?"

He lifted himself up to face her. "Esther, I've no idea what you did during the civil war, but many of us here in this lab, in this academy, were directly involved in strategic military operations. On both sides. Because we put science and knowledge ahead of politics, we work well together and the past is, thankfully, left behind."

"So what's the problem?"

She still didn't get it. Perhaps he needed to slow down again. "Esther, if Kate Braddock's encryption came from the Spacer program, she's violated the treaty conditions between the Northern Democratic Union and the Confederate States."

Esther's jaw dropped. She hadn't realized the implications at all. Perhaps it wasn't fair to expect her to, given her lack of direct involvement in the war. Most civilians enjoyed resuming their meaningless lives, establishing governance systems for the new nations, including the independent republics like California. "Marshall, that's a lot more serious than I had imagined, and I'm sorry about that. It's imperative we speak with Kate Braddock right away, before any military forces do."

Whitt nodded. "We're on some very thin ice, Esther. What began as a simple curious signal intercepted by an overzealous amateur astronomer, now has geopolitical implications in more ways than one."

She eyed him sharply. "Are you saying the signal is authentic?"

Whitt hesitated and pieced together his words carefully. "My gut says yes, it is an authentic signal. If access to the code was provided, then I'd know for sure."

"Atteberry will be over the moon happy when he hears that."

"Indeed. He barely contained his enthusiasm when he was here the other day. But, Esther," he lowered his voice, "even though I think Ross 128 is authentic, I don't know whether the sender actually transmitted atomic numbers, or whether their intention was to find water. That's what makes understanding the code vital to our next steps."

Esther looked at him closely, and he fought to keep his face straight, but he knew she could see through it.
"So the problem here is two-fold," she said. "First, we have an authentic alien signal which, as soon as that's confirmed publicly, will reignite the UN First Contact Protocol mess all over again. I think we understand Atteberry's stand on that."

"Yes we do."

"The other issue is more immediate. If Kate Braddock broke the North American Separation Treaty by using outlawed encryption codes, her actions will surely be revealed in the news about Ross 128. Militaries on both American sides will want the technology, not to mention our own congressional force. Don't forget the other nations, too. China, Russia..."

Whitt eyed her carefully. "There are spies everywhere, Esther, representing all kinds of interests. We have no idea what's going on right under our noses."

"That part isn't new, but exposing Kate Braddock as a rogue programmer will surely lead to her imprisonment."

"Or worse. There's never been a recorded breach since the signed treaty a decade ago. Both Americas have watched each other carefully to ensure the treaty remains intact."

"But we aren't the Americas."

"No, still the California government won't allow the Republic to be drawn into a diplomatic shit storm either."

Esther's indie-comm pinged. "Damn it, I've got this call with Brussels in a few minutes." She ran her fingers gently over the radio equipment, caressing the corners. "Marshall, we can't let this go public. Not yet at any rate."

"That is my position as well."

"But we also have a moral responsibility to our leadership and the world to release our findings on Ross 128. Janine and I can't keep these media people waiting much longer."

My thoughts exactly, he mused. "Let's close the circle, Esther. Just you, me and one of the techs if that's all right with you."

"Yes, of course, and Atteberry?"

Whitt grimaced. "We need vigilance. He seems chatty and eager, but I don't trust him to keep quiet given his view around first contact."

Esther hesitated. The lab was filling up with workers, and she gazed over the machines, listening to them churn to life, then back to Whitt. "Okay. But not for long, Marshall. We've got to act soon."

Whitt smiled thinly, then walked her back to the elevators in silence. He could trust Esther to keep quiet now, and that was his goal the moment he saw her in the Pi Pit.

She stepped into the elevator and disappeared. He returned to the workstation, inhaled the comforting, sweet smell of warm circuits, and thought about Kate Braddock's mysterious past. It was possible he met her years ago through the Program, who knows, there were so many of them. Didn't matter now: she was in his sights.

Whitt scrolled through his indie-comm contact list and pulled up a private link. He hadn't spoken with Levar Jackson since the war, but this was one of those urgent times they'd agreed would require a conversation. He punched in Jackson's number and exhaled.

Atteberry

A LIGHT RAIN FELL AS JIM ATTEBERRY GLIDED TO THE Terran Science Academy's main entrance in his hovercar later that Friday afternoon. The drops speckled the dusty pavement and pocked tiny puffs along the dry garden beds. He grabbed his briefcase, commanded the hovercar to park, and bounded into the TSA lobby.

Esther Tyrone waited by the security desk, her hands folded in front of her. She handed him his security pass and led him up the escalator to her office.

"Are you nervous about this meeting?" she asked, motioning him to sit on the couch.

Atteberry spied the British Scientific Romance anthology on the table and picked it up reverently. "Yes, of course, more excited than you could imagine. If the test results are poor, we wouldn't be having this conversation."

Esther sat across from him. "That's true." Her indie-comm pinged, and she glanced at it. "Dr. Whitt is on his way up with your equipment."

Atteberry only half-listened. He was browsing through the anthology when the bookmark at Forster's story caught his eye. "You like these old gems, Esther?"

"Oh, yes. They breathe innocence and foreboding, hope and dystopia."

"Like Shelley's *Frankenstein*?"

"Sure, but I prefer Wells, when the discipline of modern science emerged."

"Perhaps we should get together and talk about our favorite books one day, Doctor."

Esther smiled at him politely. Then Dr. Whitt entered her office and her smile disappeared; suddenly she looked weary.

"Mr. Jim Atteberry, welcome again." They shook hands, and he continued, "I've left your gear outside the door here."

"Thank you, Dr. Whitt, I'm eager to get listening again."

Whitt sat down beside Atteberry on the couch and undid the button on his sport coat. He also looked serious and all business. Atteberry wondered how people could do that, switch emotional gears so effortlessly. One minute, deadly professional. The next, cracking jokes with each other at the bar.

"Well, I'm happy you're sitting down, Mr. Atteberry, because what I have to say is arguably the most significant discovery in the history of mankind."

Jim Atteberry leaned forward, hands shaking and looked at Esther. She averted her gaze.

"The test results are in and they prove with remarkable certainty that the filter and algorithm you used to hear the Ross 128 signal last week work."

Atteberry clenched his fist in victory and squeezed his jaw hard. Esther studied Dr. Whitt.

"But before you get too excited, please remember the following: There are two major challenges we're facing right now."

"I know. Whether to contact the aliens or pretend they aren't there."

"Jim," Esther interrupted, "it's not that simple. Please let Dr. Whitt finish. Marshall?"

He thanked her and continued. "First, your filter pulled something out of the noise that we confirm is a coherent signal, but, there's no evidence showing that what you *heard* is the same as what was *sent*."

"Wait, how do you mean?"

"You claim you picked up a series of taps or scratches, and interpreted them as atomic numbers."

"Yes, there's no other logical explanation."

"That only makes sense, Mr. Atteberry, if what you received is precisely what was sent. It's possible the pattern recognition code introduced bias, so you got exactly what you were looking for."

Atteberry shook his head and shrugged his shoulders. "Impossible."

"It's quite common, especially in less sophisticated decryption algorithms. These programs need baseline data, a frame of reference, and that input typically comes from the programmer."

"I don't see what the problem is, Dr. Whitt."

Whitt glanced at his notes and spoke slowly. "Well, this is the reason it's critical for us to speak with Ms. Braddock so we can understand what bias exists in her code."

Atteberry's frustration replaced the joy he'd experienced a moment ago. "So, is the signal real or not?"

Whitt looked at Esther, and she picked up the conversation.

"It's like this, Jim: You heard something the other night. But whatever's responsible for it has been quiet. No one else detected anything resembling your pattern at all, just random static crashes or charted pulsars. The entire network has been focused on Ross 128, but we're still scanning all subspace frequencies for anything remotely like it, and there's nothing."

"I heard it, Esther."

"And I believe you did, Jim, I do. So we've moved on to investigating whether the signal was a random anomaly of unknown origin, or if it came from an intelligent alien life-form."

Atteberry reflected on this for a moment. It's true there had been many reports over the years of amateur radio enthusiasts detecting unknown signals. They were dismissed as noise or later refuted with new evidence. That's what happened with those Ross 128 signals in 2017. For a few days, people wondered if astronomers had found a true alien signal, but the transmissions were later attributed to Terran satellite activity.

"Okay, so what's the other problem?"

Whitt answered. "The second challenge is in the interpretation itself. Let's suppose no bias in the algorithm exists, and what you heard is what was sent. You interpreted that as atomic numbers, the chemical symbol for water. Now then, if an alien ship or world was transmitting *water*, what could that mean? No interpretation method exists for a message like that."

"Not true," Atteberry said, "this kind of relational analysis and extrapolation takes place all the time in the literary world." An awkward silence fell over the room. "Esther, Dr. Whitt, what would have to happen for you to accept the Ross 128 signal is real?"

Dr. Whitt cleared his throat. "Simple. We'd have to record that same signal again, but just as importantly, we'd have to decrypt your filter code and find what bias is in there so we can assure ourselves that it's valid."

Atteberry rubbed his beard. "There is another method to prove the signal is real without decrypting the code." He smiled, but he was deadly serious.

Whitt's voice rose. "No, we're not even going to consider a subspace transmission. You misunderstand what contravening the UN First Contact Protocol means."

"I know we can't just hide under a rock and hope that no one sees us."

"Oh, but you're wrong, Mr. Atteberry, you're so wrong about that."

Atteberry felt the tension rising in the office. He figured Dr. Whitt must be holding something back, maybe some other reason for not trying to contact the Ross 128 aliens. He briefly remembered how long it would take a conventional signal to travel back and forth to Ross 128: 22 years.

Whitt finally broke the silence that permeated the room. "Well, I—we—don't want to keep you any longer. I'm sorry I can't give you a more definitive conclusion on the testing, but the uncertainties are overwhelming. Perhaps some other day, you may receive your little signal again."

Whitt and Atteberry stood up.

"Thank you again, Dr. Whitt, for all your efforts."

"It was my pleasure. Now, please keep all this to yourself. If there's going to be an official statement made about Ross 128, it will come from us, understand?"

"Completely."

They shook hands and Whitt left. Esther remained seated on her chair. Then Atteberry pivoted. "If you have a minute, may I ask you something, Esther?"

"Of course."

He hesitated and looked over her collection of books again. "It's funny you don't have a larger collection of science fiction, you being a scientist and all."

"Well, don't misunderstand, I love science and everything about it, the discipline, the complexity, the experimental method and discovery. But I'm just not a big fan of it in fiction. I'd rather read the old Victorian stories. They speak more to my sense of..." Her voice trailed off as she watched Atteberry turn his head so he could read the spines.

"Jim, you don't honestly want to talk about my reading preferences, do you?"

He turned to face her again and the way the grey light from the grey day hit her grey eyes as she sat there made his heart jump. Atteberry, to his great surprise, blushed like he was suddenly back in high school again. "No, as much as I'd love to, it's something else."

She smiled curtly.

He continued, "Esther, I was wondering if you'd like to go for a coffee or a sandwich sometime. You know, just to talk about things. For fun."

Esther stood up without saying a word and studied his face. He noticed she did something with her thumbs and index fingers, rubbing them together lightly, a nervous habit, perhaps.

He tried to lighten the tension in the room after meeting Dr. Whitt. "What do you say, Esther? You, me, a couple of lattes and an hour to kill?" He smiled at her, but she remained resolute and stoic.

"No, Jim. Sorry."

Esther

ESTHER ESCORTED JIM BACK DOWN TO THE LOBBY without a word spoken between them. She felt it would take him forever to leave her office, but that may have been more a reflection of her own discomfort.

He looked like he'd been smacked in the head, all sad-eyed, brave-faced, silent, distant. She hated to refuse his coffee invitation, but it was the right decision to make before her emerging feelings for him impeded her objectivity.

When they arrived at the front lobby door, Esther smiled at him as warmly as possible to let him know everything was okay, an unspoken signal that everything was still good. He had difficulty meeting her eyes, which only made her feel worse. She recognized that same sensitivity in herself whenever she mustered up the courage to ask a colleague out on a date or even just an evening at a show, only to be rejected. It stung. Bad. She still wasn't used to professional criticism of her work either, but at least she could persuade herself it was all to improve the findings. How is a personal rejection the same? It's not.

Instead of going back to the office, Esther rode the elevator down to Space Ops for a quick follow-up with Marshall. She strode onto the main floor and found him talking with a couple of techs near the quantum simulator. He dismissed them, and came to meet her at an empty office where he pushed a whiteboard covered in differential equations away so they could sit.

She established her space with him, up close and personal so that Whitt had to crane his neck. Even with her modest heels, she was still several inches taller than him and knew how to use the height difference to her advantage. She pulled her shoulders back.

"So, Esther, was that a good meeting?"

"Sure, nothing unexpected. He clearly had no desire to talk about our valid concerns. Why, if we left him on his own, he'd be chatting with the aliens about his day in the classroom and sending reconnaissance vehicles to greet them."

He scrambled away from her, sat down, and threw his legs up on the table. Esther sat with her back rigid.

"Well, Atteberry is a passionate fellow, and although I don't agree with his style or his position on first contact, we need people like him out there in the field, so to speak."

"Agreed. Imagine a lab full of that enthusiasm. Harness his energy, and we'd get all kinds of new research done."

"Yes, yes, well let's see if he does anything. I don't trust him to keep quiet, but I'm hoping he'll talk to Braddock and somehow she'll come out of the cold and work with us."

An autoserver whirred by and Esther picked up an apple; Whitt took a mug of water. They conferred on what Jim Atteberry said, and how he reacted to the findings.

"Either way, Marshall, we should plan a formal announcement on Ross 128 early next week. I'll call Janine and set up a bull session for Monday when I get back upstairs."

"Perfect. Yes, I think we want to say the signal came from an unknown source, apparently in the Ross 128 system, but not likely alien intelligence. That conclusion is familiar to the media, and they'll accept it with little fuss."

"Right, well, I'll be on my way, Marshall." Esther stood up and marched toward the elevators.

"Just a moment, Esther, wait for me." Whitt jumped up and joined her part way on the floor. He touched the top of her forearm briefly with ice-cold fingers. She turned to him. *Now he invades my personal space. Clever.*

"Esther, I'm curious. What did Atteberry say after I left?"

She watched him carefully and saw the corners of his narrow eyes move. "Oh, nothing to do with this. He asked me out for a coffee and, I'm not sure why, but I refused."

"Okay, I see. Because you know, we cannot keep secrets from each other on this. No side conversations, you understand."

"Yes, Marshall. You should know me well enough by reputation if nothing else that I always put the best interests of science and the TSA above my own. Only Jim Atteberry knows what he wanted to discuss over coffee, and I wasn't interested enough to find out."

Whitt dropped his arm from hers and they continued walking to the elevator. "Good, good. I'll wait to hear from Janine about Monday, then."

When the elevator doors shut, Esther sighed deeply and relaxed her shoulders. She leaned against the shiny chrome wall. Funny how Marshall had so quickly forgotten humiliating her after he asked her out for drinks and pulled a no-show. That had all the signs of a power play, a message for her before she settled into her new position. She'd been dumped and ostracized enough, heard the boys and men snickering in hallways before she showed up and they all went silent. *No side conversations.* Indeed.

Jim Atteberry, however, did things differently.

Esther click-clacked across the lobby to the escalator and rode it back to her office. Once there, she closed the door and sat down at her desk.

"Marty?"

"Yes, Dr. Tyrone?"

"No disruptions for the next half hour please."

"Yes, Dr. Tyrone."

Questions surrounded Ross 128, and global interest in this signal was more intense than in any other event for a long time. It'll be important to keep the media informed, to be open as much as we can be with them. Whitt was right, as he often was.
They both understood the high stakes at play.

Jim thought differently on this, too. The first contact proponents like him said it was our responsibility as galactic tenants to forge ties with all alien neighbors no matter how strange. The reasoning was, she smirked, that if the bogeyman followed you, whistling in the dark would not help. So naïve.

Yet, he came breathing life into the exploration for intelligent life like none she had encountered, maybe even breathing life into her, too? *No, Esther, let's not go there.* Declining his little coffee get-together was necessary for her to keep her objectivity and focus on the work—this was no time to get distracted. Perhaps after Ross 128 blows over, she could take him up on his offer. *That's what I should have said. Damn it, Esther, how could you be so stupid sometimes? How difficult is it to take a rain-check?*

Then there's the matter of the wedding band he wears. It may mean nothing since the institution of marriage disappeared a generation ago, but it did to her. Perhaps it meant something to him too? He still hadn't mentioned a wife or girlfriend in the picture, only his daughter, Mary, and she found that out by accident. Perhaps Kate? Possibly, but not likely.

Esther, this is exactly the kind of thought train you don't want to board. You made the right decision. Now, let him go and move on.

SEVEN

Atteberry

"Earth to Captain Dad, come in, Captain Dad. Over!"
"Hm? What is it, kiddo?"
"I said: Can you pass the salad, please? Over."
Jim Atteberry handed the wooden serving bowl filled with the greens to Mary, and she smiled. "You're not entirely here, are you, Dad?"
"No, I guess not. Have you ever had one of those strange days where your mind wanders all over? Elbows off the table, please."
Mary sighed that pre-teen sigh she'd picked up at school this year. Funny the first time, not the hundredth. "Yeah, sometimes." She finished spooning the salad onto her plate. "Like when I'm

really thinking hard about something, a math or science problem, my friends laugh at how totally spaced out I look."

"Well, that's where I am now. Do you want to hear about it?"

"Sure!"

Atteberry told Mary about the meeting with Esther and Dr. Whitt, and how they both agreed the signal was real, but unlikely from aliens. He didn't mention asking Esther out for coffee. Mary focused on picking at her supper.

"So after the test to make sure the equipment worked, they still couldn't say whether the signal was from aliens."

"But you heard it, right?"

"Yup."

"And they don't know where it's from."

"Yup again. Please, Mary, elbows off." He shooed his hand at her.

Mary grinned mischievously and Atteberry rolled his eyes, exasperated.

"Well, perhaps they're right, Dad, I mean, Marjorie Welsh from Seventh Grade and her group of idiots were bugging me about it today, calling you a weirdo or something. I didn't pay much attention to it, but maybe there isn't anything there? It is a possibility, isn't it?"

Atteberry felt a spark of rage sweep to life deep in his gut, and he gently put down his knife and fork. "Mary," he said looking straight at her, "are kids at school making fun of you because of me?"

"A little, but it's no biggie, Dad. Kids tease other kids all the time. I think it's 'cause they're jelly."

"Why would they be jealous?"

"Because their dads aren't nearly as amazing as mine."

Later that evening, while Mary read in her bedroom, Atteberry sprawled out in his giant recliner in the basement,

THE CRYING OF ROSS 128

staring at the network of pipes and wires on the ceiling. The low thrum of the power supply at the radio bench was the only sound he heard, other than the odd intermittent knock and bang of the house's bones settling in for the night. It had been a heck of a week, and he finally had a chance to catch his breath.

What Mary had said over supper, about the scientists and the signal, stuck in his mind. No one else had heard it, and interest in the story was slowly waning. But if it was real, ah, if it was real, then it would completely change the way we see ourselves. It would have to.

He closed his eyes and breathed deeply. Perhaps if he could convince Kate to give her code to them, it would alter their findings; but she'd have nothing to do with that. Asking her for more help was out of the question now that he'd put their friendship in jeopardy. The weight of remorse still hung on him like Marley's shackles.

Early snippets of sleep glittered over him and his mind wandered. That weirdness with Esther was strange, too. He sensed she liked him, and what was the problem with grabbing a coffee together? Just as importantly, Mary liked Esther, too, and this wouldn't even be a date date. One thing nagged every thought he'd had the rest of the day: that old familiar awkwardness around women he hadn't experienced in years, since before Janet.

Janet, where did you go? Their evening chats together and slow walks along the Pacific were fading memories, and with Mary growing up so fast, she'll need her back soon, or at least—

The gentle signal alert interrupted his near-sleep. When he opened his eyes, the computer screen shone with brilliant lines of data scrolling top-down, along with the graphic analyzer displaying all the frequency variation, carrier wave and modulation data. The muted audio didn't stop him from recognizing the visual pattern of the one-one-eight taps.

He leapt up and cranked the audio volume. The basement filled with a massive scratching sound, like someone shoveling a pile of crushed stones.

Chicka.

Chicka.

Chicka Chicka Chicka Chicka Chicka Chicka Chicka.

Mary jumped out of bed and ran down the hall. In a second she stood beside him and grabbed his arm, and the two of them gawked at the monitor and listened to the alien signal spill through the noise from 10.8 light years away.

"Dad, is it recording?"

"Yes," he said calmly, "And look, Mary, do you see the signal frequency on the screen?"

She looked over at the graphic analyzer. "It's the same as last time, isn't it?"

"Yes, the same pattern again, too."

Atteberry's indie-comm pinged. He reached into his pocket and recognized the call code from the TSA.

"Mr. Atteberry, is that you?"

It sounded like the young tech who escorted him in to the Space Ops Lab earlier that week, the same pimply faced young man who helped with the initial testing. Was it Bart or something?

"It's Mark Jefferson from the TSA calling. We met earlier this week? I'm a grad student working with Dr. Whitt."

"Yes, Mark, do you hear this?" Atteberry raised the indie-comm and waved it around his head. Mary laughed and doubled up, her hands on her knees.

"Sir, are you there?"

"I'm here, Mark!"

"Okay, good, good. Dr. Whitt is here, and he says to come to the lab right away. We're analyzing the signal on our own quantum simulator. Can you hear it in the background?"

Atteberry covered his other ear and listened hard. It was clear, the identical one-one-eight pattern came through over the indie-comm. He picked Mary up and gave her a big spinning hug, and she laughed, raising her arms in the air, just touching the ceiling joists.

"Mr. Atteberry?" Pause. "Sir?"

"Mark, are you saying you have independently validated the Ross signal?"

"Um, yes, that's what we've done. Sir, it's a real signal, and it's the same pattern as you heard before."

Atteberry held his breath and closed his eyes, dizzy with the hundreds of images flashing through his mind. "How confident are you about that?"

There was a long pause, full of fumbling and strange noises, the clamor of people shouting, and he imagined the chaos unfolding in the cavernous lab.

Finally, Mark spoke. "One hundred percent, sir. There's no doubt about it."

EIGHT

Atteberry

CHILLS SHOT UP ATTEBERRY'S SPINE AND THE HAIRS on the back of his neck tingled like fire. His eyes filled with tears and his knees weakened. He put Mary down and she bounced over to the radio bench.

"There's one more thing too, sir," Mark added. "We're triangulating the signal and, well, it's still too early to tell, but—"

"Ross 128? Can you confirm Ross 128?"

There was another pause on the link. "Not yet, sir."

"What do you mean, Mark? Spit it out."

"We're using the ice station on Ganymede and the Martian exploration base to triangulate, but it will take several hours before we can say definitively. Still, it sure looks like it's from Ross 128."

Atteberry sat down at the radio bench and trembled. Mary squealed but it sounded like she was a football field away, his thoughts a muddle of *what ifs* and *holy shits*. His mind raced, overwhelmed with what to do next: confirm location, send messages back, determine the exact nature of the alien communications and life-form. Then what? In some ways, the easy part was done: finding concrete evidence of intelligent life in the universe. Imagining ourselves as unique or alone was over. Strangely, the story of Genesis flashed through his thoughts.

"Come on, Dad, you've gotta go to the space lab!"

"Yeah," he said as he pulled out of a daze.

"Can I come too?"

"No, I'll call Evie's parents to see if you can spend the night at her house."

"A sleepover? Yes! Let's go!"

The two Atteberrys flew up the stairs. He called Evie's parents, then pulled his briefcase together and linked his indie-comm with the radio receiver. Mary threw some pajamas and a book into her backpack while Atteberry summoned the hovercar.

He gathered his things in the hallway and opened the front door. Mary pushed past him into the night as the hovercar glided silently into the driveway. When the car's lights swept across the lawn, something ducked behind the bushes one house over. At first, he felt the urge to dismiss it, jump in the hovercar and get going, but the prehistoric part of his brain screamed at him, and he paused.

"Hurry, Dad!"

"I'll just be a second."

Atteberry strolled out towards the end of his driveway and stared down the street at the shadows. He waited, hands in pockets. Mary sang in the car, and the street pines whispered as a light evening breeze whistled by. He waited, unmoving. Watching. Listening.

There it was again.

A movement. A quick sound. More, much more, than a cat would make. Atteberry felt the adrenaline rise and course through his body, the fast-twitch muscle fibers at the ready, the full suite of his senses standing by. He ran up the street when, in front of the bushes, a dark figure lunged out—face shrouded, black gloves on—and bolted up the street until the dark night swallowed him.

Mary screamed, a chilling, unnatural sound. It filled the cool air and trailed away into silence. He tore back over the lawn and pulled her from the car, then held her tight, her body shivering, not like from the cold, but an involuntary reaction to terror.

"It's okay, Mary, it's okay. I'm here."

In a moment, she pulled her head off his chest and looked at him with raw fear in her eyes. "Who—who was that, Dad?"

"I can't say, but you're safe now. Let's stay home together tonight, okay?" He carried her back into the house and placed her gently on the living room sofa, then wrapped her in the hand-knit blanket Janet had made. But for all his stoic outward confidence, Atteberry couldn't get comfortable. He sat with his daughter for a moment, fidgeted, got up and paced around the room, stopping to peer out the big bay window from time to time until his adrenaline dissipated.

Who could be watching him? The internal motion detectors still blinked normally, so the house appeared to be secure. He didn't own a gun, never wanted one in the past, but now he was having second thoughts. If anything ever happened to Mary... He banished those thoughts.

"Can I get you anything, Mares?"

"No, thanks, Dad."

To avoid creating any more anxiety, he smiled, downplaying the event and said cheerfully, "Well, that was something different, wasn't it? I mean, really, who wants to sniff those beautiful chrysanthemums at night?"

Atteberry sank down beside her again and she snuggled in. Many groups and individuals engaged in open surveillance like this since the two Americas fell into a cold war. Each side felt threatened by the other; each side desperately struggled to control what their people read and saw. That old thinking was next to useless in an open society, but it didn't stop governments from subterfuge, sprinkling misinformation around and watching their own people. The dark figure could easily be from either of those jittery republics.

Or, perhaps the shadow represented corporate interests. The multi-national conglomerates made no secret of their desire to exploit whatever they could find in the galaxy. It was in their capitalist DNA, and they would pay handsomely to be the first consumers of a new, alien world.

Whoever it was, whatever the motives, all that was irrelevant: he had no doubt the figure poked around for one reason only, and that was Atteberry's initial discovery of a cry from space.

"I'm going to call Kate. She's super smart and will know what to do."

Mary clutched on to him when he tried to get up for his indie-comm on the table.

"I'll be right here, Mary."

Kate linked through on audio and he filled her in on the latest signal, along with the watcher in the bushes. "Thoughts?" he asked.

"Oh hell, I don't know, Jim, but I doubt anything good can come of it. What did the cops say?"

"The cops? I didn't bother reporting it. No doubt they get hundreds of useless calls like this all the time."

"It wouldn't hurt to get your encounter on the record."

Atteberry thought about that for a second and conceded she was probably right. "Okay, first thing in the morning, I'll give them a shout." Then he added, "The TSA guys validated the signal using a quantum simulator, by the way. And I have your algorithm."

Her voice perked up. "That's interesting... a quantum simulator. They must have used the Ross signal to calibrate it."

"But I thought that would add bias, wouldn't it?"

"They made an assumption, Jim. Instead of trying to validate last week's signal by analyzing my code, they assumed what you copied was true. Then they used that knowledge as input data to calibrate the Q-Sim. They needed a baseline, and your findings gave them one."

"Okay, but if there *is* bias in your code, wouldn't it just propagate through to the simulator?"

Kate snorted. "Sure it would, but there's no issue with the code, Jim. It works."

"How can you be so certain?"

"Trust me on this. Just like how I'm convinced Whitt and his cronies are behind that creeper sniffing around your home."

"What?"

"Yeah, it wouldn't surprise me one iota that your new TSA buds are keeping an eye on you. And as far as the code goes, it works, Jim. What can I say? I know what I'm doing."

Atteberry couldn't argue with that. While her background as a Spacer remained redacted across the Calnet, there was no questioning her ability as a programmer or as a teacher. She was the brightest in the department.

"So," she said after a moment of silence, "congratulations, my friend, you did it! There's proof we're not alone. That's amazing. You'll be in all the history vids now."

His thoughts returned to the scope of this discovery and how confirming extra-terrestrial life was the simple part—the next actions were critical.

"Kate, I'm not interested in that sort of thing. What drives me now is making contact. Surely, we must try to establish comms with whoever's out there. And if the signal is a plea of some kind, we've gotta help them."

"It's not Terran policy to invite bug-eyed space monsters over for drinks, remember?"

"I know, Dr. Whitt reminded me of that, but the lawmakers drafted the old policy under theoretical conditions. It's real now, Kate. Contact has been made, and that changes everything. I'll talk with Esther Tyrone again and see what she thinks. Maybe she has some pull over there to convince them of contacting Ross 128." He looked over at Mary and saw she'd fallen asleep after all the excitement. "Listen, I gotta go put Mary to bed. It's been a crazy night."

"Sure thing, my friend. Take care of yourself and Mary, okay? The first time you heard that signal, no one really believed you and it was all science fiction space opera fun and games. But it's real now, Jim, and it's obvious you're getting noticed by some powerful players. Apparently being spied on, too."

"I can handle power plays, Kate, and I can hold my own against ambitious types."

"This isn't minor league campus politics crap, Jim. You don't understand what governments and their militaries are capable of doing and justifying. No idea."

Atteberry realized, again, that Kate was right. She'd lived it before and had deep physical and emotional scars to prove it, but he believed most people were fundamentally good, even if they were prone to the evil lurking under their skin. Ross 128 was not just another civil contact/no-contact debate. This discussion carried dark undertones with it, and his family was at the center of it.

"I'll be careful."

He carried Mary off to bed and sat on the chair by the tidy dresser for a few moments, listening to her soft breathing. He really should call the Space Ops Lab and let them know he wouldn't be coming in, and that last thought bubbled through his mind until it buffeted against the tug of sleep on his eyelids, and drifted away.

Saturday, October 6
Atteberry

THERE WERE FEWER VEHICLES IN THE TSA RECHARGE AREA than he expected following confirmation of intelligent life in the universe. On his way to drop Mary off at Kate's, Jim Atteberry monitored the world news stations but there was no mention of the Ross 128 signal. His hovercar eased along the sidewalk to the main entrance and lowered gently to the ground. Atteberry stepped out, and the car ascended and whirred off to recharge with the others.

Mark, the grad tech, met him inside the lobby and escorted him down to the Space Ops Lab. Dark circles bagged his eyes and his hair was all disheveled. The elevator doors opened up in front of the lab, and Atteberry smelled low-level ozone and warm circuits immediately. He followed Mark into the huge room and through a handful of workers and strange-looking equipment to the radio astronomy workstation where he'd been the week before. This time, however, the bench held additional equipment—spectrum analyzers, scopes, a heavy duty power supply and cables running from it across the floor to a large trapezoidal prism-like machine in the center of the room.

"What's that?" Atteberry asked.

Mark followed Atteberry's gaze and said, "Oh, that's the quantum simulator. It wasn't here the last time you were."

Atteberry had heard of Q-Sims being used to scramble messages in military communications, but the technology remained mysterious.

Dr. Whitt arrived at the workstation a moment later. He also looked exhausted and there was a coffee stain on his shirt. "I'm glad you could make it, Mr. Atteberry. What an exciting 12 hours it's been around here!"

"I can imagine. I didn't sleep much last night."

"Sorry to hear your daughter wasn't feeling well. I trust she's better this morning?"

"Yes, thanks."

Whitt offered him a chair and the two men rolled up to the computer interface on the right of the main receiver. He increased the audio gain and the now familiar scratches echoed off the walls. "It hasn't stopped all night."

"I know. I've been recording it at home." He looked around the room again. "Excuse me, Doctor, but where is everybody? I mean, I thought this place would be hopping."

"Ah, yes," he said, "well, the news about Ross 128 has not been released and I've made sure that only a few others in the Academy are aware of what happened last night. To everyone else, it's just another Saturday morning."

Atteberry frowned. "Why's that? This is the most exciting news in Earth's history!"

Whitt studied his face and spoke, choosing his words carefully. "That's what makes it so dangerous as well, and the real reason I wanted you here last night."

"What are you saying?"

"Mr. Atteberry, I recognize you don't have experience working in the scientific industry so this may come as a mild shock. The moment we release this news to the world, the entire academy will likely be shut down, taken over by competing military forces or worse, destroyed by terrorists or fanatics."

Atteberry scoffed. "Surely you're paranoid. Our forces could protect the work here."

"The Republican Security Forces are no match for the two Americas, or the Chinese or the Russians or the Argentinians. Any one of those groups could take us over, not to mention the homegrown ass-wipers."

"Nations would not go to war over this. Ross 128 is cause for celebration, not conflict."

"So you're a geopolitical expert now? Come, come, Mr. Atteberry, don't be so naïve. The only reason we're here chatting today is because I haven't told anyone what we found last night. Except for these two techs," he waved his arm around the room, releasing a shot of body odor, "and you, no one else knows what happened here."

"Are you including my daughter, too?"

Dr. Whitt's eyes narrowed, and he looked over at one of the analyzers. "Yes, I suppose so."

Atteberry considered mentioning that Kate also knew, but decided against it. "What about Dr. Tyrone? After all, she's the director responsible for SETI."

"Esther doesn't know yet. I left a message earlier for her to come in today on this matter, so I'll apprise her shortly. "

Mark squeezed under the one of the workstation's side panels, and Dr. Whitt made a point of not saying anything. Atteberry agreed he didn't comprehend the kind of pressures facing scientists to find military applications of their work, but the Astronomical Society had debated the issue without resolution a few times over the years. It was an issue that only came up because of the civilian network of sky watchers who were rightly sensitive to any dangers associated with their hobby.

After Mark went back to the Q-Sim, Dr. Whitt continued. "It's extremely important that from here on out, we keep this news to ourselves. Unfortunately, Mary also heard the signal, so you must make sure she doesn't discuss it with any of her colleagues at school."

"You mean her friends."

"I believe that's what I said."

Mary was a strong, independent, and smart kid. She saw rules and instructions as guidelines rather than laws, much like him, and she wouldn't do anything to jeopardize him or their security. Atteberry said, "Sure, she'll keep it quiet if I ask her to."

"Good. Now then, I imagine you're interested in seeing how we decoded the signal with the Q-Sim. Mark will walk you through that." He got up to leave and motioned for the tech to come over. Atteberry remained seated.

"Dr. Whitt, thank you, I am thrilled about all this, but I have to ask. Does this mean you won't be sending a signal back to Ross?"

Whitt stood straight in front of him, but even so they were almost eye to eye. His pleasant, professional demeanor flickered, revealing a momentary sneer. "You already know we won't," he said. "Even if the entire planet knew about Ross 128, we wouldn't attempt to contact it. That would contravene the UN First Contact Protocol, remember?"

"Oh I remember, Doctor, but paranoid lawyers developed that protocol when intelligent alien life was just a concept, a theory, a big *what if.*" Atteberry got to his feet and looked down on the scientist. "It's real now. As human beings we can't pretend our world won't change no matter what the official UN position is. Besides, that signal is a voice, a *real* voice. The message is *water.* We have a moral duty to respond."

Dr. Whitt did not back away. Instead he leaned in. "The truth is, we will not contact the aliens. Full stop. But if you want to consider *what if* scenarios, think about this: You choose to tell the news to the world. First thing people ask is, 'What does the TSA say?', and we say, 'Well, there is no signal and this college teacher is severely under-qualified to be claiming there is.' Do you see?"

Atteberry narrowed his eyes with equal parts frustration and rage.

"They would ask other organizations about it, and the answer would be the same thing: We have heard no signal from Ross 128. Of course, that's the truth because they don't have access to the only Q-Sim on the planet calibrated to decode the message."

Atteberry's jaw worked silently for a moment before he said, "But I'd show them my equipment, and prove it that way, and you couldn't stop me."

Dr. Whitt put his hands in his pockets and rocked on his heels. "That's where you're wrong. Oh, I suppose if you really wanted to jeopardize your career and maybe even your daughter's safety, you could scream and shout from a soapbox. But you won't do that."

"Why wouldn't I?"

Whitt leaned forward, close to his shoulder, and whispered. "Because you and I both know your friend Kate Braddock used outlawed encryption codes in her algorithm that contravene key clauses in the North American Separation Treaty. I make one call to the authorities, and Ms. Braddock will never be seen or heard from again."

Atteberry's heart sank and a wave of guilt washed over him again. He couldn't believe he'd left her program with this guy, and now her life was in real danger.

"Do you understand now, Mr. Atteberry?"

He knew he was beaten. "Yes, I do."

"Good!" Dr. Whitt looked over at Mark who had been keeping his distance from the two men. "Mark, show our visitor how the Q-Sim works and walk him through how we detected the signal last night. I'm sure he'll find it fascinating."

He followed Mark and feigned interest in the simulator, but his mind focused on how to make contact without jeopardizing Mary and Kate. Suddenly, a sick feeling bubbled in his stomach that quickly overshadowed his guilt about Kate's code: he didn't remember telling Whitt his daughter's name, so *how did he know she was called Mary?*

NINE

Whitt

AT 10:29 THAT SAME MORNING, THE ALIEN TRANSMISSION ABRUPTLY ENDED. It had been received for over 14 hours and the two techs in the Space Ops Lab heaved a great *Whoop*, the customary ritual after a successful project or event. Whitt congratulated both of them, shaking their hands. They secured their work areas and went home for a rest, but not before he reminded them of their obligation to remain silent.

Esther had yet to arrive, so Whitt proceeded to inspect the Mount Sutro transmission site via remote link. He entered the Oxford Room and bio-scanned the computer to life.

THE CRYING OF ROSS 128

"TSA antenna array, Mount Sutro."

The computer pinged, and immediately a live view of the facility appeared on screen, with multiple camera viewpoint options.

Whitt found it remarkable this tower had lasted over a hundred years and still dominated the city skyline like a spindly-legged giant. He isolated the views of the highly directional UHF and VHF antennas on the north side of the apparatus. Everything looked in order from a visual inspection. Then he investigated the radio room itself at the base of the tower and punched up the operating specs of the subspace transmitter. It was running in standby mode, as usual, and all operating parameters showed normal.

Still, two years had passed since the orbiting Oxford array was used for faster than light transmissions. He punched up the array coordinates on screen and studied the eight satellites configured in a 30 by 30 kilometer honeycomb pattern. The mothersat followed about ten klicks away. It was a simple array using classic radio interferometry to target signal sources. The mothersat acted as a data collector and relay station, and the essential piece of equipment that needed regular testing for handling transmissions. The array worked efficiently for receiving and relaying subspace signals back to Earth, as evidenced by the multitude of radio operators listening in around the world, but sending faster-than-light signals into space was a more delicate operation.

Whitt ran a mock transmission by synching the subspace transmitter at Sutro with the mothersat, and calibrated both uplink and downlink comm frequencies. To send a signal to a target 11 light years away would require significant beam coherence so he computed the required array parameters. He estimated the alien signal source frequency to be 70 hertz, and that's what he chose for his simulation. A test at that ultra-low frequency had

never been performed previously, but he punched it to run for 30 seconds and the system handled it with no glitches.
So if I wanted to contact the aliens, I could do it.
Being the first man in history to communicate with alien lifeforms filled his head with grand ideas. The inevitable research money meant nothing to him: that would be a given. It was the recognition and freedom to run a fully-funded lab for a change that drove him, to be a pioneer, an influencer in the course of Terran history like no one since Jesus. But of course, he would not violate the protocol. Not yet, at any rate. Not until the time was right.
A barely audible double-ping on his indie-comm interrupted his thoughts. He'd been expecting this call.
"What can you tell me?" he demanded.
Levar Jackson's voice on the other end of the link sounded rough and tired. "Is the comm secure?"
"Yes."
"Good. The target house is now live and bein' monitored. Equipment synched, so there's nothin' he can do with his radio apparatus that we won't know about in real time. Target's indie-comm is also live and monitored. The target spotted one of our guys last night, unfortunately, but no further action is required. Operation is fully green."

Esther

ESTHER DIDN'T WANT TO LEAVE THE COMFORT OF HER BED. Marshall had pinged her at five in the blessed a.m., waking her from a dark, dreamless sleep, something about coming in to the lab as quickly as possible, but she discounted him, shaking off the dregs of last night's wine and *Moll Flanders*, and rolled back to sleep.

The other ping on her indie-comm at 9:45 got her attention. It came from Jim Atteberry, and that's when she realized they must have picked up that Ross signal again. Shit. The duvet flew off and she jumped out of bed. Within ten minutes she was in her two-seater, floating fast toward the TSA.

She dabbed on light makeup as the car glided over the hills and cruised along the flyway. Marshall's ping, well, he could wait. Jim's message said *"Urgent"* and *"Please,"* and that's the one she wanted to answer first.

"Ping Jim Atteberry"

A chime sounded as the link with Jim connected. Esther put him on video mode and saw he was also in a car, but not moving. "Hi Jim, sorry I didn't get back to you sooner. Bit of excitement this morning, hm?"

"It's really something, isn't it? Confirmation of the Ross 128 signal!"

Esther was at once surprised and not. This is exactly what she'd anticipated and concluded Marshall's message was the same. Yet she couldn't let Jim know she hadn't heard the news already and hoped her body language didn't betray her.

"Yes, Jim, it's something. Where are you now?"

"In the parking lot of a Grinders. I need to speak with you, Esther."

"Sure, come by the Academy. I'm on my way there now." But Atteberry hesitated, his face full of concern and, what else was that, fear?

"Could we chat for a few minutes here? I'll send you the coordinates."

Esther thought briefly that this could be a cynical ploy to have that coffee date she dumped back at him and her expression changed. "Okay, send them over."

The Grinders coordinates pinged in to her car and it asked her to accept the course change, which she did, and they turned right at the next intersection. Later, when she strolled into the coffee shop, the smell of roasted beans and sugar smacked her senses. Jim, wearing a golf shirt and jeans, stood up from a booth and waved her over. The autoserver scooted up to the table, and she grabbed a classic dark, heavy on the cream.

Jim looked awful. His bird-nest hair and previously trim beard were a mess. Smiling, she brushed a crumb off his face with her thumb.

"Were you up most of the night?"

"Yeah, I got the call from Dr. Whitt's assistant to get down to the lab. Mary and I were already listening to the signal at home."

"But it hasn't hit the media yet."

"No, and that's something I'd like to discuss."

Esther thought that a bit odd, given that Jim made it a point to be open and transparent in all things. At least, that's the impression she got from watching him these past couple of weeks.

"Esther, I think we need to contact the aliens despite what the protocol states."

She grimaced. This was a big juicy bone for him. "You understand the problem with that, Jim, no matter how much sense it makes?"

"So you agree with me?"

"That's not what I said. Whether we should isn't my call. The point is, as a civilian science shop reliant on government funding, we're duty-bound to follow the rules." The coffee shot through her veins, erasing the vestiges of a mild hangover, and she found her stride. "The pressure on the Republic to turn leadership of this over to India or China will be immense. Any decision about anything to do with this comes from that level, not you or me."

"Okay, but listen, we're also duty-bound as citizens of the Earth to make contact. We can't just pretend we're not here, especially if this really is a distress call."

Esther read the desperation in his face and he looked considerably older than he did last time they met. *If he's aged that quickly, imagine what I look like.* She stole a glance at one of the large wall mirrors in the shop and quickly turned away.

"It's not that simple. The arguments against first contact are sound, logical. They've all been debated ad nauseam for years."

"Esther, it's like I was telling Dr. Whitt this morning. The UN wrote the First Contact Protocol when none of this was real. It reflected war-time thinking and a great fear of the unknown. Times are different now. The signal is real and we're ten years beyond the American conflict."

"The cold war between those two is also real."

"Okay, but we're not them!" A couple eavesdroppers were watching him, so, leaning forward over the table, Atteberry lowered his voice. "What better way to demonstrate the good that can come from people working together? And what better way to show the universe what it means to be human?"

The passion he exuded over first contact appealed to her in all ways, touching her deeply. A lightness crept over her heart accompanied by a sense of conflict between her feelings and rational duty. "I get it. There's solid potential here, but don't be impatient. I totally understand Marshall's position about keeping this news quiet for now and not causing panic. It's a prudent, precautionary approach."

Jim smirked. "You sound like a civil servant."

"That's because I am one. So are you, by the way." She smiled, and they both laughed, locking eyes in a singular moment.

Jim broke away first. "There's something else going on, Esther."

"What is it?"

He hesitated, struggling with his words. "I don't know if I should tell you this."

Esther's face changed. The lightness dissipated like morning mist. Something was up and she suddenly felt the need to be vulnerable in front of him.

"It's okay, you can trust me."

Jim breathed deeply. "I'm being watched. Well, I'm pretty sure I'm being watched."

"The hell?"

"Last night, Mary and I were about to leave, and I planned to drop her off at a friend's house, then get down to the lab to analyze the signal."

"What happened?"

"Some guy was hiding in the bushes. When I confronted him, he tore up the street and disappeared."

Esther ran through a mental list of potential suspects. "I don't know what to say."

"Is it possible, Esther, that the TSA was checking up on me?"

She sipped her coffee, considering the question. That didn't sound like any TSA security operation. Their teams were open about what they did, and who they needed to check. "I doubt it, Jim, we don't operate like that. Perhaps it was corporate. You know what these tech companies are like, always sniffing around for the latest innovations. I'll bet that's who it was. Too sloppy to be a professional."

"I'm wondering if I'm safe. If Mary's safe."

"Did you call the police?"

"Not yet."

"Start there." She downed the last of her coffee and played with the mug handle. "If they do nothing, you could always hire someone to keep an eye on things, at least until the news goes public."

"Yeah, I don't think so." He cocked his head. "I'll see if anything more comes of it now that I spotted this creeper."

Esther checked the time on her indie-comm and collected her purse. "The TSA beckons, and I should check Marshall isn't drowning in paper and shit." She smiled again, and he returned it in a charming way. She'd done well to keep her cool and be professional until whenever these school girl feelings disappear. They left the booth, headed out to the pick up area and waited for their cars.

"By the way," she asked, "how is Mary? She seemed like a fun kid when we were on the link a couple days ago."

"Oh yes, she's something. All grown up one minute and the next, she's playing with her stuffies." He looked around and scratched his beard. "To tell you the truth, Esther, I'm worried. This watcher last night really shook her up, and some days, I... well, you don't need to hear my fears as a single parent."

Esther gulped.

"A dad can only do so much. It seems like every day, more and more, she aches for her mother."

The two hovercars pulled up, one after the other, Esther's in the lead.

"Jim, I don't want to sound intrusive or out of line, but I'd love to meet Mary one day." She blushed and looked down at her sneakers, waiting for the response she hoped to hear. When nothing came, she glanced up at him expectantly.

Jim fidgeted opening the car door and wouldn't meet her eyes. "I have to go."

Atteberry

ATTEBERRY GAZED OUT THE HOVERCAR WINDOW, SEEING NOTHING, thinking about Esther and Mary as he banked around corners and other cars on his way downtown to Kate's apartment. His stomach was off, and he desperately needed more sleep. The news about Ross 128 had shaken him. The implied question Esther asked about meeting Mary surprised him and added to his emotional burden.

Stepping out of the car, he stared up at the glass tower, all 48 reinforced, earthquake-resistant storeys, then entered the building. He boarded the elevator, punched 30 and held his breath until the harsh smell of cleaning solution disappeared. Kate opened her door and welcomed him in. Normally she wore no makeup, and he liked that authenticity about her, but today there was a hint of color on her lips, causing him to do a double-take. Mary was off in the other room playing on Kate's computer.

"I showed her some programming tricks I built into a game for my students," she said. Jim raised his eyebrows and smiled. "She's been chattering away in there for the past hour." Sure enough, he picked up snippets of the little conversation she was having with the computer screen.

"Kate, thanks again for watching her."

"You're welcome! I'll do it any time I can."

They walked over to the sofa and she sat cross-legged, facing him as he stretched out.

"Jim, forgive me for saying, but you're a mess. You need to get some sleep."

"Sure, but there's too much happening. I'll take a caffeine speeder in a while to help me focus."

Kate eyed him cautiously. It was those nasty little speeders he relied on too heavily last year that messed with his mind, his work.

"Don't worry, I've got this covered."

"Sure, no sweat, but you can always crash here if needed." She had an idea. "Listen, you and Mary want to stay for lunch?"

Mary, with her bionic ears, screamed from the spare room, "Yay!"

Atteberry lowered his voice and mumbled, "I don't think we can, Kate. The signal ended an hour ago and there's tons of data to review."

Kate shrugged it off and said, "What happened at the lab this morning?"

Atteberry ran his fingers through his hair, tilting his head back. "I got there and Dr. Whitt only had a couple techs working. It was eerily quiet, like a morgue or something. He said there'd be no announcement, and then all the low-key activity made sense."

"I see."

"They picked up the signal with a Q-Sim they'd calibrated using your algorithm, just like you told me. No one else in the world, presumably, received it, just me and the TSA."

"I was afraid of that."

"Why? Is that a problem?"

Kate exhaled through clenched teeth. "I'll bet Whitt told you not to tell anyone, right?"

"Right, but I said Mary was aware because she was with me when the signal started."

Kate suddenly had a fearful, unsure expression on her face.

"No, Kate, don't worry. I didn't say anything about you or last night's conversation."

She reached over and squeezed his shoulder. "That was the right decision. Whitt will hide the news as long as possible under the excuse of not being sure of the findings or not wanting to cause a panic in the streets. I've seen him do it before."

"How do you know him? Was he part of the Spacer Program or something?"

"Not exactly," she said, "but he constantly buzzed around the group like a fly, trying to jam himself into different projects. He wanted to run a team himself, but was late entering the war and never got a chance. Still, he's a brilliant physicist and a talented code-breaker, no doubts about that. He wrote virus codes for the Confederates in the early days of the cold war, too.

"But you don't trust him."

Kate stared daggers and hissed, "Not one bit. Whitt's a narcissistic creep who will do anything for power, so I hope you're being cautious."

"I am."

She frowned and stood up, admiring the view overlooking the Bay, then put her hands on her bony hips. "You know, Jim, you can see the TSA from here." He got up and joined her. "See?" The curving low-rise grew out of the Golden Gate Park like an extension of one of those massive tree canopies.

In a moment, Kate turned. "I've given this nocturnal visitor of yours more thought."

"Oh?"

"Do the police or anyone else know about it?"

"Only Esther Tyrone, and Dr. Whitt."

"Hm, you may not want to raise it with the cops after all. Not all of them are trustworthy, and when the news gets out about the alien signal, all hell will break loose on this dumb old planet, right? So you should stay close to the people you know and trust."

"Like you."

"Yes, never forget that."

Atteberry remembered the first time they'd met. It was at the campus bookstore. She was lost and broken, and he'd put her at ease, even helped her find a place to live, and asked no questions about her past.

"Thank you."

Mary suddenly whooped, and yelled, "What are you guys talking about out there?"

They both smiled and Atteberry shouted, "Super boring grown up stuff, kiddo." Then he held Kate by the shoulders, and the protruding bones beneath her shirt echoed her fragility. "I owe you so much. Whatever you need, just call."

She nodded and pursed her lips. "Jim, I have to ask how well you know Esther Tyrone? Could she be the spy?"

"We met a couple weeks ago, and I like her a lot. She's friendly and smart, loves books. Spying doesn't seem to fit."

"That makes her perfect for the espionage racket, then. Do you trust her?"

Atteberry appreciated that Kate had a knack of getting right to the questions that plagued him most and put them into words he could understand. For an English teacher, he often stumbled over them like a drop out.

"I can't say yet, but when I asked her out for coffee, she said, 'Get stuffed.'"

"Really?"

"Okay, not in so many words, but I got the distinct impression she wasn't interested. Then, with Ross 128 blowing up again, we get together for coffee before she goes to the TSA, and says she'd like to meet Mary some day. I don't get it."

Kate stared over the bay's horizon at a pair of large ocean-bound freighters crawling out from port, heading west. "I've heard nothing about any involvement in the conflict or post-war skirmishes, so I don't think she's connected to the military like Whitt."

"That's good, right?"

"It is. Still, sleepers are everywhere."

"I like her, Kate."

"Undoubtedly, and that's another reason to exercise caution." She picked up his hand, and they gazed out the window, alone in their own thoughts, with Mary giggling and chattering in the background.

Atteberry chuckled and said, "I asked Mary a while ago if she'd be okay with me dating."

"Oh, how'd that go?"

"She didn't like it at all, thinks I'm betraying Janet even though she's been gone two and a half years." Mary squealed again from the other room.

"It doesn't seem to be a problem now."

"Yeah, well, I agreed just the two of us would stick together from now on. I'd be okay to have friends, but not dates."

Kate put a hand to his cheek. "Jim, you're beautiful, and it's okay to struggle like this, but if you want to go on a date, Mary will understand. She may resist at first, but she'll come around."

"Suppose I kept it to myself?"

"No, no, don't shut her out. I remember what it was like to be a girl at her age until I wasn't any more. She worships you, and keeping secrets would end that fast."

Atteberry sighed and suddenly felt tired. "I wish Janet was here."

"I'm sure Mary does too. But Janet's gone, for whatever reason, and I doubt she'll ever be back. But even if she crawled home one day, it wouldn't be the same, would it?"

Atteberry played out the mental experiment and struggled with his own need to trust. "Probably not."

"Tell you what might work: patience! You've introduced the idea to Mary, now let her live with it. Instead of going on a date, invite Esther over for a coffee as a friend."

"That's twice today I've been told to be patient."

"Remember how much Mary loves and needs you. Honor that. A 'date' is a threat. A 'colleague,' not so much. Look at us, for example."

Kate hugged him as Mary tumbled out of the computer room, face red with excitement, eyes wild from being in the flow.

"That was the baddest thing ever, Kate. Thanks for showing me!"

"You're welcome, squirt."

"Are we staying for lunch? Please, Dad?"

Atteberry smiled and hugged Mary, full-on bear style, unable to imagine his life without her, or without Kate, who helped him stay tethered and true. It wasn't just brotherly love that he felt for her, although he certainly did care a lot. No, when Atteberry felt her breathe and touched her hand, the world seemed safer.

"Sure, Mares, sure. There's no place I'd rather be right now."

Whitt

LATER THAT SATURDAY EVENING, THE HALLWAYS OF THE Terran Science Academy were dark. However, no natural light could enter the Space Operations Lab, so day and night often melted into each other and the terms became meaningless. This was one of those nights.

Whitt paced around the Oxford Room, head down, stroking his beard, fighting off the profound lack of sleep, and ruminating. So Atteberry's keeping quiet for now, but Jackson's bug on his indie-comm showed movement. An apartment building downtown. A Grinders earlier that morning where he met up with Esther. Curious, she hadn't mentioned anything about it when she arrived at the lab.

Something on the computer screen flashed and caught his eye. The antenna satellite array icons still fluttered in near-real time since he pulled them up that morning, but the lines of data racing down a secondary monitor had stopped. The *PROCESSING* button blinked. *This is it.*

"Mark, put this on the main screen viewer."

Whitt peered out of the Oxford Room at the massive screen covering two-thirds of the lab's back wall. In a second, the image from the Oxford monitor flickered on.
And now we wait for the final confirmation.
Mark was the only tech remaining from last night's Ross 128 Discovery Team, a name Whitt coined when they decoded the signal. He shuffled over to stand beside Whitt and watch the PROCESSING button as it spun and chugged along on the large screen.

"Tell me, Mark," Whitt began, "did you ever think you'd be part of a team discovering intelligent life in the universe when you came here from Wisconsin?"

"No, sir, um, no, this is still a lot to gather in."

"Indeed. Well, I always found the trick is to stay focused on the task at hand, and keep working the problem, working the steps, and the distractions fall away."

Mark took off his glasses and cleaned them with the bottom of his lab coat. "Yes, thank you, sir. Good advice." He exhaled deeply. "This is it, eh?"

"Yes, Mark, any second now we should have the Ross 128 signal coordinates." He turned and looked up at the tech. "Any guesses where it came from? There's at least one Earth-like planet orbiting Ross, if you recall."

"That would have to be my guess, sir."

"Mine, too. It makes sense, wouldn't it?"

The two men remained silent for the next couple of minutes, watching the screen. The heavy duty power supplies feeding the massive servers hummed along, expelling faint wisps of ozone.

"What do you think the message means, Dr. Whitt?"

"The so-called *water* signal? Well, the jury's still out on that. Mr. Atteberry's deduction was rather brilliant for a non-scientist. I dare say he's probably got more talent than a lot of the idiots around this place." Mark smiled and looked away. "And at first blush, it makes sense to communicate through atomic numbers, but I really want to give it more thought before jumping to any conclusions. We don't want to release the wrong information."

"But what if it's true about being H_2O?"

"Let me ask you this, Mark." He turned to face him. "If it is true, and if we're ever permitted to contact them, what message would you send?"

Mark scraped his heel along the smooth concrete floor. After several minutes, he finally shrugged his shoulders and said, "I don't know. If the only tools we have are atoms and simple molecules, our options are severely limited."

"True, but don't give up so easily. A sentient, intelligent life out there is sending a message of water to you, so how do you respond?"

Mark scratched his head.

"Consider how toddlers learn words, Mark. Mom or Dad points to an object, perhaps a tree, and says 'tree,' then the kid says..." He opened his arms expectantly.

"Tree!"

"Excellent, you see, you don't have to over-think this. The aliens may be looking for water, drowning in water, targeting water—who knows? But if we want to assure them we can hear, we should be like little Earthling toddlers, yes?"

Mark grinned and nodded his head. He was a smart young man, Whitt thought, just needed some more confidence.

"I suppose we could also send back another simple molecule. Perhaps something with carbon in it to let them know that we understand chemistry, too."

"Now you're getting it. We send back H_2O first to establish contact. Then maybe a simple carbohydrate molecule—CH_2O or something. A chemical bread crumb, so to speak."

The computer in the Oxford Room behind them pinged and their attention returned to the big screen. A three-dimensional model of the Ross 128 dwarf star system appeared and a thick red triangle glowed next to the Ross 128b planet, colored green. At first, Whitt figured they were right, and the signal was coming from that rocky world, but then the triangle shifted positions.

"Mark, is that drift due to spatial corrections?"

"No, sir. We expect minor variances, but not on this order of magnitude. I can zoom in for a closer look but we'll lose some resolution."

"Yes, do it, Mark. We need to figure out what we're looking at here."

Mark skipped to another computer he'd been working on earlier. The image faded, followed by a representation of the 128b planet's curved horizon appearing against the backdrop of the dwarf star. The icon hovered over the planet.

"Is that a spacecraft in orbit, Mark?"

"It has all the signatures of a craft, yes, sir!" Mark shouted from his workstation.

"It doesn't appear to be in a fixed orbit, however."

"Oh? What's it doing?"

Mark checked his data, punching codes into the computer. "It seems to be adrift, sir."

The triangle continued its random path through the space between the planet and the dwarf star. Mark re-joined Whitt and stared agape at the screen.

"Now what do we do, Dr. Whitt?"

"Nothing for the moment, Mark. We wait."

Concern snapped across Mark's face, and he said, "Should we contact them? I mean, if it is a ship that's adrift, crying out for water, shouldn't we try to help?"

Whitt felt his cheeks burn, and he faced the young tech. "In time, we will contact them. But only when it's safe to do so. Think, Mark. This could also be a ruse, a trick to find out where we are. Perhaps their intention is to do us harm."

"The protocol."

"Indeed."

"Got it. Okay, I'll call Jim Atteberry and tell him we've identified the source." Mark turned toward his workstation but Whitt grabbed his arm, stopping him.

"There's no rush for that, Mark," he whispered.

"But—"

"Come, let's work the problem of targeting a transmission back to that craft together." And he led the tech into the Oxford Room, outlining a list of things to accomplish prior to responding to the distant cry of Ross 128.

Sunday, October 7
Atteberry

JIM ATTEBERRY STARED OVER A STEAMING MUG OF COFFEE at the pile of overdue, unmarked writing assignments sitting on his kitchen table. Sunday mornings often eased into the day, running some errands, spending time with Mary and, when necessary, catching up on marking. But not today. This morning, he felt panicky.

His inability to focus on real work grew from the Ross 128 excitement, and he told himself that once the discovery became public, he'd be able to recommit to his work. That same reasoning told him the international governing bodies responsible for such important announcements would not keep this news quiet for long. The most challenging personal conflict facing him now was withholding the truth from others. Keeping secrets required enormous amounts of energy.

Mary padded into the room, rubbing her eyes, and sat down beside him. "You have to mark all those?" No good morning, just straight into the day's set of questions.

"Yes, but I'm having trouble getting started. I'm more interested in thinking what the aliens look like, how they talk, where they've been. Say," he smiled, "your jammies are inside out." She laughed and rocked back and forth on the chair.

"Mary, you remember what I said about keeping the alien signal to ourselves, right?"

"Yup."

"And you know how I hate having to keep secrets?"

"I do."

"Okay, so for a little while, it's super important to keep the aliens to ourselves even if it's a bit dishonest."

"Dad, I know already."

"Just checking, kiddo."

Mary got up and grabbed a bowl and the cereal box, made a mess pouring half the contents on the counter, and carried her breakfast to the table. Then she found milk in the fridge and poured a good measure of it on her place mat before hitting the bowl. "Don't look at me like that, Dad, I'm still waking up!"

"I'm going to have some cereal, too," he said.

They chatted about not much of anything while eating their breakfast. Mary came to life and bounced around, looking for her tablet, then, upon finding it, planted herself on the living room sofa in a blanket of fall sunshine streaming into the house. Atteberry took his pile of assignments and trudged down the stairs to his work space.

The power supply for the radio apparatus hummed along and Atteberry caught the sweep of the filter scanning the bands. Nothing had come in overnight. Work beckoned, and he sat down at the desk, picked a paper from the middle of the pile, and frowned at the title: *Moby Dick: A Whale of a Tale of Hope*. Goodness. Where to start with this mess? He stuffed it at the bottom of the pile and walked across the floor to the radio station.

THE CRYING OF ROSS 128

The Ross 128 signal dominated his thoughts. Were these creatures from the Earth-like planet in that system? What did they look like? Did they need help? How soon could one of our ships get there at normal space velocities? The answer to that last question was 11 years, give or take, at light speed, and we hadn't figured out how to compress space-time yet for travel. A rescue mission was out of the question, presumably, but if the aliens had subspace travel capability, then they could come here. We certainly had lots of water.

The lights on the receiver blinked faintly, but just enough to pull Atteberry's thoughts away from his daydream. The filter swept along the bands, data scrolled across the computer screen, and a few minutes later, the lights flickered again as if the entire system hiccupped. He timed the cycle on the computer clock.

The radio blinked again, same interval.

"Mares, are you there?"

"Yup!"

"Can you come here for a sec?"

She fell off the sofa and banged down the stairs.

"Have you been monkeying around on the radio?"

"No, Dad. Why?"

"Watch this."

The main VFO readout dial displayed the changing frequencies as the filter swept by, then it flickered and returned to normal.

"What is that?" Mary asked.

"I'm not sure. I wanted to check if maybe you'd been on it."

"Nope. Can I go back upstairs now? It's freezing down here!"

Atteberry nodded, and she raced back up to the sunshine. One thing he'd learned as a homeowner is that strange noises that appear suddenly were always caused by something, and they don't disappear just because they're ignored. He remembered the time a squirrel squeezed into the attic by chewing the crap out of the roof vent.

What caused the glitch in the equipment? He stopped scanning for signals and punched up a diagnostic algorithm on the computer.

"Full system check?"

"Yes."

"Processing."

The problem didn't take long to find: someone had introduced a line of blank code into the filter sweep function, or at least, a line of code he could not see. At first, he passed it off as a random artifact of interfacing with the TSA's equipment, but then believed it was something else. A virus, perhaps?

Kate was slow answering his call on the indie-comm. After several attempts, she appeared, audio only, and said in a slow, labored voice, "Jim, *Jesus*, what's up? I'm not even awake yet."

He'd forgotten she was a late sleeper. "Sorry, Kate, but listen, something's going on with my radio, possibly a virus. There's a mysterious, hidden line of code that I can't read, so I wondered if you could run some of your fancy remote diagnostics on it for me."

"Yeah, sure, as soon as I'm up I'll have a look at it. Send me your passcodes and I'll run it from here."

Atteberry fired off his access codes.

"Thanks. I'll give you a shout soon."

He went upstairs to get another coffee, and after he'd tackled a handful of papers, his indie-comm pinged. Kate again.

"That was fast," he said, "you find anything?"

"What you've got is a line of tracer code, Jim." She sounded like her normal self and was on the televiewer, appearing with glasses on and a big blue sweater.

"What's a tracer code?"

"Nothing inherently dangerous, just a common bug found in a lot of marketing subroutines, consumer machinery and such. The code tracks and records a user's activity, then transmits it to a third party."

Atteberry understood immediately what this meant. "So everything I've been doing on the radio, monitoring the stars, finding the Ross signal, it's all being seen by someone else?"

"That's my guess. I thought the glitch could be a nasty sleeper virus, so I looked into that but, no, it's definitely a tracer."

"Could this have happened when the TSA had my gear a couple weeks ago?"

"I doubt it. To place this code in a system, you either have to access the system remotely through all your security walls, or else *in situ*."

"You mean, physically where the system is, at my home?"

"Yes."

"But no one's been here. Why don't you think Whitt or one of his techs could have done this when they had your algorithm?"

"For the same reason they couldn't access my code. It's encrypted to hell and back. They wouldn't have a clue where to begin, not even Whitt."

Atteberry felt his heart race and his fingers shook a bit when he lifted his coffee mug and drank.

"I'll tell you what I think, Jim." Her notes flashed in front of the screen. "You remember that late night creeper fellow you scared away?"

"Sure."

"Perhaps Creeper Boy came back when you were gone, broke into your house, and planted the code on your system."

"No way, I've got security cameras and motion detectors everywhere. I would've seen something."

"Jim," she said calmly, "I could easily bypass your security if I wanted to. Those things are designed to dissuade teenagers and

Neanderthals from arbitrarily breaking in, not those of us who know what we're doing."

"I see."

"Listen, I'll come over in a while once I'm dressed and bring my sniffer gear to clean up your radio and computers. In the meantime, you'd better check your equipment again for anything missing."

Atteberry shook his head. A wave of anger, humiliation and fear washed over him. He kept putting Mary's safety at risk, and Kate's as well, and for what? Chasing an unknown signal across the sky? Time to drop this crazy business. His gut told him, however, that Marshall Whitt was behind it all, and he needed to find out why.

"Thanks, Kate, talk soon."

He cut the link and held his face in his palms. The ripples of this event kept pushing outward into the dark corners, and there was nothing he could do to stop it's spread.

TEN

Sunday, October 7

Esther

LATER THAT AFTERNOON, ESTHER TYRONE PACED in her small apartment like a caged animal, listening to Vivaldi in a sad attempt at self-distraction. Yesterday's brief meeting with Marshall at the Space Ops Lab kept playing over in her mind. When she'd entered the lab after recovering from Jim's abrupt dismissal of her idea to meet his daughter, everything was quiet, just like he'd said. Marshall puttered around in the Oxford Room overlooking the satellite antenna array and ran a series of simulations. A normal day, perhaps, except that it was Saturday when everyone other than grad students and post-docs were off doing other things. Marshall had been more aloof than ever, if that was possible, and her intuition screamed caution and to choose her words wisely.

Esther stopped pacing. So far so good. She hurried out to her small galley kitchen and made some tea, then splashed a good measure of rum in it.

Why can't you find someone, Esther? You're not making much of an effort. The rum-spiked drink went down easily. *Too old and tired, maybe. You put it off too long.*

"Increase music volume."

The concerto grew louder until she drowned in it, sat down on a chair, got back up again, and fixed her hair that no one would ever see in the front hall mirror.

They had spoken in the Oxford Room; that's when she officially heard about the discovery. Marshall reported all kinds of things about the Ross 128 signal, but how much of it was true, she didn't know.

He had insisted that he and Mark had it all under control, and that her job was appeasing the media and feigning a business-as-usual posture. Fine. But this manipulation of the Q-Sim, now calibrated to Jim's code—or Kate Braddock's code, really—as a way to work around the problem of encryption was brilliant, yes, and entirely underhanded. Marshall's desire to keep things as quiet as possible—even within the Academy—was not normal. No clear need for this level of secrecy existed. And what was Jim's role in it all?

"Stop playing."

The music immediately ceased.

"Play Chopin nocturnes."

Esther marveled at the grace and fluidity of the challenging melodies, and between the new music and the rum hitting her empty stomach, she finally relaxed and flopped on the large sofa.

THE CRYING OF ROSS 128

What bothered her most was the need to keep this discovery quiet. The significance of maintaining secrecy wasn't the issue. Rather, to hold this information from Dr. Kapour was, in her view, unwise. Kapour directed the damn Academy. He needed to know.

There was a time when post-detection protocols failed miserably, no matter how well-intentioned, because they weren't binding on nations or individuals, and astronomers couldn't be trusted to keep their yapping maws shut. In all the first contact scenarios played out in the '20s and '30s, individuals always defaulted to their own positions, resulting in a "Me first, the world second" attitude. Until the UN finally achieved acceptance of the new protocol in international law—and it took the Second American Civil War to make that happen—the search for alien signals harkened back to the gold rush days of nineteenth century America.

Those were dark days on the continent. Even though she hadn't been directly involved in the conflict, many of her colleagues were. The one lover she took in Paris—a frumpy biochemist named Levitsky—was pleasant enough but refused to discuss his work, yet enjoyed peppering her with a million daily questions. He lasted a month. When he got transferred to Buenos Aires and left without telling her, she celebrated quietly with a fine Merlot. It saved them both from going through the ridiculous ritual of breaking it off, pretending to be hurt, remorseful, and so on.

Esther downed the last of her tea.

"Stop playing." The apartment went quiet immediately.

"Ping Marshall Whitt."

Marshall's woolly face appeared on the televiewer. Behind him were several parked hovercars and vegetable stalls in the distance.

"Hello, Esther. How are you?" He didn't smile but continued to pack his bags into the car.

"Good, Marshall. Listen, quick question for you: it's something you said yesterday."

"Careful, Esther, I'm not sure the link is secure."

"Right." She cleared her throat. "I was just wondering why so much of this... event needs to be kept under wraps. I really think we ought to at least discuss this further with others in the Academy, perhaps beyond."

Whitt stopped what he was doing and looked at her through his indie-comm. "No, Esther, we've been over this. You know the risks. But if you want to talk about it more tomorrow, I'd be happy to meet you for coffee in the Pi Pit."

"I'd like that, Marshall. Thank you."

"It'll do us good to make sure we're fully committed to this course of action."

"Okay. I'll see you then."

Before she ended the link, he interrupted her.

"Esther, a moment, please. I'm curious."

"Oh?"

"Did Jim Atteberry ask you to call?"

Esther felt her cheeks blush and wished the call was on audio only. "No, why?"

"I wonder about such things, you know how I am. And you and Mr. Atteberry seem to enjoy each other's company, so perhaps you two had been chatting."

She felt defensive suddenly and stood up. "Marshall, what are you talking about?"

"I think you know, Esther. I'm sure it'll come to you, maybe over a coffee." The nasty, toothy smile told her that *he knew*, like he could read her thoughts.

"I'll see you tomorrow, Marshall." She cut the link before he could respond. *It's time to pick a side, girl.*

Had her comms been compromised? she wondered, because it appeared Whitt was watching her. The TSA-issued indie-comm looked normal and passed her quick diagnostic test. These were the most secure comms devices on the planet, but not beyond Marshall's influence. He seemed to have his pudgy little fingers in everything. Still, if he took the path of least resistance, it would be infinitely easier to watch her through Jim Atteberry's movements.

An overwhelming need to see him again sprung up, yet the sting of being rebuffed at Grinders remained fresh. What the hell, she'd call him in the morning.

Perhaps it was the drink that gave her the confidence, perhaps it was her heart's last gasp for intimacy. Either way, the day's curtain drew to a close for her even though it was the middle of the afternoon.

"Play from where it left off," she said, and pulled herself away from the televiewer. Music filled her apartment again, and she poured herself another cup. This time, without the tea.

Monday, October 8, 2085
Atteberry

HEAVY RAINS SLASHED ACROSS THE CITY, RUMBLING IN FROM the Pacific and rolling over the hills and bay. Jim Atteberry dropped Mary off at school, watched her splash through the puddles in her bright pink coat and hippo rain boots, then flew towards the Terran Science Academy. He taught at 11 and had a departmental meeting over lunch, so time mattered.

A long stream of hovercars released their riders at the front of the TSA, so Atteberry had to wait his turn. Thank god for Kate. She'd come over yesterday and cleaned out the code that caused the flickering in his radio equipment. Then she'd spent several hours with the computers, hunting for sleepers and tracers and anything else that looked suspicious, but there was nothing more. Whoever planted the bug in his gear focused on the radio alone, it seemed. Atteberry hadn't changed his mind about Whitt being behind it all.

In the short ten-second run from his car to the lobby, Atteberry got drenched. The wind whipped around the curved architecture in a compressed burst, and those with umbrellas found them to be useless accessories. He walked gingerly on the wet marble floor to the security desk. A new guy was there today, big, buzz-cut hair, no neck, and all business.

"May I help you, sir." Not a question. An order.

Atteberry brushed the water from his face and attempted a smile. "Yes. I'd like to see Dr. Whitt if he's available."

"Do you have an appointment."

"No, I was hoping I could talk with him for a few minutes. The name is Atteberry."

The security guard clicked away on his computer, punching the screen, entering things. After a brief moment he looked up and said, "Unfortunately, Dr. Whitt is unavailable today. Perhaps I can ask his assistant to arrange another time. We don't often accommodate drop-ins, you understand."

Atteberry grunted in frustration. A couple other visitors queued up behind him, shaking rain off their umbrellas, brushing their coats, waiting to get their access cards.

"Look, I'm pretty sure he'll see me. Would you please send a message that it's Jim Atteberry, and I only need a few minutes of his time."

"I'm sorry, sir, but like I said: Dr. Whitt is not available today. He's blocked off his entire day and isn't seeing anyone."

"You don't understand. I must speak with him." Then he lowered his voice. "Please, it's important."

Another man joined the line behind him. Busy place on a Monday morning. Atteberry briefly wondered if the news had gone out yet, then dismissed it.

"I'll send him a message that you're here, but I can't guarantee anything. If you'd like to wait in reception, sir, I'll get back to you if I hear from him." The guard peered past him to the woman in the hunter green raincoat next in line. Atteberry didn't move at first, then gave way to her as she pushed ahead of him.

He gazed around the lobby, up the escalators to the third floor, then called to the guard, interrupting his bio-scan for the green coat. "What about Dr. Tyrone? Is she available to meet?"

"Sir, please, I'll check in a moment." He finished giving the access card to the woman, and she squeaked off to the elevators. After poking his screen, the guard lifted his eyes to Atteberry and said, "Dr. Tyrone is unavailable as well." Then he added tersely, "Sir, please wait over there and I'll let you know if Dr. Whitt can see you."

With that, Atteberry shuffled carefully over to the large waiting area. The marble floors were soaked, and the cleaners had yet to mop the front of the lobby. He sank into a high-backed chair and pulled out some damp papers to read.

Half an hour ticked by, people blew in and ran out through the main doors, and then the rush slowed down. When Atteberry saw the security guard was no longer busy, he walked over and asked if he'd heard anything.

"Not yet, sir. I'll send another message right now to inform him you're still here."

"Wait, do you mean he knows I'm here?"

"Yes, sir. He acknowledged my first message immediately."

Atteberry chewed his lip. *Why doesn't he want to meet? If he was deep into the signal analysis, I should be there to help.*

"Good news. Dr. Whitt is sending someone up to escort you to the lab." He drew up the bio-card information on file and gave him a pass. "Please wait here."

Mark stepped off the elevator a moment later, and they shook hands. The car began its smooth descent to the Space Operations Lab, and Atteberry turned to the student and said, "So what's new, Mark? Have you started the analysis yet?"

Mark stared straight ahead, then at his shoes, and mumbled, "I—I can't really say."

Atteberry snorted, "What do you mean? You're working on this, aren't you?"

"Yes, but I'm not allowed to discuss the project with anyone."

"I'm not anyone. And not to put too fine a point on it, but I discovered the damn thing."

Mark's face twitched, and he scratched his head. "Yeah, still, Dr. Whitt made it super clear. I'd like to, but—"

"So he's threatened you, too."

The student remained awkwardly silent. The doors whooshed open, and he swiped his access card over the lab door reader, and they entered.

Dr. Whitt was in the Oxford Room, fiddling with the guts of an old school computer.

"Thank you, Mark," he said, "You may go now." Mark left the two men alone and closed the door behind him.

"Dr. Whitt," Atteberry began, "I need to be completely frank with you."

Whitt looked up from his work and removed his glasses.

"Someone has been watching me, or at least they were a few days ago. That was bad enough. Then I find someone's hacked into my radio gear, leaving tracer code in it." He'd said this a little too quickly, and tried hard to suppress his true desire to shout at someone.

THE CRYING OF ROSS 128

Whitt's expression did not change. He remained cool and distant, staring at him with his dark eyes.

"Dr. Whitt, I have to ask: Are you behind any of this?"

Whitt took a handkerchief from his lab coat pocket and cleaned his glasses. "Let me get this straight," he said in a slow voice. "Are you accusing me of putting some tracking virus in your radio equipment? Is that right?" His narrow gaze bore straight into Atteberry's head.

"I—I, like I said, I have to ask."

"Why do you think I had something to do with it?"

Atteberry swallowed hard and took a half step toward him. "I'm not sure. I don't know who else would be interested in my radio habits. And you did threaten me about going public with Ross, remember? Threatening Kate?"

"Oh yes, that. Don't tell me you're still sore about that! You understand—and I have no doubt Esther told you, too—we must follow the protocol on these events. I just needed to protect you."

Atteberry shrugged his shoulders, fighting to keep calm. "Protect me from what?"

"From yourself, of course. Your words and actions, even the most innocuous ones, can have massive international repercussions. You do understand that, don't you? Butterfly effect and such?"

Atteberry realized the discovery had already put his family and Kate at risk, despite little action taken. "Yes, I suppose so."

"Well then," Whitt said, "let's not argue about that and instead, shall we consider your surveillance problem? For indeed, that's what it sounds like you've got."

Atteberry grabbed a stool behind him and sat down, not feeling any better for having confronted the lab weasel.

"First, I can assure you I have nothing to do with tracer codes or spies or whatever else is going on. We're colleagues, in a sense, aren't we? We both know that at some point, the UN will likely give us the go-ahead to contact Ross 128. Subterfuge on my part is completely unnecessary and illogical."

"Okay," Atteberry considered, not entirely convinced.

"So if it's not me or anyone at the TSA, the real question, the one you should be asking, is: Who would want to stop you in this? Who are your personal enemies? What other groups in the world may wish to either steal your subspace filtering algorithm for themselves, or otherwise undermine your attempts at first contact?"

Atteberry thought about it. He had no enemies he could think of. There were some jealousies around the department, but nothing related to his amateur radio astronomy work. It made no sense.

"If someone wanted to steal Kate's code, why not just take it if they already broke into my house?"

"A good question, you have the instincts of a scientist." Whitt flashed a quick grin. "I wouldn't know, Mr. Atteberry, I don't play in those shadows." He put his glasses back on and bent over his open computer again. "If it were me, I'd consider how the discovery of Ross 128 and whatever contact comes out of that would help strategically, economically, politically or militarily. I can think of a number of different groups who would love to control this event for their own gain."

"You mean, like other space agencies?"

"Of course! But we expect that on all things. There's a certain rush from our friendly competition with the Indians and the Europeans." He picked up a screwdriver and began wiring a connector to the motherboard. "But there are many other groups and individuals who are not so pleasant. Many others."

Atteberry guessed he meant global military outfits. Historically, they had always had an interest in leading the exploration and colonization of space. This discovery could be their pathway to controlling a larger universe.

Whitt continued talking while he worked. "So, there are the two Americas, our own government of course, the Russians, Indians, Chinese... not to mention those terrorist groups out there who would love to exploit our human fears about hostile aliens and such."

"I hadn't thought about all that."

"I'm sure if you spend any time at all on this question, you'd come up with a list of 50 organizations all wanting to know how you discovered the signal, and how to use that for their own goals."

Whitt replaced the cover on the computer and wiped his hands on his coat. "There's someone else you may want to consider, too. Someone closer to home as it were."

"Who's that?"

"I hesitate to say because I recognize how close you are." He put his tools back in a small pouch.

"Who is it, Dr. Whitt?"

"How well do you know Kate Braddock? I mean, how well do you *really* know her?"

Atteberry threw his head back and laughed. "That's insane! I trust her more than anyone in the world."

"Oh, I understand, truly, I do. But the work she did in the past was highly specialized and top secret. Where does she come from? What kind of dubious alliances has she forged over the years? In short, she may have been playing you all along."

"No, no, I don't believe that for a second."

"Fair enough, Mr. Atteberry, but if you're considering who could be behind this mysterious tracer, I think you have to consider all possibilities. Even the ones that appear impossible."

ELEVEN

Whitt

FOR THE REST OF THAT MORNING, MARSHALL WHITT CONFINED HIMSELF to the dim lights and warmth of the Oxford Room, running additional subspace transmission simulations and plotting his next moves. The only time he left was to check up on the progress of his students and researchers in their respective projects. During one of those breaks, Mark asked him discreetly about Ross 128, and he assured him the tests were progressing smoothly under his direction, thanks for asking.

A message arrived from Esther shortly after lunch. She'd been managing the remaining media—the latecomers and conspiracy theorists—and their questions about Atteberry's initial claims. The official TSA statement on Ross 128 focused on continuing the analysis with nothing conclusive to report. She updated Whitt on enquiries and also mentioned her monthly meeting with Kapour next week, a not-so-subtle reminder of her position on internal communications. He ignored that.

On his way back to the Oxford Room to check the final simulation results, Whitt picked up a mug of tea from a nearby autoserver. The program hadn't completed its full test run yet, so he waited patiently in front of the screen and thought about the growing problem known as Jim Atteberry.

That fellow was nothing if not persistent, but his fear and suspicion of being watched was totally understandable. Jackson had mentioned his man being spotted that night. No need to remind him to be careful though, as Levar probably had him transferred elsewhere already. The data stream from Atteberry's radio had also stopped, thanks to his whacked-out friend's diagnostics, but that wouldn't matter in a few minutes.

However, much to his delight, Whitt did discover that Atteberry and his daughter's indie-comms were still active. He could continue tracking their movements and comms freely, so whatever stealth code Jackson put on them was undetected during Braddock's clean up. That was a bonus.

The computer chimed and the data streaming across his monitor stopped. The simulation was complete *sans* glitches. The final tests of various models where the satellite antenna array focused its transmission beam toward Ross 128 were finished. The impact on signal strength from small tuning adjustments designed to minimize scatter from spatial bodies was evaluated. The variables also accounted for effects of atmospheric ionization and other possible sources of interference. Given the extremely long wavelength of the transmissions, however, his concern over scattering was hardly warranted. This last simulation proved that, once sent, the signal should arrive in the Ross 128 system intact and stronger than the ambient cosmic noise. Whoever, or whatever, was out there could not miss it or mistake it for something other than a responding intelligent signal.

Esther's concerns over hiding the discovery had been easily managed to date; her own sense of ethical duty and responsibility made sure of that. But Atteberry, ah yes, Atteberry. Well, he was another type of animal. His suspicions kept simmering along with his frustration over the secrecy of the event. He was—without question—a risk. Part of the solution was to sow the seed of doubt in his mind about Braddock. However small, that uncertainty would be enough to keep him on edge until the plan rolled out to its logical conclusion.

It was time to hedge his bets.

"Call Levar Jackson. Secure comms."

A moment later, Jackson came through Whitt's indie-comm, audio only. "What can I do for you, Marshall?"

"I'll be brief," he said. "Once the discovery goes public, our friend may become more problematic given his philosophical views on access to information. I'm open to suggestions on managing him, as long as it's peaceful."

"I see." Jackson paused momentarily. "Well, there were plenty of tactics we used durin' the conflict to undermine authority and credibility, and lots of new ways to achieve that now. We could start there."

"Perfect." Whitt terminated the simulation. "I'm listening."

"The target is an open access proponent, so I'll plant the idea through the astronomy community, the media, that he's a public danger and a nuisance, bent on invitin' disease-carryin', hostile aliens to Earth with his "Let's-all-be-friends" approach. Any marginal sympathizers he has will reject him because fear trumps logic every time, right?"

"Indeed it does, but we've seen those open access, alien-hugging characters before. I need more than that."

"Patience, Marshall, I'm gettin' to it. See, not only is he a danger to the entire planet—that's bad enough—but he's also a direct and immediate threat to each one of his students. I'd even go so far as thinkin' he's not fit to care for his own kid. Know what I mean?"

Whitt played with a pencil on the computer table. Jackson's *thinkin'* was positively delicious. Undermining the man was helpful, but painting him as a personal menace to individuals under his care was gold. The daughter, too, could provide additional unforeseen leverage.

"I like that approach a lot. Can you prepare a step-by-step outline for me and send it on this secure link? Not all the details, of course, just the main points, times, expected results, risks."

"Will do. How about later today?"

"Yes, that'll be fine." He peered at the screen over his glasses and reconfigured the antenna array coordinates from *simulation* mode to *live*. "Oh, one other thing. I don't want the daughter, Mary, harmed in any way."

"Understood."

Atteberry

"I DON'T GET IT, KATE. WHAT'S WITH ALL THESE STRANGE LOOKS?"

He took a bite of his ham sandwich and looked at her for an answer. Kate wrestled with a stick of cheese in a bag and gazed around the college cafeteria at the groups of students and instructors who stared at them, some snickering, others resentful.

"It's like this," she said. "There are rumors circulating about you becoming unhinged over the alien signal. Take a gander.

People aren't sure how to react. Some are frightened, like that girl in the grey blouse over there—don't look yet, don't be so obvious, Jim—and others like the guys near the bin, all laughing to hide their fear."

Atteberry put the sandwich down and coolly surveyed the room. Not everyone stole looks, of course, but too many did. "What are they saying, did you hear?"

Kate grinned matter-of-factly. "I did." She faced him and shook her short-cropped hair, as if shivering. "There's two bits of gossip. The first is that you're becoming a public nuisance, a threat."

"Why?"

"Because of your behavior lately over the signal. No one knows about that discovery officially, right, but they remember your initial presentation to the Astronomical Society and how everyone shit all over you."

"Come on, Kate, how is that threatening?" An autoserver in need of repair coughed by, grabbing garbage off a nearby table with its mechanical arms.

"It's the whole first contact thing again, Jim. Social media's been hit with story after story, reigniting the fears people have about aliens coming to Earth. Never mind they could be hostile: the problem is cultural and health-related."

Atteberry considered how first contact between peoples in Earth's own history often resulted in death and disease, collapse of local economies and social structures as one culture steamrolled over another.

"So," she continued, "no one actually believes there are aliens, but because you've been pre-occupied lately, your work is suffering—"

He leaned back, folding his arms across his chest. "No it isn't!"

"Yes, it is." Her gaze bore into him like a red hot poker.

Atteberry pushed the sandwich away.

"The whole 'Do we invite E.T. for lunch or don't we?' thing is being fanned into massive flames," she added.

"That's happened before with others who claimed to hear signals, so it's not a big deal."

"Perhaps," she said, lightheartedly, "but another more powerful, personal reason exists for each student."

"What's that?"

"Word is you're mentally unstable and could snap in front of them."

"What do you mean?"

Kate stared at him with intense bewilderment. "Meaning they don't feel safe in your classroom, Jim. Serious business. Kids, parents, the administration won't have that."

"But it's not true!"

"Of course not, but there's a perception being propagated by rumor and, like it or not, the stories are out there."

Atteberry looked down at the remains of his lunch and shuddered. He'd suddenly lost his appetite. "What about you, Kate, what do you think?" he asked quietly.

"Well, you're an amazing, completely badass, incredible teacher and one of the few decent human beings on this wretched planet without soul-killing flaws." She sipped her juice. "The rumors will pass in time. Just ride out the weirdness and stay focused on teaching. If students refuse to come to class, that's their business. But, listen carefully," she said, staring intently into his eyes, "if your work and commitment continue to slip, that's the college's business. So wake up and pay more attention."

"Sure, thanks."

Kate bit into an apple and looked around the room again.

"I confronted Whitt yesterday."

"Oh? About the tracer code?"

"Uh huh. He denied knowing anything about it."

"Of course."

"He also suggested other possible groups who might have an interest in controlling first contact, your algorithm, space research."

Kate smirked. "What did he say about me?"

Atteberry flinched, startled. "How do you know he mentioned you?"

"I told you, I know him."

Atteberry inhaled deeply. "He asked me how well I know and trust you, given your past in that program, the war."

"Me?"

"Yes, he hinted you might be working for some third party, some foreign power. To what end, I don't have a clue."

Her eyes narrowed. "Do you believe him?"

"No, no, of course not, but it makes me wonder what the hell he's up to."

"Forget him," Kate said, "Whitt's an asshole. Just be careful around him. There's always an ulterior motive for everything he says and does."

The struggling autoserver whirred by and Atteberry picked up a coffee. "I'm also worried about Mary. She seems okay, but it's hard for me to tell, and she really needs her mother, or at least another woman to talk to."

Kate reached across the table and put her hand on his. "No doubt she does, and I wish I could help."

"Why can't you? She loves you, Kate, and looks up to you like no one else, not even her teachers."

"I think the world of her too, you know that, Jim, but I just can't help with some things, like her first period... Boys... Girls..."

For the second time, Atteberry felt truly inadequate as a parent. The first had occurred when he and Janet brought baby Mary home from the birthing station, plunked her in the middle of the living room in her travel carrier and wondered what the hell to do next.

"Maybe I could try, if that helps."

"Thanks, Kate. Some days I wish Janet were here, even if we weren't together, you know? It'd be great if Mary could see her mom."

Kate finished her apple, wiped her hands and folded her arms across her flat chest. "What really happened with her? There must be more to the story."

Atteberry chewed his lip and remained silent. He'd never talked about it, not even with Mary. Perhaps he would have sooner if he'd understood why Janet left in the first place, but there was no obvious cause, no answer given. Sometimes people act without a reason, and often clues aren't forthcoming for this or that behavior. But he'd loved Janet with all his heart—at least he thought he did—and had a beautiful child with her. They'd started building a life together, and then one day she simply wasn't there.

"There's not much to tell, Kate. We met at some rally when I was a grad student at Berkeley and hit it off right away. In fact, she introduced herself to me first." The memory of that chance encounter played over again in his mind. "I was awkward around other people, but she made me feel secure and happy like no one else. We began dating and fell in love."

Kate smiled at him and lifted her eyebrows. "What did she study?"

"Economics. She was fascinated by the ebb and flow of labor markets, competing systems, the link to national and international policy. Not really my thing, but I supported her."

"Did she work anywhere?"

"Oh, yes. At first, she did independent market research for a policy shop in Washington, and that evolved into other strategic projects here."

"Contract gigs, then?"

"Uh huh. Janet hated the idea of being tied to one institution like I was." He smiled, and then his face dropped. "It was a Sunday morning, when Mary was seven and a half, I woke up and she's not in bed, not downstairs, not outside, and her indie-comm is gone along with a handful of clothes from the closet."

"I remember when that happened. It was just after I arrived, if I'm not mistaken. You were crazy worried."

"Yeah, I called the police the next day and, last I checked, the missing person file is still open but there was never any trail at all."

"Could she have been kidnapped or something?"

"The cops thought so initially, but without signs of a struggle, no ransom call, nothing, they dropped that idea. She just disappeared. At one point, they even suspected me, but their investigation turned up nothing."

Kate cocked her head to one side and ran her finger over the table top, pushing a crumb around. "But she contacted you later, right?"

"Yeah, she sent me a note saying don't try finding her. That was it. No 'Sorry it didn't work out' or 'Give my love to Mary'... nothing like that." He became lost in thought. "The poor kid really took it hard as you can imagine. Cried for the longest time. Actually, we both did."

He was thankful Kate gave him this moment to reflect in silence as the scabs were ripped off those old emotions. Then he said, "Life goes on, and we're happier now. She misses her mother terribly, as do I, but I'm at the point where I need to let her go and accept that, for whatever reason, she couldn't be with us any more. It's time to move on."

Kate grinned. "And that's where Esther Tyrone comes in."

"Yeah."

"Tell me, Jim, what do you like about her? I mean, she's a bit older than you for one thing. Why her and not someone else around here for example? Someone younger?"

Atteberry downed the last of his coffee. "Age is irrelevant, Kate. It's just not important. What I like is how warm she is, and welcoming, her love of books and science, her smile."

"What else? That's little info right there."

In fact, he hadn't thought about it, but in his heart he enjoyed being near her. It was this emotion he had that drove him, and it was nothing logical; as if, odd and cynical as it may sound, there was an understanding between them that didn't rely on words, a comforting connection in their silences together that vanished when they spoke.

"It's a mystery, Kate, I can't explain it."

She smiled and checked the time. They got up and Atteberry noticed the large number of students and faculty watching them leave.

Kate said, "I understand exactly what you're talking about, Jim. Many times, my Spacer colleagues and I just sensed each other's thoughts." They walked towards the exit, and as they squeezed through the heavy glass doors, she added, "Give her a call, Jim."

Esther

Esther Tyrone's hovercar sped silently over the traditional roadway, two feet above ground. The call from Jim Atteberry late yesterday afternoon inviting her over for supper and to talk stars and space came as a complete surprise, especially after the awkward departure at Grinders on the weekend. This could not possibly be a good idea, yet she convinced herself that, indeed, meeting him would be helpful to the Academy, and to her. She'd wanted to see his amateur radio astronomy station for some time.

The vehicle glided effortlessly to a stop in Jim's driveway, the anti-grav thrusters lowering it softly to the ground. Esther checked herself one last moment in the mirror, played with a loose strand of hair, then exited and rang the doorbell. The hovercar purred away to the neighborhood recharge paddock.

Jim Atteberry opened the door with a big smile on his face. "Welcome, Esther! I'm glad you could make it."

A strong scent of freshly-baked bread and Mexican spices greeted her as she stepped into the modest home and took off her jacket.

"You come straight from work?"

"Yes, it was easier that way. Sorry if I look a little ragged. It's a little crazy right now."

"Au contraire, you look great." Then, catching himself, he added, "I didn't mean, er, well..."

"That's quite alright." Esther smiled and changed the subject quickly, "Something sure smells good!"

Jim invited her in and showed her to the kitchen. Mary sat at the table, working on her tablet, and took off her earphones when their guest walked in.

"Hi, I'm Esther. We talked on the phone a while ago, remember?" She held out her hand and Mary shook it.

"Hello, are you here to see my dad's station?"

"You bet, and lucky enough to be invited for supper, too." Jim offered her a glass of wine which she took, and he poured himself a small one as well.

Mary gathered her things up from the table and put them in her backpack that lay at her feet. "You're in for a treat, Esther. Dad's made some of his fartolicious chili tonight."

"Mary!"

"What?"

"Mares, that's quite enough of that." Jim gave her that eye, the one emoting *You are amazing and funny and I love you to death* combined with *I can't believe you just said that!* She giggled and smiled at Esther, who winked back.

"Okay, Mares, go wash your hands for supper, please."

"They're not dirty," she complained.

"Yes they are. I can see the germy little germs wriggling all over them from here, all nasty and gross." She took her backpack down to her room and in a moment, Esther heard the water running. Mary sang as she cleaned up.

"Is she always this happy and funny?"

"Most of the time. Like any of us, she has her days and her moments, but I've really been blessed. That kid brings so much joy into the house." They chatted for a few minutes before he spooned out some chili from the crockpot into their bowls and put them on the dining room table. Esther brought out the bread, and Mary, with freshly-cleaned hands, came in with salad.

Over supper, the girls did most of the talking. Esther had learned a long time ago that the best way to engage strangers, especially kids, is to ask questions, and lots of them; get them chatting and show genuine interest. So the conversation migrated from school to space, friends to boys, clothes to hairstyles, sports—especially basketball—and books. The two of them shared a keen fascination with how differently eighteenth century girls were portrayed compared to those in today's novels. Esther also pointed out that boys were different, too. They agreed on that, chattering about characters from *Nicholas Nickelby* and other Dickens' stories.

After supper, Jim and Esther cleared the table and Mary took off to do her homework.

"You two hit off."

"She's a lovely child, just like I imagined." She emptied her wineglass. "May I ask you something?"

"Sure."

"Why did you invite me here tonight? The other day after coffee I got the sense you didn't want me to meet Mary."

Jim peered up sheepishly from the dishes, started covering the salad with cellophane. "Yeah, sorry about that, but I didn't know how to respond to you. The personal-professional boundaries are blurring for me."

"My, you are bold after half a glass of wine."

He laughed. "Oh, it's not that, rest assured. Kate Braddock—you remember her? She encouraged me to call you back, and was right: I'm glad you're here."

Esther blushed and closed her eyes briefly. *He likes you, Esther. For god sakes don't blow it.* "Well, I'm happy you called." Then she added quickly, "So, how about you show me your setup?"

On the way down to the basement, he asked Mary if she'd like to join them but she was deep into her special science project for the high school and needed to finish it.

When Jim threw on the lights, Esther stopped in her tracks to take it all in. The station was massive, occupying almost the entire opposite side of the room. She recognized the Yaesu receivers, conventional transceivers for the normal space-time radio bands, two power supplies, scopes, monitors, a high-end computer and, further along, a work area with various circuit boards in disarray. It reminded her so much of her own father's radio shack when she was growing up. The smell of warm circuits triggered happy memories of being with her own dad.

To the right of her was a massive built-in bookcase. He'd arranged it across two sections: one for science and radio-related books, the other for fiction.

THE CRYING OF ROSS 128

"It must have taken you years to collect these," she said, eyeing the older editions.

"I've had some my entire life, and the ones you see here are those I like the best. There are more boxes in storage." He pointed to a closed-off room. "In there by the washing machine."

There was a desk with a stack of papers on it, a large recliner not far from that, and an area in darkness. "What's over there?"

"Oh, that. I'll show you if you promise not to laugh." He walked her over and turned on a separate set of lights that flooded the space, exposing a small table top, easel, dozens of canvasses—some painted, others not—and a shelf of acrylic paints and a handful of brushes. A supply of paper plates, plastic bowls and a couple of binders were also there.

"So you're a painter, too," she said. "Will you show some to me?"

"Sure, as long as you don't expect Monet or Rembrandt." He pulled out some of the canvasses and placed them on the table and the easel. They were colorful and... Well, colorful. Sorry attempts at landscapes that tilted out of proper perspective, Esther thought, yet full of energy if nothing else.

"These are... interesting, Jim."

He chuckled. "Yes, that's the word for it. I picked it up shortly after I became a single parent since I had a lot more time on my hands, and Mary was painting one day and asked me to join her. I'm the first to admit my talents lie elsewhere."

Esther held up a small 24-by-20 inch abstract and a smile broke over her face as she attempted to suppress a laugh. "This is... a horse?"

"A dog, actually," he snorted.

"I figured it must have been one or the other. Or a sasquatch." Esther giggled and put the canvas down.

"Come on, I'll show you my real hobby."

They sat down at the radio astronomy station, and Jim demonstrated the setup, which gear did what—which she already knew—and the log of recorded cosmic events dating back years, including the two times he heard the Ross 128 signal.

A photograph of him, a young Mary, and a beautiful blonde-haired woman with piercing blue eyes perched on the far side of the bench. It was taken by the ocean, and they seemed to be a happy family enjoying a late afternoon together.

She gathered her courage and, nodding to the photograph, asked, "Is that your wife?"

"Yes, that's Janet."

"How did she pass away?"

Jim turned his full attention to her with a puzzled expression on his face. "Hm? Janet's not dead, Esther. At least, as far as I know."

Esther's cheeks burned, and she lowered her gaze. Her disappointment was palpable. "I'm so sorry, I thought—I completely mistook—"

"It's okay," he smiled. "She left us about two and a half years ago, shortly after that picture was taken, and we haven't seen her since."

Esther's entire body was on fire, partly from the wine but mostly from embarrassment and a sharp unexpected pain in her side. *How could she be so stupid?*

"In case you're wondering, we're still technically married, or separated, or... I don't know the marriage rules any more. But we're definitely not together."

Esther's shoulders slumped, and she held on to the edge of the radio bench to steady herself. *Maybe not a couple, but clearly not single. Another unresolved relationship, and you're on the outside looking in.*

Whitt

MARSHALL WHITT CUT THE FINAL TRANSMISSION CHECKLIST short and finished translating the array input data. He initiated the uplink to transfer the beam coordinates to the relay mothersat.

"Commence array reconfiguration."

"Input security code required."

Whitt punched the Space Ops coding sequence into the computer.

"Access enabled."

The uplink connection was established and the new coordinates streamed up to the orbiting array. Over the next several minutes, Whitt saw the satellite icons on his screen slowly maneuver into position.

He attached the outgoing transmission content to the Q-Sim encrypter. It was the same, simple continuous wave signal that the Ross aliens had sent—a message that we acknowledge you. One-one-eight, repeated over and over again for several minutes. A more robust communication would come later.

With the encrypted signal, Whitt recognized that no one else on the planet, except for Atteberry, would be able to receive it since it followed the same coded pattern as that established by Braddock's detection algorithm. Other stations listening to deep space would only hear cosmic noise. Moreover, because the outgoing signal was generated in the UHF range, it would be detected here as yet another noisy transmission to a satellite, a frequent occurrence.

This reminded him that something would have to be done with Atteberry's equipment if he wanted to keep him in the dark. Or maybe not.

A new idea hatched in his mind, quite opposite to his conventional approach. Perhaps there was a role for him to play on the team...

"Engage subspace transmitter."

"Identification required."

Whitt entered his own secure ID code.

"Secure access code required."

He punched the alpha-numeric sequence into the computer. The protocol for engaging the subspace transmitter was lengthy, and the entire process took slightly over 15 minutes to complete.

On the screen, a green icon appeared with *TX* written on it. This is it. A rare subspace transmission was set to be unleashed on Ross 128. Whitt stared at the button for a moment and thought he should mark this occasion somehow. The absence of witnesses and fanfare made his intended action as exciting as picking up a loaf of bread at the corner store. He bowed his head and prayed to the god of his understanding, asking forgiveness and mercy, peace for his kids, and success if it be his will, amen. He looked up again at all the checks reading green on the monitor, and his finger hovered over the *TX* button. Not bad for a mechanic's son. He wished he could be with his dad again, just to share this special time together, to see his face, his eyes, his fear. History in the making. He exhaled deeply.

Whitt played the sequence out in his mind one final time. He imagined the transmission working its way through space. Beginning as a UHF signal at Mount Sutro, then uplinked to the Oxford Antenna Array's relay satellite where it would be converted to ELF waves and beamed toward that drifting vehicle near the planet Ross 128b.

The array was set to pump out a continuous string of one-one-eight pulses. At this subspace frequency, it would take mere moments to arrive at its intended destination, and then, who knows?

Whitt leaned forward in his chair and watched the satellite icons dance on his screen. *It's time to change the course of mankind. And I'm the person who's going to do it.*

"You want water?" he said to no one in particular. "Here you go."

He pressed the transmit button and closed his eyes.

Atteberry

ATTEBERRY'S EMOTIONS SWIRLED THROUGH HIS BODY, causing him to sense in one moment as if he would float away, and in the other, like he was drowning under the weight of an ocean. He'd experienced this feeling only once before, with Janet, when they made love on the pier the night she proposed.

Something was happening between them, filling his consciousness, lingering in his mind, and totally alien to him. But a change fell over Esther immediately when Janet's ghost appeared. Not unexpected, since he hadn't opened up about her before tonight. The truth was, he had no idea if she was dead or alive, and he tried to convince himself that it wouldn't matter either way. Yet deep inside, where the soul and body merge, he still loved her deeply, at least he thought he did, at least a part of him did. The lines blurred.

The quiet alert from the computer brought them both back from their own reveries. Data began scrolling across the screen and Atteberry smiled.

"Is it... is it Ross 128?"

"Different frequency. This is a normal space-time signal."

Atteberry put one side of the headphones to his ear and listened. He fine-tuned the filter and then his face relaxed. "Listen to this," he said. He unplugged the phones and increased the audio gain, and they both leaned in toward the speaker.

It sounded like a small helicopter or single-stroke piston engine.

Esther smiled and looked at him. "That's the Crab Nebula pulsar, isn't it?"

"Yes, chugging along like an old school lawn mower." Atteberry turned the volume up louder until the chopping sound filled the basement. Mary came running down the stairs.

"That's not the alien signal, is it?"

"No, Mares," Atteberry shouted over the racket.

"It's a pulsar, right, Dad?"

"Yes it is!" Atteberry decreased the gain, and they all shared a laugh. Mary turned to Esther, "He does that, you know, turns that stuff up way loud and sits there listening to it."

"My father used to do that with his radio station, too, except he wasn't listening to space. He searched for rare Morse code signals."

Mary skipped up to the bench and pointed to the brass telegraph key. "Dad does that sometimes, too, but mostly he listens to space music. Have you heard the creepy sound that Saturn makes?"

Esther and Mary started in on another conversation, and each time they mentioned the sounds of planets and stars, Atteberry would pull up audio files so they could all listen together. Mary had taken a real shine to Esther, and he wondered if perhaps she was the woman who could be a confidant and teacher for his daughter. Maybe even more for him. She looked beautiful in her tight maroon sweater and skirt, and Atteberry tumbled along to a riot of emotions he hadn't felt for some time.

"Mary, is your homework all done?"

She rolled her eyes like the teenager she would soon become. "Yes, Dad."

THE CRYING OF ROSS 128

"Great! Do you want to show Esther what you're doing to—"

He was interrupted by a new alert chiming over the sounds of Neptune fluttering in the background. The main tuning dial was back on the Ross 128 subspace frequency. He killed the planetary opera and the now familiar one-one-eight pattern blasted out.

"Oh my god," Esther whispered, "it's the alien signal!"

Atteberry ensured the recorder was on and working, then turned up the audio gain but quickly knocked it down again as the noise overloaded the speaker.

"What the heck..."

"What is it, Jim?"

"Something's weird. This transmission is incredibly strong."

Mary covered her ears and smiled. Her excitement filled the space between the three of them, but Atteberry remained concerned.

"Either whatever produced it is now here in orbit, or else this is a Terran source."

"Terran?" Esther said, her face quickly losing its glow.

"There's no doubt about it. Is that your colleague, Esther?" Atteberry's voice was harder than he intended it to be, and he wondered if she'd accepted his supper invitation so quickly to distract him from Whitt's dirty work.

She answered softly. "It could be, likely is. Perhaps he got permission to engage the aliens."

Atteberry knew enough about bureaucracy to realize it was unlikely Whitt had authority from anyone.

"The only other subspace transmitter is in Mumbai, but it's not operational."

"Are you sure?"

"Yes, Jim," she said with annoyance, "I am sure. I was just speaking with the director there yesterday."

"Sorry." The data continued scrolling by and the column indicating signal strength remained off the charts. Atteberry wondered why, if true, Whitt would take the risk of contacting Ross 128 without permission when anyone with a subspace receiver could—

He looked at Esther and he knew she'd figured it out at the same time he did. Nobody else on the planet could hear this signal. It was effectively camouflaged because no one had Kate's filtering algorithm or, in the case of the TSA, had a quantum simulator calibrated to that operational frequency. Anyone listening would only hear a strong, but garbled, encrypted message and would assume it to be some kind of random event.

"I'm sure Whitt was doing something with the Oxford antenna array," Atteberry said. "I saw him there doing it when I confronted him about the—" He looked at Mary who stared back at him, wide-eyed.

Esther piped up. "Running simulations is normal, but to actually transmit requires access codes that he doesn't have. In fact, the UN Security Council changes them up frequently to prevent possible leaks, and only stable governments are barely allowed close enough to get a whiff of them."

"Then how did Whitt do it?"

"I don't know, but I need to ask him, and until I do, let's give him the benefit of the doubt. It may not be him, after all, or he could be working under duress; but if it is Marshall acting on his own, he's breaking the protocol and that's a dangerous game. We could have more than our own security forces to deal with."

Mary interrupted them. "Dad, what's going on?"

Atteberry hugged her and said, "We're not sure, kiddo, but we'll find out. Either way, there's nothing for us to fear." He thought she gripped him a little too strongly.

The transmission ended abruptly, replaced by low-level noise and static crashes. The trio remained silent for several minutes, waiting to see if anything more would come. It didn't.

"Hey, Mary," Esther finally said, "do you have any hot chocolate?"

Atteberry looked at her quizzically. Mary turned with a huge smile on her face.

"Yes we do!" she squealed, "and marshmallows!"

Atteberry joined in. "Tell you what, Mares, you run upstairs and find some mugs for us, and the hot chocolate, and we'll be there in a minute. I want to set the radio up for scanning again."

"Sweet!" She bounced over to the basement stairs and hopped up each one like a rabbit.

With Mary gone, Atteberry whispered, "We have to discover what's going on. This could be dangerous and destabilize the peace—or whatever it is—between the two Americas."

"Yes, but we must be prudent. I've got to understand what he's up to... why he's putting the TSA at risk."

Atteberry had another thought as he put the frequency sweep on automation. "What if your leadership is complicit in it?"

Esther scoffed. "And not tell me? Unlikely."

"But possible."

"How do you figure?"

Atteberry dimmed the screen and squelched the audio gain so only alerts would come through. He switched the recorder to stand by, then turned to her. "Look, I understand why *I'm* being kept in the dark. I'm an outsider. But if you're not being included in the decision-making loop, that raises a different problem completely. It means," he said with deep concern, "that someone there doesn't trust you."

Esther's face suddenly looked tired and defeated. "You jump to conclusions quickly, Jim, and even though you may be right, I'd appreciate a little more credit and respect."

He grimaced. "We ought to head over there as soon as we've had our hot chocolate. I'll call Kate and see if she can come over and stay with Mary."

"No, please don't do that." Esther put her hand on Atteberry's arm and stared deeply into his eyes. "You can't get more involved."

"Why not? I'm already up to my neck in it."

"Because it's one thing for me to ask Marshall about his activities—that's what colleagues do, we challenge each other. But like you said, you're a civilian, an interloper; you may be portrayed as one of several TSA enemies."

"Enemies? I'm no enemy."

"Not to me, you aren't, but what about how Marshall sees you?"

Atteberry muttered and stood up. They walked to the stairs. He motioned for her to go up first and he followed behind. Then Esther paused and faced him. He felt dangerously close.

"Jim, do you realize he has the authority to lock up trespassers or *persons of interest* almost indefinitely if he thinks they're a threat to the Academy and its work?"

"I didn't know."

"Well, he does. I do, too, for your information, as does each member of the executive, so let me speak with him. I'll return to the TSA tonight and tell you what I find." Esther continued climbing the stairs and called out, "How about some of that hot chocolate!"

Mary squealed with delight from the kitchen. Atteberry sighed and rubbed his eyes, following her a moment later.

TWELVE

Atteberry

HALF AN HOUR LATER, ATTEBERRY RETRIEVED ESTHER'S COAT for her at the front door. Mary sat on the nearby stool they used for tying up their shoes and boots.

Esther knelt down and smiled at her. "Well, it was a lot of fun talking with you tonight. I learned all kinds of new things."

"Thank you for coming over."

Atteberry took Esther's hand and went through the motions of helping her stand, but his mind was elsewhere. Then he patted Mary on the head. "Go get ready for bed, Mares."

"Okay, bye!" She slid off the stool and dawdled down the hall, tapping her fingers along the wall.

When Mary was in her room, Atteberry whispered, "So you and Whitt aren't just scientists?"

"We are researchers first and foremost, but our jobs comprise more than just space programming and the lecture circuit."

"The politics, you mean."

"Jim," Esther looked him straight in the eye, "at this level—probably at any level, really—doing the science for its own beauty is rare. There are always other interested parties paying close attention to what we do: politicians, militaries, corporations, terrorists, and who knows who else."

"I suppose that's why someone was watching the house the other night?"

"I have no doubt. It happens more frequently than you might think."

"But I don't understand this other power you and Whitt have to arrest people. What's that about?"

She hesitated, a hardened look on her face, then said, "It wasn't always this way, but the war changed everything. The top scientists were all in bed with various generals and powerful leaders. They demanded, and got, these additional legal powers to curtail suspected espionage. It helped stop the infighting and allowed organizations like the TSA to operate without fear."

Atteberry bit his lip. "Have you ever...?"

"Arrested someone? Yes, I have. At my previous job. A lunatic who kept showing up at the oddest times claiming to have been abducted. As I recall, he was a pretty smart mathematician, but snapped somewhere along the way."

"What happened?"

"I had the security guards hold him in the detention cells at the lab. Left him there three months while the in-house shrinks looked him over. It was some kind of imbalance with his meds in the end, or so they believed. I wasn't convinced."

"And when you released him?"

"I haven't authorized his release yet."

Gazing up at him, her eyes suddenly teared and her face showed great pain. Atteberry squeezed her shoulder and rubbed it gently, and she leaned toward him ever so slightly, then pulled away.

She attempted a smile but her lower lip trembled. "Thank you for a wonderful evening. I'd love to do it again sometime. Would that be okay?"

Atteberry's confusion dampened his excitement, and he was about to agree with her when the familiar sound of the radio alert chimed from the basement.

"Do you hear that?"

Esther cocked her head and dabbed her eye. "I do. Is it Marshall again?"

"There's a way to find out. Come on." As they descended the stairs, Atteberry shouted, "Another one, Mares!" She thumped down the hall and fell in behind Esther.

He cranked the audio gain and immediately recognized the true Ross 128 signal again. Esther shook her head in disbelief, and a huge grin spread over her face. She'd never heard it come in live; she sat down at the workstation staring at the speaker and wept openly. Mary hopped around in time with the *chicka chicka* and Atteberry assumed a business-like attitude, verifying the equipment, monitoring the frequency and the recording of it. Yet for all his check-listing and seriousness, he too couldn't stop smiling like a kid with a big bowl of ice cream.

Then, after a series of the one-one-eight pulses, the pattern changed significantly. Something new. Atteberry scratched down the unfamiliar tap codes on his notepad, but the strength of this signal barely pushed above the background noise and static. Solar activity must be interfering with it.

He wrote out the sequences with a view to analyze them later, perhaps even with Esther. He caught a glimpse of her face as she rose from the chair and smiled.

When the crash at the front door came, it almost disappeared into the chaos and excitement of the radio room and Ross 128 pounding in. Esther and Mary noticed it first and looked toward the stairs. Atteberry cut the audio gain and listened. The house was silent, other than the circulation fan and gentle hum of the equipment.

Mary's eyes suddenly grew wide with terror. She was about to say something when Atteberry put his finger to his lips. Esther held on to her while he tiptoed silently across the room.

It was dark in the front hall. He strained his eyes to catch any kind of movement or shadow, but there was nothing. Only the normal, regular sounds of the house. After a couple of minutes, he relaxed and sauntered back to the radio bench.
"Could've been a car door slamming."

At that point four large men flew down the stairs, moving deftly and taking positions in front of them. Mary screamed and held on to Esther.
Atteberry stood his ground and demanded, "Who the hell are you? Get out of my house!" He pushed the smaller one up against the wall, raising him off his feet.

"That's enough, Mr. Atteberry." The voice was smooth and deep. It echoed as its owner thumped slowly down the stairs.

The balding man behind the voice smirked hastily at him. He stood at least a foot taller than the stranger, but the fellow easily weighed 20 kilograms more. A small handgun pointed at Atteberry's head. Wearing an off-the-rack suit, the man could have been mistaken for an accountant or non-descript office worker.

THE CRYING OF ROSS 128

"Mr. Atteberry, I apologize for the intrusion and for this." He waved the gun around. "We don't mean to scare you or your daughter." Mary and Esther clung to each other, terrified. "Dr. Tyrone, I'm a bit surprised to see you here, but that makes no difference." Returning his attention to Atteberry, he stashed the weapon in his jacket pocket. Atteberry shot a glance at Esther that screamed *Is this what you meant?*

"Who are you," he growled.

"Always wanting to know everything, aren't you?" The man said. "Well, if you truly must, my colleagues and I are in the business of tying up loose ends. And you, sir, are a big loose end."

"Did Whitt put you up to this?"

"Heh, you have no idea what you're doing. Or what you've done. I suppose the thought never occurred to you that whoever masters alien communications also controls space itself, hm? You are a global security risk, sir, one that needs to be contained."

Atteberry stood between the man and the radio where Mary and Esther held each other. "I'm calling the cops." He motioned toward the bench where his indie-comm sat, but two of the goons blocked him.

"The police? Really? And what are they going to do?"

"Stop me from tearing your eyes out, you piece of—"

"Tut, tut. There's no need for that. As long as you cooperate, no one will be harmed."

"What do you want?"

"As I said," the man whispered, "I'm here to fix up some, er, untidiness. It isn't much, but I can tell you that your days as an amateur radio astronomer listening to bug-eyed aliens are now over."

Atteberry's breathing was shallow, and the adrenaline poured through him like whiskey on a cold night. Clenching his fists, he uttered each word carefully, "Get the hell out of my house."

"We will." Then turning to the goons, the man ordered, "Take everything, gentlemen, all the equipment you see on this bench, including the notepads." Then, staring intently at Mary, he said, "I have no doubt that Mr. Atteberry will be extremely cooperative."

The other men moved like cats, ripping the radio station apart and silently hauling the gear away. In less than a minute they were done, leaving Atteberry, Mary and Esther in a state of shock and disbelief.

As the man turned to ascend the stairs, he said, "Thank you for your cooperation, Mr. Atteberry."

"You hardly gave me a choice," he croaked.

"Don't take it so personally. You knew this would happen, didn't you? Understand me well: there will be no more radios for you, sir. No more signal-watching. No more Ross 128. No more searching for extra-terrestrial life." Then, glancing at Esther, the little accountant said, "And I suggest if you want to stay safe and not be inconvenienced again, you mark my words too, yes?"

As quickly as they had stormed his house, the men quietly disappeared into the cool night.

THIRTEEN

Atteberry

ATTEBERRY KNELT AND HUGGED HIS DAUGHTER IN THE DARK BASEMENT.
"Are you okay, Mares?"
She whimpered.
"I'm so sorry this happened. I got you into this. Both of you." Atteberry looked up at Esther, confused, angry. Her eyes were wide, and she fought back tears, her hands trembling. When he stood up again, she grabbed him and held him tightly.

"I feared this might happen," she whispered. "But I hoped, foolishly it turns out, that maybe you'd be spared."

Rage washed over him that he could no longer suppress. "I don't understand, Esther. Did you know something about this?"

"Oh god, no! It's just that—I've heard stories about this sort of thing before, especially in the days after the civil war. Some of my colleagues had their research stolen, computers confiscated, and they were forced to sign non-disclosure agreements under the threat of imprisonment. I wondered if some group might target you, briefly, but dismissed it because I thought we'd grown beyond this kind of cloak-and-dagger crap."

Mary interrupted them. "Dad, I want to go upstairs."

Atteberry glared at Esther, then scooped Mary up and carried her to her room. He stayed there, comforting her until she finally, mercifully fell asleep. When he came out several minutes later, Esther had gone.

ATTEBERRY STARED AT THE VACANT RADIO BENCH, noting how much bigger it seemed without any equipment on it. The creeps had taken everything except for his indie-comm and a couple pencils. The receivers, HF transceiver, power supplies, scopes, monitors, cables—all confiscated. That gear could be replaced easily enough, but they'd also swiped the subspace filter containing Kate's pattern recognition algorithm. In fact, now that he replayed the entire scene in his mind, it was the first piece of equipment they grabbed. They'd known exactly what to look for.

His anger over this violation slowly subsided. Mary was asleep, but he knew her well; she was prone to having nightmares ever since Janet left, so because of that and the encounter with whoever it was, he expected another sleepless night. He flopped into his recliner, still staring at the empty bench.

The evening had started great, with a comforting tug of a full family warming him, and especially how well Mary and Esther got along. So what had happened? Whitt's transmission blasted in, assuming it was his. Esther seemed to be enjoying herself until talk of Janet began. He learned how dangerous his discovery was in the most humiliating, frightening way, and somehow Esther thought this sort of break-in could happen, but hadn't warned him. Then she'd left without saying goodbye. Throughout it all, his emotions sloshed around inside like rainwater in a moving barrel, sometimes light and full of riotous pleasure that early love brings, other times quelled by the reality of putting his daughter in danger.

First item of business in the morning: get a new security system, pronto.

Atteberry desperately wanted to talk this violation through with Kate, but decided against it. He considered calling Esther to... *to do what, blame her somehow?* That was his default manner of handling personal attacks and humiliations in the past: lash out at everyone closest to him. Janet helped him overcome and manage that knee-jerk reaction and give things time, give himself time, to calm down.

It frustrated him, scraping his nerves raw, that this historical discovery—intelligent life in the universe—had turned into a secretive, shadowy, geo-political monster when it should be a celebration of global joy. What was going on?

That asshole Whitt must be pulling the strings. Kate was right: he wasn't trustworthy at all, and now he had the only equipment in the world capable of hearing the alien signal *and returning their transmissions.* What was it that beady-eyed accountant jerk said? *Whoever controls communications with aliens, rules space itself.* That made Whitt a... a what? Surely this was more than just a narcissistic, vainglorious scientist yearning for public recognition.

He reclined some more and turned his gaze longingly to his books. Just looking at them brought him a small measure of comfort. Kate said that Whitt used to be connected with the military and loosely with the program that recruited her. If his actions were not strictly personal, it stood to reason his past affiliations could now be involved too, if not orchestrating the whole affair. But why? What's the end game?

Mary stirred in her sleep but settled down again quickly. Whatever the reasons behind the break-in, the subterfuge, one conclusion was clear: he would never forget that terrified look in Mary's eyes when those creeps stormed the basement. And if some military or private security force was taking over comms with Ross 128, this was no longer simply about his own family's safety. This had global ramifications, perhaps even affecting the future of Earth and all the other Marys around the world.

He hauled himself out of the chair, climbed upstairs to the kitchen, and poured himself a whiskey. Tomorrow, he'd call Esther. He had to find a way to stop Whitt and whoever else was behind this without exposing Mary or Kate to more harm. He needed to expose the Ross 128 aliens to the world. It was his only hope to save it.

But tonight, he would break his rule and drink until he passed out. He lifted the glass to his lips, then, surprising himself, poured the contents into the sink and went to bed.

Esther

The following afternoon, Esther paced in her office, stopping every few minutes to gaze out the large window facing the grey Pacific. Jim's message came in bright and early that morning on her indie-comm: *Meet me at that coffee shop again at 3:00. Please?* She hadn't responded, and he hadn't followed up, but she assumed he would be there at the Grinders waiting, and she'd have to decide soon: Go now, tell him you'll be late, or ignore him. Esther leaned toward the latter.

On her way home from Jim's, she had stopped at the TSA to speak with Marshall, but he was no longer there. Mark was the only person in the lab other than a couple of security guards patrolling the corridors. She had nodded at the grad student and left. Once she arrived at her apartment, sleep remained elusive as she rehearsed what to say to her colleague.

But when she reached her office this morning, confronting Marshall had all the appeal of leprosy. So she buried herself in busy work and asked not to be disturbed.

She liked Jim Atteberry with an instinct as ancient as the universe itself. Maybe this feeling was love, because no matter how wonderfully nebulous and present, it dominated her thoughts and shunted her around in an infinite number of directions. Intellectually, any kind of relationship with Jim, other than a professional one, would be risky, dangerously exposing her deepest fears. Yet, it was her heart speaking, pleading with her head to take the chance, regardless of what would happen, and to overcome her damned logic. It was madness, of course.

Adding to this inward, beautiful misery, that photo of Janet gutted her. Mistaking her for being dead, okay, that was an honest faux pas, words being what they are with all their limitations and subtexts. But Janet was young, strikingly good-looking, with high cheekbones and that golden hair flowing over slender shoulders. Esther realized she simply couldn't compete with that. Suppose she never returned, her memory would always be with him and he would unwittingly compare them if they ever kissed, or... So what could she offer him? Older, plainer, more insecure than she let on to anybody. What did he see in her, if anything, other than an entry to the TSA? To top it off, Janet was Mary's mother.

Nevertheless, as long as the relationship between Jim and Janet remained unresolved, she couldn't get involved with him, for that would only lead to heart break, the inevitable, historically accurate, perfectly predictable result. So leaving when she did last night was the logical decision, the best course of action given the happenings—both good and bad.

You should have left him a note. Now he must think you're heartless.

At 1:45, her hovercar hummed around to meet her in front of the lobby. The hell with it, she owed him an apology for abandoning him like that at the very least, and she also wanted to tell him she hadn't spoken with Marshall yet.

Before leaving her office, Esther told her computer to reschedule any appointments that afternoon to another date. Following a brief tidying up, she raced down the escalator, hopped into her waiting car, and flew out of the TSA campus towards Grinders.

Jim was just sitting down at the same booth they had shared a week ago. She tried to be as professional as possible but her lack of sleep and itchy emotions betrayed her. Fortunately, the lines on Jim's face and the bags under his eyes told her he hadn't slept much either.

"Thank you for coming. I wasn't sure you would."

She looked down at the table. "Me neither. Listen, about last night... abandoning you without saying anything... it was rude and disrespectful."

"Oh, don't apologize, Esther. That was crazy for all of us, but I'm the one who's sorry." They sat in silence for a few minutes, picking drinks off the autoserver and looking around the café.

"How is Mary?" Esther asked.

Jim stirred his mug. "Mary, yes. I think okay. She was very quiet this morning and didn't want to discuss it, but perked up a bit when I dropped her off at school."

"Please let me know if I can help... like if she wants to talk or something?"

"Thanks." Jim sipped his drink, "She had so much fun with you before the... you know."

"Glad to hear it. Hanging out with kids isn't my forte. My sister has a couple but they're much younger, toddler age, smell funny and collect worms. At least with Mary I can have a grown up conversation." She brushed her hair back. "Jim, why did you ask me out here this afternoon? Have you had more visits?"

"No, nothing like that. Oddly, it's been a normal day. Quiet. No, the reason I wanted to speak with you is to apologize for last night, and to solicit your help if you're willing."

"My help? I guess it depends on what you need?"

He leaned forward, arms locked in front on the table. "My gut tells me that Whitt was behind the break-in last night. This seems like rather over the top behavior for a man who is only interested in self-glorification."

"Agreed."

"So what outfit is giving him direction, and why? If he's not in it just for personal glory, he must be working for someone."

Esther considered the idea for a moment. Countless scientists, good and bad, had sold out to commercial interests since the early days of smelting and alchemy, chasing fortune or fame. For Marshall to do the same thing wouldn't be a surprise: his character oozed ambition. "It's definitely possible."

"What puzzles me, though, is the end game. Consider this: Whitt is now the only one in the world capable of communicating with the Ross 128 aliens. The only one."

"True, although Kate Braddock could produce another copy of her algorithm and—"

"Nah, I don't think so. There's a reason why I haven't simply gone to the media or the cops with all this."

"Oh?"

Jim leaned in more and whispered, "Whitt recognized the encryption signature from his days in military research. It's a code the Spacers used during the war, but once the treaty was signed, they were forced to give up all their coding machines, algorithms, project data, you name it. And to keep using that material would violate the agreement and be punishable with imprisonment or even execution, depending on the seriousness of the crime."

Esther's face darkened. "I had no idea. And you think Whitt is holding this over Kate?"

"There's no doubt in my mind. He even threatened me, saying if I mention anything about Ross 128 to anyone, he would expose the code, and Kate, and have her arrested for treaty violation." He took a sip of coffee and glanced around. "Now, combined with what you told me about his authority to detain people last night, I'm finally understanding how dangerous this is." Jim looked her in the eyes and said, "He must be stopped, Esther. The alien signal belongs to everyone, and our duty is to find out why he's being so secretive."

She grimaced. "Wouldn't that just put Kate's life at risk?"

"The opposite, actually. It would protect her, and here's why: If a handful of people hear the aliens, then the threat to Kate is real. However, suppose every nation learns about alien contact at the same time, then he can't do anything. The crying of Ross 128 is a big, harsh light to his shadowy ways."

Esther smiled thinly. "I'm not sure about that, but I do understand how public exposure could, in theory, reduce the risk." After a young couple eased by their booth, she quickly added, "What does Kate think?"

"I haven't said word one about it to her."

Esther's back stiffened. "You have to discuss it with her, Jim. It's her life that's most at stake."

"Sure, and I will. But first, consider this."

She looked at him eagerly, returning his gaze.

THE CRYING OF ROSS 128

"I need you to help me gain access to the subspace transmitter and the Oxford antenna array. I want to broadcast the Ross 128 signals live to the world, without any signal encryption."

Esther's jaw dropped, and she flicked her gaze nervously around the room. "You don't know what you're suggesting, Jim."

"Oh, I do. I'm asking you to go behind your colleagues' backs, commit a crime by giving me unauthorized access to the Space Ops Lab and transmitter, and jeopardize your career because of it."

Esther gulped hard. Her head spun. Everything she'd worked for her entire life flashed before her, and it could all be lost because of this man and his fervent open transparency doctrine. Yet, she admired how he protected Kate and Mary, and yearned for the same.

"That's an unfair request, Jim," she uttered. "I don't understand you at all. Last night, some guy pointed a gun at you, scared the crap out of Mary and me, and stole all your radio gear. Now you want me to get *more* involved in this dark business?" Fear and anger swelled in her chest as she searched for the words and, after a couple of false starts, she said, "You have some nerve asking me to flush my career and life down the toilet for... for what, anyway? Sorry, I see no need for shouting alien drivel from the mountaintops. So what if Marshall gets the glory in the end? Who cares?"

"This is bigger than Whitt's ego, don't you see? Someone else must be behind him, and it's clear whoever it is, they're hell-bent on keeping Ross 128 to themselves."

Esther's face relaxed and her breathing settled down.

"Why do you think that is, Esther?"

"I—I really don't know."

"Hm, me neither, but I doubt it has anything to do with the old 'contact-versus-no-contact' arguments. I mean, we're not even having that debate publicly."

Jim could be persuasive, and his logic appealed to Esther. Marshall was involved in something heavy behind the scenes, but what that was remained mysterious. Did she have sufficient courage to get deeper into it, with all the associated risks?

They finished their drinks in silence. When she put her empty cup down, Esther looked at him sympathetically, yet determinedly, and said, "I'm afraid I can't help you with this, Jim."

He was about to protest when she quickly added, "But as a concession, would you care to take a little drive?"

Atteberry

HER TWO-SEATER SPED OVER THE TRADITIONAL ROADWAY towards UC San Francisco, located in the shadow of Mount Sutro. Atteberry left his car at the recharge station near Grinders and accepted Esther's invitation to travel with her.

It was a bit of a tight squeeze for his long legs, but not uncomfortable, and the smell of the interior was an intoxicating mix of Esther's perfume and new upholstery. Because of the size, their thighs and shoulders kept brushing up against each other. Atteberry felt her trying to wriggle some space between them to no avail, finally accepting that they would be close for this short trip—not that he minded.

"What's at the university?" he asked.

"Actually, we're going behind it to the Mount Sutro Tower."

Atteberry realized this must be the location of the subspace transmitter. It made sense, after all, that the uplinks to the satellite antenna array would share space with all the other communications organizations.

The car flew over Frederick Street to Clayton, Clarendon, and then veered left onto Dellbrook and La Avanzada. From there, it crawled toward the base of the massive tower while all kinds of proximity alerts sounded until Esther voice-commanded them off.

Atteberry had never been this close to the tower before. As they neared it, he saw the area was completely encircled by barbed wire and concertina, at least ten meters high and three meters thick, and interlaced with vines and thick shrubs. The only visible entrance through the wire came with a guardhouse and security gate. As they glided to a stop, an armed, uniformed guard approached them, one hand raised, the other on his holster. He stood about a meter away from the vehicle.

"Drive window down," Esther said, and the hovercar complied.

"Identify yourselves," the guard barked.

"Doctor Esther Tyrone, Terran Science Academy." She produced her identification and access card. Pulling a bio-scanner from his hip pocket, he approached her warily, held it at face level, and stared into the small screen until it blinked green.

"Welcome, Dr. Tyrone. It's good to see you again." He peered past her into the vehicle. "Who's that?"

"This is Jim Atteberry. He doesn't have an access card but you'll find him in the system. He's been working with me and Marshall Whitt on a SETI project. I thought I'd give him a quick tour of the transmitter site."

The guard punched the bio-scanner and a second later, he smiled and said, "Welcome, Mr. Atteberry." Turning to Esther he asked, "Will you be here long, ma'am?"

"No, just a few minutes I expect."

"Very well, pass on through."

He pressed a button on his shirt collar and the security arm rose. The hovercar floated through and pulled up to a single doorway at a tiny out building, bereft of any signage except for the word *Entrance* stenciled on it. No outward markings at all to indicate this held one of the most important pieces of communications equipment in the entire world.

Esther pressed her hand against the bio-lock and the door clicked open. She flicked the lights on and Atteberry followed her inside. The room was windowless, and the walls were about half a meter thick and reinforced with some kind of coarse, dark material. The smell of low-level ozone and dust hit him immediately, and the slumped ceiling caused him to duck even though there was plenty of clearance.

A couple of pegs poked out from the wall to the right of the entrance. One had a stained baseball cap on it and the other had what looked like a spare TSA access card—the same kind he saw when he visited the Space Ops Lab. A small, thick wooden table sat on the other side of the room, and he recognized a subspace receiver on it along with a speaker and an operating computer with a darkened screen. Left of the receiver was another piece of strange gear.

"Is that the transmitter?"

"Part of it," Esther said. "The rest is under the table and within the walls.

Atteberry bent over and studied the space below. What he thought was part of the wall turned out to be a large, thin box with one manual key switch on top of it and thick power cables running out the side. The largest cable was connected to the other unit on the bench.

"I get it," he said. "The guts are underneath, but this box is the interface."

"Yes, that's right."

"The computer's linked to the TSA?"

"Right again. There's also a remote link to New York, and another to Kyoto."

Atteberry took a closer look at the arrangement. "You mean people in Japan can access the transmitter? Amazing."

"It's no different than any number of remote applications, other than the security gates, firewalls, encrypted codes and so on."

Atteberry smiled and imagined the hoops someone would have to jump through to transmit a subspace signal, and realized that's the reason she'd brought him here. This wasn't a cozy little info-tour. She knew it would be a deterrent. "Is the transmitter on now?"

"In permanent stand-by mode, yes. If the unit's cold it takes about 15 minutes to warm up to operational conditions and go through all its internal checks." She grabbed a couple of stools from the side of the bench and offered one to Atteberry. They sat down in front of the equipment.

"So, if Whitt fired up the transmitter last night, could you confirm that?"

"Yeah," she said, shifting her weight on the stool, "but I'd have to run the computer logs. That would tell us the GPS and network coordinates of the incoming commands. If Marshall did send them, we'd know right away. But consider this," she added, "it could have been someone else at the TSA running it. Doubtful, but possible."

Atteberry's indie-comm vibrated and he checked it. Mary was home from school and wondering when he'd be back. He excused himself and returned her message.

"Mary?"

"Yes," he said. "She's home, so I'll need to get going."

"I'm happy to drop you off, Jim, if you want to send your car home on its own."

"Thanks, I'll take you up on that." Clearing his throat, he asked, "Is it possible to physically transmit from here? I get that it's linked remotely, but if there was an emergency or something, could you run it directly from here?"

Esther considered the question. "I don't believe so. I know it sounds odd for a piece of equipment to require remote access only, but this isn't just any old device. The security protocols are designed so that even if someone did break into this room, they wouldn't be able to operate the transmitter. In fact, it's wired so that if someone even tried to tamper with it, the unit would self-immobilize. It's an added measure to make sure it remains functional only for a select few."

"Fascinating," Atteberry said. "But if it's such an important piece of equipment, why is there only one guard? Shouldn't there be a small army?"

"Careful, Jim. We only *saw* the one. That doesn't mean there aren't others around and, by the way," she said, pointing to the four ceiling corners, "we're being watched by some of them right now."

Atteberry peered into the dark. He hadn't even noticed the tiny cameras mounted there. His stomach sank. "And Whitt? Is he one of those watching us now?"

Esther rose from the stool and flattened her skirt. "Could be. He's not supposed to be monitoring this site since it's really the responsibility of our own Republican Security Force. But you never know with him."

Atteberry got up, still hunching over.

"Would that bother you if he was?"

"Yes, it would."

Esther looked at him coyly, mischievously, and said, "Sometimes being open and transparent has its drawbacks." She gave a quick look around the room. "Come on, let's get you home."

She led him to the door, opened it and flicked off the lights. Late afternoon sunshine hit them sharply, and she put her hand to her eyes as the daylight temporarily blinded her. When she hesitated a moment for her eyes to adjust, Atteberry deftly lifted the spare access card from the coat peg and dropped it in his pocket.

Once outside, Esther turned and leaned against the heavy door, pushing it shut. He heard it hiss and bolt twice. Then, as they walked to her car, Atteberry sent a command to his own hovercar to drive home.

He had no idea if he could gain access to this room again through all the security measures in place, but he knew that if anyone could hack their way through encrypted computer system firewalls, it was Kate Braddock.

FOURTEEN

Friday, October 13, 2085

Whitt

DR. MARSHALL WHITT ARRIVED AT THE SPACE OPERATIONS LAB early the next day humming an old John Philip Sousa march he'd heard on a documentary video. An autoserver waited for him as he approached his office and he poured a coffee and sat down at his desk. That's when he noticed a small alert icon flashing on the computer screen.

"Open."

THE CRYING OF ROSS 128

The security report blinked on. Jim Atteberry's name had been highlighted in two places. The first appeared when he'd been signed in to the remote subspace transmitter site at Mount Sutro. The second, when he left. Whitt did not fail to notice Esther Tyrone's name there too.

Shit.

"Contact Jackson, secure line."

His indie-comm chimed and in a couple of seconds Levar Jackson's deep baritone voice answered gruffly.

"Jackson here."

"Levar, I'm looking at a routine security report from yesterday and wondering why I'm learning about Jim Atteberry's trip to Mount Sutro now instead of from you when it happened. Explain, please."

Jackson coughed and cleared his throat. "Sure, we noticed that, but didn't think it unusual, so I let it go."

Whitt felt the slow burn rise. "Not unusual? A civilian—*this* civilian—rummaging around one of the most strategic comms sites on the planet?"

"I'm gonna push back here, Marshall. Your man has been all over the TSA, includin' the space lab, several times since this Ross 128 thing came to light. I have no idea what you two are doin' together, and frankly, I don't care. In my professional judgment, if he and Tyrone took a tour of that precious comms site, it's completely consistent with everythin' else he's been doin' with you guys."

Whitt pursed his lips and stroked his beard. Jackson was right, Atteberry had been everywhere. But with his equipment confiscated and what appeared to be a growing friendship with Esther, he was becoming a bigger risk, a potential cancer. More and better attention was necessary.

"Your point is taken, and I haven't kept you up to date with some other events either, and that's on me. Where's Atteberry now?"

"Hang on a second."

Whitt heard shuffling in the background and Jackson's breathing over the indie-comm.

"He's on his way to the college, it looks like. Just dropped the daughter off at school."

"Are you sure about the girl?"

"Yes, her device is active. She's there alright."

"Okay, I'd like you to keep a very close eye on Atteberry. If and when he contacts Esther Tyrone or Kate Braddock, I want to know immediately, and I also want transcripts of any of their calls. Understood?"

"Got it, Marshall." There was a lengthy pause, and then Jackson said, "You realize this goes beyond the scope of the initial task and is goin' to cost more."

"Yes, yes, understood. Keep track of your expenses and then tell me where we're at by the end of next week, okay?"

"Sure, I'll confirm through a secure message later this mornin'."

Whitt cut the link and sank into the chair, tenting his fingers in front of him. The loss of equipment should have put a massive scare into Jim Atteberry, but clearly hadn't. He rocked back and forth, watching others enter the lab through the main door across the room, planning multiple moves. Another idea slithered into his mind, one he'd been mulling over, that was less dramatic and might appeal to Atteberry's sense of open access for all. It required additional brainwork, a proposal of sorts; then he made a mental note to contact Major Tanner in New Houston.

First, however, was this other matter.

"Has Esther Tyrone arrived yet?"

"Dr. Tyrone is in her office," the computer voice responded.

THE CRYING OF ROSS 128

WHEN HE KNOCKED AT HER DOOR AND ENTERED, Esther was reading on the couch. She had a notebook beside her, coffee on the table in front, and a stack of files and technical manuals on her lap. Whitt liked the outfit she wore this morning, a dark green skirt and jacket, and hair pulled back with a band.

"Marshall," she smiled, "you're just the man I want to see."

"What a coincidence. I'm anxious to speak with you, too."

He closed the door, crossed the room and sat down in a chair opposite her. She moved the files from her lap to the table. "You go first."

"Alright. There's a lot happening, as you well know." He paused, choosing his words carefully.

"Could you be more specific?"

"I'm talking about Ross 128, the discovery of alien intelligence in the universe. The fact that this will change the direction of mankind forever. All our philosophies, religions, scientific pursuits, history books. Everything."

Esther sipped her coffee. "No doubt, and you've made contact with them."

"Yes, I transmitted a message the other night, which I believe you're aware of."

"The alien beings signaled back too, just before Jim Atteberry's home was invaded and his station dismantled by a bunch of thugs." She stared at him, narrowing her eyes. "You wouldn't happen to have any insights about that, would you?"

Marshall raised his eyebrows and sighed deeply. "Of course I do. I ordered the equipment confiscated. It's sitting all nice and cozy in a secure room in the lab."

"I see. Was it also your idea to scare the shit out of a little girl, and me too?"

He maintained his poker face, suppressing an overwhelming desire to lash out. "That, Esther, was unfortunate. They didn't expect to see you at Atteberry's home, and the daughter, Mary? Yes, that was simply bad timing."

"She's okay, by the way."

Marshall reflected on that evening for a moment, sat up straight and put his hands on his knees. "As long as we're being open and frank, let's get everything out on the table, shall we?"

"I'd like that." Before he had a chance to say anything, she fired off a series of questions: "When will Dr. Kapour be informed, the UN, the California government, your own Academy colleagues?"

Whitt scowled and raised his voice ever so slightly, just enough to take control of the conversation. "Please, what I'm doing is prudent and in our best interests. I will tell Kieran as soon as he needs to know, but in the meantime, it's critical that he be protected from all of this, you see?"

"I'm afraid I don't."

Whitt spoke more slowly. "There's a lot of unknowns surrounding what we're dealing with. The message from Ross 128 is still being analyzed. I can't fully make out the intention, the meaning, and I owe it to you, to Kapour and indeed to the whole planet, to find that out before going public."

"A precautionary approach, Marshall?"

"Exactly." He leaned forward. "Please bear with me a little while longer, then we can go together to Kieran, the other directors and anyone else."

"I can't understand why we don't do that right now. What's the problem sharing this event with as many others as we can?"

"It's quite simple: I don't trust them."

"*You* don't trust *them?* That's rich."

"Perhaps." He recalled briefly that time a few months ago when he stood her up and recognized the folly of his words. "Look, what concerns me most is Atteberry's—or Braddock's—pattern recognition program falling into the wrong hands, military hands, other enemies. I can't count on him to be responsible and keep quiet, given his much-publicized hippie views on open access. That's why I acted the way I did. You would do likewise in my position."

She leaned back and crossed her legs. "When, Marshall? When will you go public with this?"

How much longer could he keep her quiet and more or less in line was the real question... a week? A few days? "Tell you what, Esther, if nothing changes by the twentieth, we'll brief Dr. Kapour on everything together. He'll be mad as hell, of course, but I'm confident he'll come on side quickly because he listens to you."

Her expression did not change.

"In the meantime, allow me to finish the work I've started and determine the intentions of this alien ship, and—"

"It's a ship, eh?"

"Yes, and it's adrift around 128b."

"The planet?"

"Uh huh, but doesn't appear to be in a standard orbit. The analysis isn't complete, and we're refining the triangulation parameters, but the vessel seems to be drifting in free space, floating randomly through the Ross 128 system."

Esther glanced out the window at the sky, so Whitt continued. "Once I determine the intentions of this ship—that is, whether a distress call or something else—then we'll go public, or at least inform the leadership here and give them some options."

She turned to him again with determination and impatience in her eyes.

"One week, Esther. That's all I ask. And, if you like, we could both analyze the most recent signal."

"With a condition or two, I imagine."

"Of course. You would have to keep it from Jim Atteberry. He cannot know what's going on."

"Why not? He discovered the damn thing."

"Hm, well, to protect him and his daughter, primarily. I have no doubt that others are interested in this transmission and its strategic importance, too. You understand this well. If others suspect he knows key information, someone will go after him."

She flashed an angry look.

"Or Mary. He may not accept this approach, but you do. This is for his own protection."

Esther rose and put her hands on her hips. "Let me think about it, Marshall. Working with you on the project would be helpful and exciting, but I want more time to consider the implications."

"One week, Esther. That's all I need."

"One week."

He opened the door and just as he stepped out of Tyrone's office, glanced back at her standing at the window, staring out toward the ocean. "One other thing. Did you and Atteberry enjoy your time at the transmitter site yesterday?"

She glared in shock at his reflection in the pane, then dropped her gaze to the floor.

Esther

THE OFFICE DOOR CLICKED SHUT, AND ESTHER LET HER GUARD DOWN. She brushed a hand over her forehead and clenched her teeth. *The bastard knew.* He was making a point, a threat, without even saying the words. *Smart* bastard. She'd heard the stories about him before, how he could play politics and manipulative games, but until now she hadn't really seen it in action except for the date that wasn't. But then, how did the TSA and Whitt differ from any other organization she'd worked for, with ego-driven, power-hungry individuals who did this sort of thing for sport?

THE CRYING OF ROSS 128

So he'd caught her. All he'd need to do is make a phone call to Kieran Kapour, and she'd catch major shit. It was a well-known fact within the TSA that civilians were absolutely forbidden to enter the transmitter zone, but that didn't stop her from taking Jim there under the false pretense that he was part of the team. In truth, it was a concession, a weak excuse to buy his friendship. Mind you, he did have security clearance—for now—but that didn't change the rules and she was not in the habit of breaking rules of any kind.

What the hell got into you?

Esther flopped on the couch and picked up the pile of manila folders. She leafed through them but couldn't concentrate. Why hadn't Marshall already gone to Kieran? If he wanted her temporarily out of the picture, it would be so easy. She'd be suspended for lack of judgment and putting the TSA at risk—maybe a week, certainly no more than two. Yet, he didn't play that card. Clearly, he intended something else for her.

Was this a *"Keep your friends close and your enemies closer"* thing? If so, was she friend or foe? Curious, too: How did he know she took Jim to the site? Routine security report? That seemed unlikely. Although there were records of every kind of activity kept, especially around sensitive areas, these were generally logged and filed unless an incident occurred. Replaying yesterday's tour, she couldn't see anything out of the ordinary. This meant he must have flagged Jim Atteberry's name with security. Or hers.

She threw the folders back down on the table, took out the compact mirror from her nearby purse and checked her face. *Is this what you're turning into, Esther? A rule-breaker in pursuit of an ambiguous love that simply can't work?*

She shook her head. She had crossed a line she had no business crossing, putting her own selfish desires before her duties, responsibilities and obligations for the Academy. This must stop.

Esther vowed to take a giant step away from Jim Atteberry before she became completely swept up in his vortex, and to focus instead on helping Marshall, no matter what his end game was. The TSA and her career must not be jeopardized.

Atteberry

THE OCTOBER BREEZE WHISPERED IN FROM THE OCEAN under a perfect blue sky, sweeping over the downtown core and through the campus buildings at City College. It was late afternoon right before the weekend. Jim Atteberry and Kate Braddock meandered along the path beside Cloud Circle, speaking in hushed voices. Mary's principal had left a message that morning for him, and it plagued his thoughts.

"Apparently, she's been writing some pretty dark stuff in her school journal. The teacher wondered if everything was okay at home and I told her about the break-in and how it shook us up. What else could I say?"

"But Mary's all right?"

"Yeah, quieter... and a bit restless and clingy. But other than that, she's keeping up with her schoolwork and chatting with friends over the indie-comm. I tried to get her to open up about it, but she didn't want to, so I'll give her the space she needs until she's ready."

Kate put her hands in her pockets and scuffled over the concrete path. "Did you find out officially who grabbed your gear?"

"No, but I'm convinced it's that asshole Whitt. You were totally right about him, Kate. Can't be trusted at all. Esther doesn't even know what he's up to, so I doubt it's official TSA policy, whatever it is."

She stopped and touched his shoulder. Her hair was a mess, and she had huge dark circles under her eyes from lack of sleep.

A fresh scratch appeared on her left cheek, too. "Jim," she said, "what'll you do now?"

"I'm really torn. I can't risk putting Mary through any more of this, and all my instincts scream 'Protect her!' But I have this feeling that whatever Whitt is up to, it'll put a lot more lives in danger."

"What do you mean? Have you found out something more?"

"Not exactly." They began walking again. "I've been trying to figure out who else is behind Whitt's desire to be the only human being capable of communicating with the Ross 128 aliens. Seriously, it's got to be more than just wanting the glory for himself, right?"

Kate shrugged.

"So the question plaguing me is: Who's *really* driving the bus?"

"And who do you think it is?"

He reflected for a moment, piecing together the bits of logic. "If I go back through history, there's always been a close connection between science and the military. So, following that pattern, it makes sense that some kind of military organization is behind this as well."

"Uh huh, many of those TSA scientists were involved in the civil war one way or another. I suppose they might still have connections." Then she thought some more.
"Could it be our own Republican Force?"
Atteberry shook his head. "There'd be no point. It's not like we're preparing for battle or anything. California broke away from that nonsense the moment the first bombs were detonated."

"Still, some never drift too far from conflict, do they?"

"Yeah, you're right about that. It's hardly a stretch to see how the Chinese, Russians, or even the two American Republics could benefit from controlling strategic space comms. But like Whitt said, several organizations the world over are interested in this technology."

They stopped at a bench and rested. Kate leaned back and closed her eyes, facing the warm sunshine. Atteberry caught himself staring at her thin body in an oversized white blouse and denim jacket. She seemed to be losing even more weight these days. She liked to fast, but this was different, more frightening. Prying wasn't in his nature, so he didn't ask.

"Perhaps," she said finally, "it doesn't matter who's behind Whitt, if anyone at all." She opened her eyes. "The danger to you is real."

"Well, not so much now that my gear's been stolen. Not that I'm still bitter."

"You really think so? Look, it's looming pretty large for me too, Jim. Whitt knows I could always set you up with another pattern recognition algorithm and you'd be back in business. As long as I'm alive, I'm a threat. Actually, it's surprising he hasn't arrested me yet."

"Is that why you're losing sleep?"

Kate studied his face briefly, and appeared to be on the verge of tears. Then just as quickly, she reined her emotions in so that he doubted what he saw.

"Sorry, that wasn't fair." He returned to the subject. "Don't you think if he'd wanted you gone, he would've done something by now?"

"Yeah, who knows what's rattling around in that pointy little head of his."

"The thing is, Kate, I truly feel the only way to stop whatever it is he's doing is to expose the Ross 128 aliens to the rest of the world. And the sooner the better. Once the news is made public, the threats, the dangers, disappear."

She laughed. "You're a nut," she said, smiling.

"That's why we get along."

THE CRYING OF ROSS 128

"Yeah, well, if you went to the media or any scientific authority, you'd be ridiculed. You know that, right? There's no proof any more. No one else can hear the signal unless I give you another code. And all Whitt or your Esther have to say is 'We're studying the situation,' and paint you as one of those crackers they're always dealing with." She popped a piece of gum in her mouth. "Meanwhile, you may as well put a target on your back—and Mary's, too—if you did that." She lifted her face to the sun again, chewing. "Doesn't sound like a good idea to me."

Atteberry considered her words and watched the hovercars glide by on the Circle. Way off in the distance, ship horns sang. "Well, I have a plan to get around that."

"Figures."

"It involves you, Kate."

"Oh?" She sat up and eyed him intently. "What is it?"

"I saw the subspace transmitting station yesterday with Esther. It's up near Mount Sutro by the tower. A one-room deal, but heavily guarded with wire and cameras and who knows what else."

"Shit, Jim."

"But listen. The transmitter is activated remotely. There are links to the TSA here, of course, but also ties with New York and Japan."

"And you're planning... what? Fly to the Big Apple, figure out where the link is, and contact Ross 128 yourself?"

"Not exactly. Since it's a remote access network linked to computers, it could be hacked, right? We find a way into the system, fire up the transmitter, and expose the signals to the world by making your algorithm completely accessible. Anyone anywhere with a subspace receiver could hear it."

Kate bowed her head and shivered, remaining silent for several minutes. Atteberry understood her well enough to give her the time to think it through on her own. If she had questions, she would ask.

Finally, she said, "Come on, let's keep walking."

They left the bench and headed back toward the main building. She held his hand; it was cold and fragile in his. She stopped him in the shade of a large palm tree.

"You know I don't—can't understand love at all," she whispered, "and there's nothing I wouldn't do for you or Mary." She looked down before lifting her head and meeting his eyes. "But I can't do this, Jim, sorry. Please forgive me."

Kate stroked his hand, then left him and melted into a stream of students entering the building.

Atteberry checked the time on his indie-comm and glanced toward Batmale Hall. He scanned the crowd coming and going and, to his surprise, imagined a young man, not quite fitting in as a student, staring right at him. Before he could take a second look, the fellow had disappeared.

FIFTEEN

Whitt

MARSHALL WHITT DOODLED ON A NOTEPAD IN HIS OFFICE at the Space Operations Lab. The signal he'd received back from the alien ship on Wednesday night confused him and, for a brief moment, he wondered if Jim Atteberry would be able to solve it. Possibly, but the game had barely started, and patience was the key. The full Atteberry card had yet to be played.

He'd sent back the one-one-eight pattern to the Ross 128 co-ordinates and experienced the thrill that all communicators feel when a distant voice responds. The magic of radio, he called it as a young man. A signal, transmitted through space on equipment you built, acknowledged by some remote station. However, analysis of this one proved challenging.

Ross 128 had responded with one-one-eight. After that, another element was added to the pattern. Six pulses which, if the atomic number theory was true, meant the aliens were now transmitting CH_2O: formaldehyde. Whitt understood the importance of that chemical as a precursor to many other organic compounds. Moreover, interstellar formaldehyde was abundant throughout the galaxy. So what could this new signal mean? What did the alien ship hope to convey?

Shortly after, the pattern grew to include nitrogen and, along with the familiar one-one-eight for water, various other molecules that Whitt realized must represent protein structures. However, within these were other mysterious, confusing pulses and, after studying the chemical compounds, he couldn't draw any conclusions. There were too many missing pieces. After several challenging minutes, the alien transmission ended. Whitt had yet to send anything back.

He sketched some of these chemicals out since doodling helped him think better. So many questions. What he needed was a team, a proper team with funding and computational power and the best cryptographers on the planet under his direction. He put his pencil down, took off his glasses and rubbed his eyes. It was time.

"Contact Major Suvo Tanner, New Houston. Secure line."

As he waited for the Major to connect, Whitt gazed around the empty lab. The lights were dimmed half-way, the day's activities now mere echoes. He looked forward to going home after this call.

The video link flickered and a middle-aged woman in a sharp blue uniform stood in front of a clean desk. "Hello, Marshall, you look tired. How are you?"

"Major Tanner, it's been a hectic few days here and, as you can appreciate, when we're chasing new discoveries and such, we can't ask the universe to take a break."

She chuckled. "Much like the military, if you remember."

"I do, Major, I certainly do." He flashed a mirthless smile. "I wonder if you've given any further consideration to the proposal I sent yesterday. I'm anxious to resolve the matter and attend to the business at hand."

She turned and picked up a red folder from her desk. "I've had a chance to review your idea and discuss it with my colleagues here."

"Yes?"

"Short answer is we'd love to have you join us in the new Space Exploration Agency. We could benefit from your recent experience at the TSA and your knowledge of military ops would clearly be helpful."

Whitt expected as much. He hadn't been looking for a change in career, but with the discovery of Ross 128 aliens, an opportunity presented itself for him to work on something truly remarkable, and to have the resources of a national military behind him.

"But I am curious, Marshall," Major Tanner continued. "Why now? Why all of a sudden this change of heart? We first approached you over six months ago and at the time you said something like, er, 'Never,' in response to the offer." She slapped the folder back on her desk. "So what's changed, without any doublespeak if that's okay."

Whitt inhaled deeply. "Major, accepting your offer is predicated on a couple of things, of course. I will need to assemble a first-rate team of my choosing."

"Yes, I read your proposal, and we're okay with that as long as some of our own people are on it. So what's the second thing? Did I miss it?"

"Major," he began, "do you remember the old Spacer Program back in the days before the civil war broke out?"
Tanner eyed him carefully. "Yes, what about it?"
"There's no need to be coy, Major, we both know the program still exists under a different name, fresh objectives. But the essence of it remains the same; that is, recruiting genius level programmers and scientists for delicate, strategic projects."
"Go on."
"Well, I would like a unit of my own. Just a few operators, enough to handle the kind of space experiments I've got planned."
Tanner removed her glasses and began cleaning them. Then she looked up and said, "Marshall, our program objectives have already been established and approved. We're not about to change those."
"Oh yes, I understand. But what I'm telling you is that I intend to focus all projects on subspace travel, including manned flight. And the Spacers—or whatever you call them these days—are perfect for this kind of work. We need extremely bright, well-trained people for this."
"That's highly ambitious. We're on a 20-year track with FTL travel. It's one of several—"
"I know, but I intend to push most of the resources into it. Once I join your outfit, that is."
The screen flickered. A grey line scrolled across the top indicating the secure link functioned normally. Major Tanner glanced off-screen numerous times before turning her attention back to Marshall Whitt. There was someone else in the room now joining her, perhaps a superior.
"Our budget here is surprisingly robust, but it's not a huge unlimited pot, and we are accountable to our political masters. The emphasis of our program is on achieving some short-term successes. They may not be as sexy as *Star Trek* but they're certainly viable and less risky on the whole." She glanced off-screen

again. "What you're looking for is a tough sell and I highly doubt we'd be able to accommodate your request for a Spacer unit. So has anything changed in the last few months to prompt this request?"

Whitt hesitated and cleared his throat. *This is as public as it gets.* "Major Tanner, and whoever else is with you, I have developed a subspace pattern recognition algorithm capable of detecting coherent signals in cosmic noise."

"We already do that, Marshall."

"I'm sorry to disagree with you, Major, but your technology is only able to find signals above the noise level. I can pull them out of the noise itself. This opens up unlimited spectral possibilities."

Tanner hit the mute on her comm link and discussed something with her mysterious colleague. Momentarily, she came back on. "Do you have proof of this, Marshall? We've had others claim pattern recognition apps before and the results were uninspiring if not altogether fraudulent. Has yours been validated by others?"

"Major, I have irrefutable evidence the technology works, and I'm prepared to bring it all with me since it was not developed at the TSA."

"Oh? I'm listening."

Whitt overlaid a chart of the Ross 128 dwarf star system on the screen. "Do you see this graphic, Major?"

"Yes, but I'm not familiar with it."

"Quite alright. It hasn't enjoyed the kind of global interest of popularity as, say, Ganymede. Not yet at any rate." He took a sip of his tea and continued. "This is the Ross 128 system, a dwarf star about 11 light years from us. A few weeks ago, we used our pattern recognition algorithm on the subspace radio bands and picked up a signal from this system."

"Like a quasar or something?"

"Not exactly. Major Tanner, what we received was coherent and intelligent. Our analysis indicates that whoever sent the signal was searching for water. I won't go into the details now of how we came to that conclusion, but the key point is: We are not alone in the universe."

Whitt expected Major Tanner to pepper him with a thousand questions. Instead, she leaned back on the edge of her desk, arms crossed, gazing at the floor in front of her, and turning to her colleague from time to time, listening.

"Do you understand the significance of this, Major?" She finally answered. "Yes, I do, Marshall. But tell me, why haven't we heard anything about this?"

"Simple, because I have not informed anyone. You are the first. What I plan to do is bring my technology with me, establish a new unit to work on communicating with the alien life-form, and begin right away on accelerating the subspace travel projects."

"This is going to take a while to sink in. We'll need to discuss the strategic ramifications of first contact, the UN protocol, how to position this politically. Marshall, do the Northern Democrats know anything about this?"

"No, Major, my allegiance is and always has been with the South."

"Understood. My colleague and I will review this right now and I'll be in touch shortly."

"I take it you would like to move forward then?"

"Yes, the sooner you can get down to New Houston, the better. This will change the course of the cold war, and more. Well done, Doctor."

"Will I get my Spacer unit, Major?"

"Affirmative. I'll call you soon. Tanner out."

The screen blinked and was replaced by an image of his two children playing in the backyard when they were young, before they'd been recruited. Before they disappeared forever.

THE CRYING OF ROSS 128

Atteberry

THE WEEKEND PASSED ABOUT AS NORMALLY AS JIM ATTEBERRY could have imagined, except the time he usually reserved for listening in on the amateur radio astronomy bands was filled with reading and sorry attempts at painting. Out of curiosity, on Saturday he'd contacted a few friends in the Astronomical Society about borrowing their equipment but the reaction varied from direct refusal to grave uncertainty. The stigma surrounding his earlier proclamation about life in the universe still hung over the group like a bad smell.

So here it was, early Sunday evening, and Atteberry had made a decision. The accountant thug was right: his listening days were over—at least for now—and he needed to get back to normality. A stack of mid-term exams awaited grading, and he wanted to spend as much time as possible with Mary doing fun father-daughter stuff.

They were downstairs in the basement, Mary lying on the floor reading Kafka of all things ("Dad, he actually turned into a bug! A real bug!"), and Atteberry reclining in his chair struggling through a brutal essay, soft music humming in the background. That's when his indie-comm pinged. He leaned over and was surprised to see Esther Tyrone's name appear.

"Hi Esther, how are you?"

Mary glanced up and smiled mischievously.

"Still at the office catching up on some work for tomorrow morning, but I was just wondering how you and Mary were doing?"

"Good." Atteberry called over to his daughter. "Esther wants to know how you're doing."

"Awesome!"

"Listen, I'm glad you called. I was hoping to speak with you and—say, crazy thought here, but would you like to come over after you're finished work? We could make up some hot chocolate?"

Mary's head snapped up, and she grinned. She shouted, "Say yes!"

"Did you catch that?"

Esther laughed and said in a warm voice, "Sounds perfect, and I can be over in 20 minutes or so."

"Great, see you then." He cut the link. "Mares, we'd better get those supper dishes cleaned up pronto. Come on!"

They dropped their papers, Mary climbed on his back and they clambered up the stairs to tackle the kitchen. As they finished up the dishes, the doorbell chimed.

"Come on in, Esther, and welcome again!"

"Thanks, I'm hardly dressed appropriately so I hope you don't mind."

She wore jeans, sneakers, a white tee shirt and navy jacket, hair loose and flung around her face.

"Actually, you look great."

Mary peered out from the kitchen corner with a big smile. Atteberry hadn't seen her that happy since, well, the last time Esther was here. Before the insanity.

"How are you, Mary, Daughter of Jim?"

Mary walked over and gave her a hug, much to Esther's surprise. She eyed her dad with a puzzled expression. Atteberry shrugged.

"What's new with you?"

"You wanna see my room?"

"Sure!"

Mary dragged her down the hall and shut the bedroom door. Girl time, Atteberry figured, and returned to the kitchen to put

away the remaining dishes. When he finished, he picked up a book from one of the shelves and flopped on to the sofa.
An hour later, they emerged.
"Dad, we're thirsty for hot chocolate!"
"Okay, kiddo!"
The trio gathered around the kitchen island. Mary pulled a bag of marshmallows out from the pantry and Atteberry boiled the water.
"You two were awfully quiet."
They exchanged secret smiles. "Girl talk, Jim." And giggled.
After their drinks were poured, they took their mugs to the living room and sat down, Mary and Esther beside each other on the sofa, and Atteberry in the Queen Anne.
"So, Mr. Atteberry," Esther began, "what's on your mind?"
Atteberry felt a bit awkward raising this in front of his daughter, especially since she was so happy now, but proceeded nonetheless. "I've made a decision." He put his mug down on the side table and leaned forward. "It's about the alien signal."
Mary flashed him a confused look.
"Look, I've been thinking a lot, and there's too much risk and danger to the people I love most to pursue this any more."
"So what does this mean?" Esther asked, her voice colored with a hint of nervousness.
"Just that I want to lead a regular life again. Spend time with you, Mares. Read good books and teach. Basically not invite trouble, because I've learned if you go searching for trouble, it'll find you. I need us to be safe."
Esther turned to Mary and asked, "What do you think?"
Atteberry fully expected her to be overjoyed. He felt this decision would signal a new, clear measure of security. Instead, Mary softly said, "Dad, you can't quit like that."
Atteberry straightened and looked back and forth between Mary and Esther. "It's not about quitting. The aliens will be public

knowledge soon, then all this rubbish will surely be over. If I put you in danger like what happened the other night. I'm just not..." he paused, "If anything..."
Mary scrambled off the sofa and hugged him. She had tears in her eyes.
"I love you, Daddy."
"I love you too, Mares."
Then she said, "But Dad, listen, I can help you. Maybe Esther can, too." She stared over at her, and Esther nodded imperceptibly. "You don't have to fight bad guys all alone. Besides," she added, "we've been talking and both think you're great, so just tell us how to help."

Even in the soft, muted light of the house, Atteberry saw Esther blushing. She turned her face to the side to hide it.
"How about I'll give it some more thought but keep in mind that safety always comes first, okay?"
"Okay!"
Mary's indie-comm pinged from her room so she scrambled down the hallway. In a moment, she shouted, "It's Evie. Can I talk to her for a bit?"
"Sure, kiddo!"
The door closed again and Atteberry listened to Mary's voice rise and fall but couldn't make out what she was saying. He peered at Esther, who had recovered, and moved to sit down beside her.
"Is that what you were chatting about forever?"

Esther smiled. "Oh, not only that, all kinds of things. Boys mostly, but also some school and girl stuff." She studied him closely. "We talked about her mom a bit, too."

"Oh?"

"She misses her, of course, but said she was getting used to life without her. Oh, and she adores Kate, but you knew that. Started asking some odd questions about her though."

"What do you mean?"

"Well, things like why she sometimes dressed as a boy instead of a girl, and why she doesn't have breasts."

"What did you tell her?"

"The truth... that Kate was part of a special program years ago and had to undergo surgery to protect herself, but that it didn't change who she was on the inside."

Atteberry raised his eyebrows. "I'm not sure she would entirely agree, but thank you for that. I wouldn't have known where to start."

"She hasn't asked about her before?"

"Nothing like that."

They sat in silence for a few moments, sipping hot chocolate.

"Anyway," Esther finally said, "are you serious about dropping Ross 128 after everything that's happened?"

"Yes, *because* of everything that's happened."

"See, I know Marshall's planning something, and if Kate supplied a new copy of that algorithm, I could—"

"No, Esther, no, no, I can't do that. Good idea, but Kate's life is at stake, and I'm finally clueing in that she may disappear tomorrow and never be heard from again. Whitt just needs to say the word."

"Okay, but he hasn't actually done anything. For that matter, he could have me suspended, too, but hasn't, so I think whatever he's up to, it doesn't involve reprimands and could be more for show than anything else."

Atteberry sighed deeply and shook his head. "Who knows? But I'm also worried about Kate's health. She doesn't seem well these days, I mean, she's always been light and fragile but you should've seen her on Friday. Not good at all."

There was a pause. "Jim, I'm sorry I brought up her code again. I understand how important she is to you and Mary, and I shouldn't have said anything."

"That's okay. It's an odd relationship, but one I cherish."

She checked her wristwatch, a rare piece of jewelry these days. "I should get home... big day tomorrow."
Atteberry walked her to the front door and opened it. Their eyes met and held each other for a moment until she nervously glanced away.
"Goodnight, Esther, and thanks for coming over and talking with Mary."
"Say bye to her for me."

Esther

THE ANTIQUE CLOCK ON THE MANTEL ABOVE THE GAS FIREPLACE chimed 11 times and Esther, who was on her second glass of wine, folded her book closed and sunk into the loveseat. What was it young Mary said? Oh yes, *Do you like my dad?* She was bright and direct and curious about relationships of all kinds. And she'd made it clear she didn't care for the idea of her father dating or having a new mom and that's why she liked *her* so much.

Jesus, kid, why not just twist that knife a little more, hm?

For whatever reason, Mary wasn't threatened by her and that was okay. Some of her own friends back in grade school had gone through family splits that took years for the healing to occur. Her one friend, Tara, confided some time ago that she'd never resolved the pain, and possibly as a result of that, left a trail of broken relationships piled like dog shit in the park along the way.

Still, Esther felt hurt that Mary didn't see her as that kind of friend for her dear old dad. She'd answered with an off the cuff, *Sure I like him, he's fun,* remark but knew Mary thought there was more to it by that curious, penetrating look she gave her. So she told her the full truth: that he was handsome and smart, that she liked being with him, and around Mary, too. Anything more than that, well, they'd all have to wait and see. And that satisfied her to the extent that she opened right up about everything: what's it like to really kiss a boy? To have your period (can boys tell)? To be a real scientist? To travel to space? And she was not about to let some idiot goons push her around, either.

Esther reached over and grabbed the tablet off the table. The most puzzling thing was this strange friendship he had with Kate Braddock. She knew Kate was part of the old Spacer Program, along with thousands of other genius level kids, and that her training was obviously in programming. Whitt recognized her signature encryption code, so she was probably in one of those units that developed coding, planting viruses in enemy satellites, whoever that enemy happened to be at the time. But what was her connection to Jim? Other than helping her out when she arrived on campus, he didn't say anything else.

"Search all information available on Kate Braddock, instructor at City College, San Francisco."

The tablet pinged and Esther pulled it in front of her, but all of Kate's personal data was protected under various privacy firewalls, some of which were itemized on the screen. She thought of another way.

"Find everything there is on the Spacer Program, circa '26."
New information scrolled across the tablet screen.
"Read it out."

"Spacer Program. Formally launched in June '26 under Major-General Paul Laviolette, Pentagon, former United States of America. Objective: to undertake high-level science and engineering experiments in physically dangerous environments. Program continued during the Second American Civil War under various authorities. Officially disbanded in September 2075."

"Stop. How many children did the program recruit?"
"Data classified."

Esther scrolled down the tablet. There was a picture of Laviolette, some non-interesting colonels, and a list of several pre-war projects the Spacers were involved in.
"Provide all information on recruit Kate Braddock."
"Data classified."
Interesting. If she hadn't known Kate was a Spacer, she'd have nothing on her at all. She considered a different tack. "Provide any information on any random Spacer."
"Data classified."
Whitt suspected Kate could be working for someone, but that might have simply been a red herring for her benefit. Still, if she was involved in espionage, it would completely make sense for Jim to be in the dark, seeing as how that's the nature of the business. A mole, perhaps, but whose?
Esther, you're becoming paranoid.
"The cold war will do that to a person," she muttered.
The idea clung to her mind like a Vermont burr in the fall. If Kate's intentions were sinister and she had somehow worked herself into Jim's life, he could be more vulnerable than he realized. Esther had to acquire more information on Kate and, if anything indicated a potential threat to Jim, she had to tell him.
But the Newnet offered up nothing. Kate was fully protected by privacy shields. However, the ancient worldwide web might have information if she risked looking there.

Esther did not believe in pure good or evil, but if something could change her mind, it was the chaos, vulgarity and insanity of the global internet that used to be the go-to global source of data, communications, information... everything in the world when it was first introduced. The only people who accessed it now were the despotic leaders, sexual predators, terror cells and anonymous sickos. There was a reason why it was outlawed, especially for someone in her position in a government-funded, quasi-international agency. Lack of privacy, checks and balances,

security, you name it. Thank god for the more civilized, if sometimes frustrating, Newnet.
If Kate Braddock had a past, it would likely be there.
"Access internet four."
The tablet pinged and the familiar digital voice said, *"Warning. Access to Global Internets one through four contravenes International Law Article 217. Warning. Access to—"*
"Understood." Her heart thumped loudly in her chest and she put her device down, wishing there was some other way to learn more about Kate.
Yet, the penalties for illegally accessing this internet included prison and, unlike its regular users, she had no clue about how to mask herself. And for her, getting caught would surely end a solid career that was already toeing the legal line.
Esther bit her lip. "Access internet four."
"Warning. Acc—"
"Understood."
Moment of truth, Esther. *Are you willing to put your career at risk over this?*
"Continue with access to internet four."
The screen darkened momentarily and a new alert appeared with a concise statement: *You are about to enter Global Internet Four in violation of International Law Article 217. Do you agree to continue?* At the bottom of the screen were two buttons: *I agree,* and *I do not agree.* Esther took a deep breath and placed her right index finger over the former button. This is it, she thought. She closed her eyes and pictured Jim in front of her with his warm smile, his love for Mary...
Mary.
Esther slammed the tablet on the floor and the screen went blank. She held her face in her hands and burst out crying with a painful moan that crept up from a soul-chilling well.

Atteberry

AT BREAKFAST THE NEXT MORNING, ATTEBERRY REMARKED how Mary was back to her old self: happy, humming away, spilling cereal all over the kitchen table and conveniently expecting him to clean it up. Whatever magic Esther performed last night, it certainly worked.

He dropped her off at school and watched her run up to the large glass doors where she turned and waved at him, then ducked inside with a swarm of other kids. He continued on to campus where he planned to finish marking those mid-terms and getting the grades loaded into the system before noon.

The hovercar released him in front of Batmale Hall and glided away as another car purred in to take its spot. That's when Atteberry saw the black, middle-aged man staring at him beside the main doors, wearing a dark suit and tie, tan overcoat, and gloves. His short cropped hair, steel-rimmed glasses and straight posture told him this fellow was one hundred percent military.

"Jim Atteberry?"

"Yes? Have we met?"

"No, sir, but may I take a minute of your time?"

Slight southern accent. Polite enough, that's encouraging. "Sure, there's a table inside the foyer. Shall we chat there?"

They entered the hall and found an open spot by the main windows. The man kept his coat on, which was also encouraging.

"My name's Colonel DeShawn Piper."

"Cal Rep Forces, or...?"

Piper grinned coldly. "No, sir. Confederate."

"I see," Atteberry frowned. He hadn't chosen sides in their war and didn't really care if the North and South wanted to bash each other's brains in as long as they remained east of California. "What brings a Confederate military man to Frisco, Colonel?"

Piper removed his gloves and placed them neatly on the table. "As a matter of fact, sir, *you* do."

"Me? Are you here to try intimidating me and my kid again? Take more of my stuff?"

"Please, Mr. Atteberry, I had nothing to do with that," he said softly. "I'm here to make you a job offer."

Atteberry shook his head. "Er, no thanks. I hope you didn't completely waste a trip from wherever home is, but whatever you're offering, the answer is no."

Atteberry got up to leave when Piper said, "We'd like you to join our Space Exploration Agency in New Houston."

Atteberry's jaw dropped, and he slumped back into the chair. "Your what?"

"I understand you know a thing or two about recognizing alien signal patterns. Subspace filtering and such. Now, I don't pretend to know all the technical aspects of communicating with space vessels, but I can say we are in the middle of assembling a top team of scientists and thinkers to pursue alien comms, FTL travel, and—"

"What? Space vessels?" he blurted out. A couple of students glanced over, then moved on. "Faster than light travel? Is that what you're working on?"

"It's what we will be working on, sir, yes. And your name has come up as someone who knows about subspace comms, signal analysis, pattern recognition. You were, after all, the first Earthling to record a coherent alien signal, no?"

"Ah, sure, I guess so." Atteberry's head was spinning.

Colonel Piper, expression unchanged, continued. "See, we understand how frustrated you must be watching others communicate with the Ross 128 vessel while you sit on the sidelines and have your equipment removed."

"Confused and upset, more like it. Your goons scared us good last week."

"Not Confederates, I assure you. But I do know who they were, and I can tell you they will never frighten you or anyone else ever again."

"That sounds rather ominous, Colonel."

"Mr. Atteberry, we recognize the importance of your discovery and how significant a contribution you can make to science and, indeed, to all humankind. Sometimes, in order to protect the freedom to explore and discover, we must stop the lunatics from interfering. Fight fire with fire, so to speak."

"I see. Tell me, Colonel, what do you know about this alien ship? This is the first I've heard of it."

Piper took a small notebook from his inside jacket pocket and leafed through it, stopping mid-way. "Well, it's all a bit uncertain at this stage, but we believe the ship is a relatively small craft, anywhere from 50 to 75 meters in length, about 20 meters across. Looks like a flattened cylinder, at least that's what the egg-heads—pardon the expression, sir—in the lab think."

"What do they base that on?"

"Hell, sir, I wouldn't know."

"What else is there?"

Piper licked his thumb and brushed through the notepad again, flipping pages back and forth. "Seems as if they've been incommunicado since last Wednesday. ET's running silent at the moment."

Atteberry swallowed hard. So he hadn't missed much, just that final transmission, the one with other irregular pulses in it.

Staring the colonel in the eye, he said, "Question: Where is Dr. Marshall Whitt in all of this? I'm sure he arranged the classless theft of my stuff, and he's undoubtedly behind the Terran transmission to the aliens. I find it hard to believe you wouldn't be speaking to him too."

"Well you're right about Dr. Whitt. He will be playing a large role in the new space program."

"I'm out then."
"Now wait a minute, sir, don't be so hasty with your decision. It was Dr. Whitt, in fact, who insisted I speak with you and make this offer to join his team."
"Are you serious?"
Piper glared at him with a blank, deadpan expression. "Do I look like the kind of man who makes jokes?"
"Okay, what exactly is the offer you're talking about?"
"It's a position in his research group. He will lead the entire exploration program, but naturally needs help. And he specifically wants you to head up the signal analysis group because, as he said to me, 'Atteberry gets it.' His exact words. Picture this: you'll be working with top-notch scientists, cryptographers, astronomers and technicians and your primary objective is to put in place a comms protocol with Ross 128."
"So we can communicate with each other?"
"Precisely."
A thought burst in his mind that Kate might like to join him. "May I hire some of my own people?"
Piper said, "I'm not in a position to answer yes or no. You'd need to discuss that further with Dr. Whitt."
"I see, of course. And I suppose I'd have to travel to New Houston from time to time as well."
"Actually, you and your family would have to relocate to New Houston at your earliest convenience."
Atteberry slumped his shoulders. The decision to accept this offer suddenly became more difficult. He had no desire to move from San Francisco and, truthfully, didn't want to give up his teaching either. Mary's friends were all here, and she liked her school. Asking her to leave all that and start anew would be hard. Then there was Kate. And increasingly, there was Esther.
"How soon do you need a decision on this, Colonel?"

"I'll be in town until noon tomorrow when I fly back. I'd like your answer one way or another by then."

"Why the rush, if you don't mind my asking?"

"Time marches on, sir. We'd like to outfit one of our light spaceships with subspace capability as quickly as we can and explore Ross 128 before anyone else."

"And if I decide not to join you?"

"Then we never had this conversation." Piper's gaze bore into him like a laser, as if to imply *You really must say yes*.

Atteberry stood, followed by Piper, and they shook hands. "Thank you, Colonel. I'll give it serious consideration and call you early tomorrow morning."

"Very well." Piper pulled a business card out of his pocket, and a folded piece of paper. "Reach me on my personal indie-comm at this number. Here's the formal job offer to look over." As he turned to leave, he cleared his throat and said, "Keep this to yourself, please. Discuss it only with your family. No one else."

SIXTEEN

Whitt

MARSHALL WHITT CRUNCHED INTO A RED DELICIOUS APPLE, wiped the juice on his sleeve, and waited in the TSA lobby for Piper's arrival. He felt oddly exposed in the open foyer, and wished the colonel would hurry up so he could return to the cozy confines of his office. The message he'd already checked five times had, unsurprisingly, not changed on the sixth; still, he thought there must be a hidden subtext but all the note said was *On my way* followed by the initials *D.P.* Whitt also studied the picture of his visitor so he'd recognize him in civilian clothing.

The apple was sweet and crisp, and after finishing it he tossed the core in the composter and was cleaning his fingers when Colonel DeShawn Piper strolled in, a slight frown on his face. Piper was a bit taller, and by the way he dressed, screamed *Government Agent.* Whitt found that amusing, and snickered to himself just before they shook hands and introduced each other.

"I trust your flight was uneventful, Colonel?"

"Yes, precisely the way I like it. I got in late last night after you and the Major briefed me. You're doing some remarkable work here, Doctor."

"Thank you." Whitt showed him to the elevators, and they descended. "I'm anxious to know what our friend's response was to my offer."

"Heh, that. I think you already suspect the outcome."

"An imminent move to New Houston to join the team, I'm hoping."

They marched through the Space Ops Lab towards Whitt's private office. On the way, Mark and a couple other curious techs stopped what they were doing, and watched. Whitt ignored them.

Colonel Piper removed his coat and hung it on the rack. He placed his gloves in one of the pockets and took a seat opposite Whitt. The autoserver flew by and the two men dispensed coffee.

Whitt sat on the edge of the desk, facing his guest, stirring his drink. "So, Colonel, how did it go?"

Piper blew on his coffee to cool it down with limited success and burned his lip. He grimaced. "There's no doubt in my mind he's going to make the move, Doctor. Jim Atteberry was surprised by my visit, of course, but his excitement trumped any personal problem—if I may call it that—he had with you."

"Good, so he'll come aboard?"

"He didn't exactly say that yet. He wants to discuss the offer with his family and contact me in the morning with a decision."

"Perfect, but you think he's already made up his mind."

"I do. He was thrilled to hear about a new agency dedicated to exploring and communicating with Ross 128, and showed no reservations about working under you. In fact, he could hardly contain his excitement." He took another cautious sip. "There was one challenge, however."

"Oh? What was that?"

"The move to New Houston."

"But you told him about the research center there, didn't you? The generous funding?"

Piper dangled the mug between his thumb and index finger. "Not exactly. Atteberry seemed pressed for time. It may be worthwhile for the two of you to travel there and take a formal tour together."

Whitt did not like that idea. Not one bit. A road trip now would set off alarm bells with Esther and the others at the Academy, so, no, he'd pass on that.

"Maybe one day, Colonel, but not before he's committed first." He pulled himself off the desk and sat down behind it. Piper took in his surroundings, eyeing his degrees, the famous photographs, and science awards on the wall. He loved these moments of intellectual superiority, and smiled.

"Colonel, can you tell me again what Major Tanner told you? I admit I was half asleep when you pinged this morning."

"My orders were to, er, connect with you and make the job offer to Atteberry on behalf of the armed forces." He took another sip. "Then haul my ass back home ASAP."

Whitt raised his eyes and tented his fingers. "It's this connection part that baffles me, Colonel."

"Oh that. Well she wants you to know your decision to return to the Confederate program is resonating nicely across the system. She also confirmed the initial operating budget for next fiscal which, I believe, you already have."

"Yes, but did she mention anything about the new Spacer unit I requested? There's nothing in the financials."

Piper coughed and wiped his mouth, then pulled his notebook out and leafed through it. "Your proposed unit is approved with caveats that she says you already discussed, but for obvious reasons, it won't appear in the numbers as a line item."

"Okay, thanks. I suspected she agreed but I wanted reassurance since I haven't seen paper on this yet."

The colonel smiled. "Papering decisions, Doctor, is not what we do best. That could take a couple of weeks. In fact, we were lucky Atteberry's job description and offer came together as fast as they did."

Whitt's familiarity with military systems, procedures and bureaucracy helped him understand the time frames. A week or two was nothing in the grand scheme, and he was prepared to wait longer, if necessary. Besides, he still needed to complete the analysis of the last Ross signal he received and find his replacement. Mental note to self: recommend that Esther take over leadership of the lab until a new director can be hired.

"So what do we do now? I'd like to begin working on the new space program as soon as I can, but there are some tasks I have to finish here first."

"Sure, I expected as much, and I need to hear from Jim Atteberry. If he agrees to the offer, then one of my corporals will follow up on the logistics of the job, moving, timing and so on. If he turns it down, well, that would set in motion any number of alternative actions."

Whitt felt a sudden, anxious shiver. "He can't be allowed to simply walk around free with the knowledge he has about the aliens."

"There's a contingency plan for that scenario, if it should materialize." Piper rocked back on the chair legs. "But I'm confident

THE CRYING OF ROSS 128

he'll join us." He flashed Whitt a strange, ominous look which didn't help the scientist relax at all.

"I guess we wait for his decision in the morning."

"Yes. In the interim, he may try contacting you to discuss the offer, the work, the military connection and if that happens, feel free to have that conversation."

"That's safe to do?"

"A verbal commitment is all I need. Then he's ours." Piper stared hard at Whitt in that uncomfortable, non-descript way again.

"Understood."

"Be careful, though, not to talk salary or budget with him. We haven't worked out all those details yet."

"Colonel, there is no need for concern."

Piper slapped his thighs and stood up. "Fantastic! Then our work—my work, I should say—is done." Surveying the lab, he said "If you'll point me to the exit, I'll take my leave."

"Here, Colonel, let me walk you to the lobby."

They left Whitt's office and on the way to the elevator, he showed the colonel a couple of the projects being undertaken, and pointed out the quantum simulator that hummed quietly in front of the radio benches. Piper's monotone expression remained unchanged throughout the mini-tour. Whitt figured he must have been born sucking on a lemon instead of his mother's breasts.

They rode the elevator to the lobby and Whitt escorted him to the main doors.

"Thanks again, Doctor. It has been a pleasure chatting with you."

"I look forward to hearing from you as soon as you've talked with our friend."

Piper nodded and put on his coat. He turned for the door and was about to leave when Whitt grabbed his arm. "Colonel, you said the move to New Houston caused him some heartburn, yes?"

"That's right."

"But you still feel he'll accept the offer."

"I do." He checked the time on his indie-comm. "Is there anything else, Doctor?"

"Sorry, yes, one last thing. Did he mention his daughter Mary, and whether she'd be moving, too?"

"All he said was he'd have to discuss the matter with his family. I assumed he meant for her to join him. The mother's dead or something, isn't she?"

Whitt scratched his beard and waved his arm dismissively. "The history there is murky, but irrelevant. We don't want to break up that little father-daughter unit, you understand."

"A family man, Doctor? I like that! Good day, sir." For the first time since arriving at the Academy that morning, Colonel Piper smiled broadly.

Atteberry

THE REST OF THE DAY BLEW PAST IN A BLUR. Atteberry completed his marking with renewed enthusiasm, met with a couple of students worried about their mid-terms, and attended a mandatory health and safety meeting that failed to grasp his attention. As per the colonel's direction, he did not speak with anyone about the offer. When Mary pinged that she was home, he dumped his papers into his briefcase and headed out the door.

Mary sat at the kitchen table drawing stick characters on her tablet.

"Whatcha doing, kiddo?"

THE CRYING OF ROSS 128

"Hi Dad, I'm making up a cartoon. Evie and I are writing stories and putting scenes together with stupid stick people. Mine have crazy eyes." She looked at him and giggled. "I can't draw real humans either."

Atteberry laughed and took the chair beside her, moving a bunch of books and the school bag aside. "Mary, I'd like to talk with you about something that happened to me today."

She stopped drawing and her eyes, filled with curiosity, widened.

"Not a bad thing, Mares. A man approached me from a space exploration center and wants me to work with them."

"Sweet! Will you be studying the alien signal?"

"Yes and also looking at how ships can travel faster than light. Part of a science team."

Mary leaned over and wrapped her arms around his neck. "Let's get a pizza and celebrate!"

Atteberry untangled himself and stroked her head. "Not so fast, Mares. There's a catch. The job isn't here in San Fran."

"Where is it? Pasadena?"

"It's not even in California."

Mary's face dropped, and she studied her suddenly fascinating drawings.

"It's at the Space Exploration Agency in New Houston. We'd have to move there. That's what I need to talk to you about it, Mary, because this is a family decision. If either one of us doesn't want to go, we won't go.

Mary said quietly, "My friends are all here, Dad. And what about school? And we were planning to study the aliens together, with Esther, too. What about your teaching?"

He tried to gauge her mood, but she hid it well. "All good questions, Mares. That's why we both need to consider this offer together. We both have to agree to it, not just me."

Mary saved her cartoon and searched New Houston on her tablet. She read out loud some of the aspects of the city. Three hundred thousand inhabitants, established 2077 after the civil war, primarily a research center for the space sciences but also a growing arts community, well-serviced by monorail, supersonic air travel, lots of green areas.

"What do you think, Dad? It's a lot smaller than San Fran."

"It is."

Then she said, trying to hide a smile. "Dad, would I be able to work with you on some projects? Like, could I help find the aliens?"

Atteberry felt a deep sense of pride and excitement. Wouldn't it be something to have her follow in his footsteps? Perhaps she could have a small task to investigate as part of a school project.

"I tell you what. If you're allowed to study some things with me, would you like to go?"

She didn't hesitate at all. "Yes! Oh yes, Daddy!" She rocked back and forth in the chair, mouthing *Pizza pizza* with a huge smile on her face.

"Then let's do it, kiddo! And if it doesn't work out for any reason, I mean, if you or I hate it after we've tried it for a while, we can always come home. Agreed?"

"Agreed!" They shook hands, nodded at each other and laughed. "Mares, ping that pizza place!"

AFTER SUPPER, MARY FINISHED HER HOMEWORK and together they scanned the Newnet for information on New Houston. The schools and neighborhoods were mostly all constructed in the last decade, a city built from the rubble of the war. Mary chattered away, humming and surfing through homes for sale ("That one... no *that* one..."), full of enthusiasm.

THE CRYING OF ROSS 128

Her reaction came as a complete surprise. He'd counted on there being a lot more concern, especially over her friends, but she mentioned how the technology made it so easy to stay in touch with her group and reminded him of Cassie who moved away two years ago and still talked with her regularly.

In the stillness of his thoughts, Atteberry would explode if he didn't talk to Esther. He wrestled with the colonel's suggestion *cum* order not to mention the offer to anyone except Mary, and he would have complied with that if she'd wanted to stay. But since the decision was now made, he needed to speak with her. "I'm going to call Esther," he said, picking up the indie-comm from the kitchen table and sitting down in the living room.

Esther's face appeared in a moment. She smiled, took off her reading glasses, and placed them on her desk. The telescope behind her sparkled in the light.

"You're still at the office?"

"Yes, but not exactly working. This book fell off my shelf, and I started reading, and I feel like stargazing later tonight. How are you?"

"Great! Listen, I have something I want to share with you. Do you have a few minutes?" He relayed everything that happened that day from the time he met Colonel Piper on campus to the celebratory pizza party with Mary. He did all the talking and as he finished up, a guarded expression hardened on her face.

She toyed with a pen. "Let me understand this, Jim. You're going to New Houston to work with Marshall on some kind of Ross project?"

"Yes."

"Well this is no small surprise. He hasn't said squat about moving on. In fact, I think Marshall's still in the lab working out the signal analysis with Mark what's-his-name, so I'm more than a bit confused with this sudden news. You weren't exactly on speaking terms with each other."

Atteberry rubbed his forehead. "It does sound odd, right? But think of it, Esther, I could be part of the first team to establish contact with an alien ship. This means I could help spread the right message of openness."

Her mouth twisted into a funny expression and she tossed the pen on her desk. "Jim, I think you're being naïve. Marshall is not exactly an open access fellow, and I highly doubt he'd want to apprise the world of his research. But suppose this offer is legit for a second." She hesitated and stared at the ceiling. "If he takes this on and you decide to join him, what about all the practical considerations of your life here? There's Mary to think about first—"

"Oh we've already talked."

"Please, Jim, let me finish. Mary and her friends, teaching at the college, Kate. Whether you like it or not, she is implicated in any decision you make. And then there's..."

"What, Esther? What else?"

She sighed deeply and blurted out, "There's me, too. Jim, maybe this sounds silly and totally up the pole and way too fast, but I... I hoped we'd—oh, it doesn't matter. Never mind."

Atteberry hadn't thought about her or Kate and suddenly felt a wave of guilt wash over him. "Esther, I'm sorry, you're right. I haven't discussed this with Kate yet and I really shouldn't be talking to you about it. The colonel wanted me to keep it quiet. But Mary likes the idea, and we spent the last hour exploring New Houston and all kinds of things together."

"I see." Esther leaned closer to the screen. "I would've liked to join you."

An awkward silence filled the space and the darkness between them.

"I'm sorry, Es—"

"Don't say it. Don't keep saying you're sorry when you don't mean it." Then she added quickly, "I have to go, but promise me one thing, okay? That you'll gather all the facts about the job before you make a decision. Talk it over with Kate, too, despite what that military guy wagged on about. She needs to know." Esther cut the link and Atteberry's indie-comm went blank. What she'd said made sense, and he kicked himself for not having the courage to be more open and trusting, but how could he tell her his mind had already been made up?

SEVENTEEN

Esther

THE COOL, RECYCLED AIR IN THE CORRIDOR LEADING from the elevator bank to the entrance of the Space Operations Lab felt refreshing as she hurried to speak with Marshall Whitt. He was chatting with Mark in front of a smart screen, pouring over various chemical symbols, their atomic numbers and configurations. They looked up as she approached, smiled and greeted them warmly.

"Sorry Mark, I'd like to steal Dr. Whitt for a moment or two if that's okay with you, Marshall?"

"Certainly." He handed the optic pen to his student. "Come to my office. There's a little more privacy there."

They walked in silence past the workbenches and, once inside his office, he closed the door. Esther sat down and he took the chair behind the desk. "What's on your mind?"

"Marshall, I can't put this delicately at all, so I apologize in advance if this comes across as rude or disrespectful. My intention is simply to get at the truth."

"By all means."

"Are you leaving the TSA for New Houston?"

His eyes never blinked. "Yes, that's true. Not right away, mind, but I hope to clear up my projects here quickly and move on to greater challenges."

"With the military?"

"Sort of. It's the Space Exploration Agency where I'll be working. And yes, it's funded by the their military and reports up through a strategic command structure, but I remain a civilian as will most members on my research teams."

She felt optimistic with how forthcoming Marshall expressed himself. Still, she eyed him with suspicion. "And Jim Atteberry will join your team? Working for you?"

Whitt interlaced his fingers on the desk. "Mr. Atteberry has not given his decision, but an offer was made, yes." He raised a hand. "Before you say anything, Esther, here's why: As strange as it may seem, I want him on my team when we go public with Ross 128. After all, he did hear the message first, and it's only fitting he should be recognized for it."

"That sounds a tad too generous for you, Marshall. What's the real reason? Surely, he could perform your PR work here in San Francisco, at the TSA?"

Whitt grinned coldly. "The real reason, hm? I need his untrained approach to signal analysis, his enthusiasm, and ability to speak about first contact without using equations and jargon. Obviously he lacks scientific training, but I feel he brings a certain understanding and insight to research that is missing in, say, Mark or the other young researchers around. Would you agree?"

Esther recalled her own experiences working with implacable scientists, each with their own personal doctrine, likes and dislikes. Often, what drew people into science was lost once they became employees at a job like any other working stiff. "There's definitely a culture that could benefit from an outsider's perspective, I give you that."

"So Atteberry is perfect. Look, I know it sounds strange after all he's been through and my little 'Secret Squirrel' act, but I recognize when I need to admit I'm wrong about someone."

"But why New Houston, Marshall? It just seems out of the blue."

"Honestly, I wasn't looking for a change, but when Ross 128 appeared, I realized how much I wanted the freedom, the funding, and the control that a large budget, focused operation could provide. I had some connections there and made a call, and proposed a research team."

"Marshall, seriously? Don't you think because that agency is funded with military dollars you'll just be answering to different bosses? Bosses. Not colleagues like you have here."

Whitt leaned back and stretched, putting his arms behind his head. "I have no problem with that, Esther. We all have our roles to play."

"One thing's for sure. Kieran Kapour will never give you permission to take the Ross 128 research to New Houston. It belongs to the Academy right here."

"That's a battle that won't ever materialize."

"Oh?"

"You see, I'm the only human being who can actually, physically communicate with the alien ship so when I leave, that capability goes where I go."

"What about Kate Braddock's algorithm, the code you ghosted? Nothing's stopping her from sharing that with us or anyone else.

"In theory, but you're forgetting that unfortunate breach of treaty non-disclosure requirements. She *could* share her tech with others, no question. But she *won't.*"

Whitt was right. He'd planned it all through and then some. It was accepted practice since the end of the war for researchers jumping from one organization to another to take all their data with them. Corporate intellectual property policies for these scientists were just as ridiculous as asking them to stop breathing.

"So that's that?"

"Yes. I don't have an exact timeframe for the move, but I hope to be down there and established within a few weeks."

"A few weeks! Marshall, that's not enough time for the rest of us to find a replacement for you, or at least a couple contractors to manage your projects."

"I'm recommending that you take over the lab here. Perhaps consider merging it with SETI. Would you agree that makes sense?

Esther did. It made a whole lot of sense and in the back of her mind, establishing closer connections between the two areas would create something she wanted to accomplish while at the TSA, merging the softer *search* for alien intelligence protocols with the more practical *contact* aspects.

"You're an interesting, unpredictable man, Marshall."

He grinned in that annoying, contemptuous way of his and said, "And you are unpredictable too, Esther."

She had nothing more to say, so she strolled back to her office mulling over Marshall's words. In terms of his leaving for a new research team, she argued it was inevitable given his desire for more power and control over space exploration. That was not surprising. The carrot he dangled about bringing the two directorates was particularly enticing and touched her own ambitious goals for the Academy. Did he propose this possible merger on purpose? Of course. Marshall Whitt knew exactly how to bring her onside. The one anomaly, however, was the recruitment of Jim Atteberry. A non-scientist. A political opposite. She had not figured out his end game with Atteberry.

The daily scuffles and noises of the third floor had long disappeared for the day when Esther returned to her office. She stood in front of the large window overlooking the dark grey Pacific and kicked her shoes off.

Two events were poised to bring a storm of questions and media coverage. The first? Marshall's public announcement—whenever that happened—about Ross 128 and the alien ship. The second? His departure from the TSA in favor of a Confederate agency. No doubt, that would raise Northern Democratic eyebrows, not to mention those in California who supported his work. Kieran wouldn't be happy about that decision or the political repercussions either.

She needed to clear her head and think, and the best way to accomplish this stood right in front of her.

She killed the office lights and opened one of the window panels to study the sky through her old telescope. The night blushed darkness, perfect for stargazing since there was a waning moon that almost disappeared into complete black. She searched deftly for Aries the Ram, then focused on Seven Iris glowing through the constellation. In so doing, the subtext of building a case for the merger of SETI and Space Ops ran in her mind's background. She also considered how to convince Jim Atteberry to remain in San Francisco. Logic wouldn't do it. Despite his interest in radio science, he clearly didn't have the well-honed methodical approach to decision-making that scientists had, focusing on facts, advantages and disadvantages, consequences of even the slightest action, methodological precision. No, logic wouldn't convince him to do anything, she suspected. But love might.

Whitt

"Do you know," Whitt reflected that same evening as they entered the last of the message code into the transmitter relay program, "what the majority of people wanted to say to aliens, if given a chance, a hundred years ago?"

Mark peered up from the computer screen and shrugged. "Not a clue, sir."

"Have a guess. What's the most popular message people chose to send?"

Mark hemmed and hawed, eventually muttering something about being a peaceful planet, possibly relaying our spatial coordinates in the solar system. Whitt was hardly impressed.

"You should take the time to learn the history of space communications, Mark. It will be extremely useful." They continued entering the code, line by line, checking and double checking each entry against their notes.

"So, what was it, sir?"

"Oh yes, the message. It was very simple. 'Help us.' Can you imagine?"

"Seems odd," Mark said. "Help us how? Why?"

Whitt finished verifying the line of code before responding. "It reflected the times. People worried about climate change, armed conflict, nuclear weapons, overpopulation. The world was in a highly charged state of anxiety." Then he added, "Ready for the next quantum?"

He and Mark continued coding. When Marshall paused to call the autoserver, Mark said, "Most of those problems have been fixed though, haven't they? Except for conflict which, I guess, will always be with us."

"True. As long as we humans are what we are, it's impossible and ridiculous to deny our violence-based evolution. 'Survival of the fittest' is not the most caring doctrine, hm?" The autoserver spun by their workbench and they both took coffee. "But this leads to an interesting question. We have established contact with an alien ship. All we've done to date is return the *water* message. Their most recent transmission remains incomplete, so communicating is a real challenge." He stood up and stretched. "But we'll figure the comms out soon enough, and when we do establish a common protocol, what then should we send? Our own cry for help like our ancestors wanted?"

Mark looked up from his stool. "I guess I'd begin with what we look like, our coordinates around Sol, and that we are a peaceful planet." His expression changed suddenly. "Or 'Save us'?"

"That's as good as any other message, I suppose, but the aliens are searching for water. Perhaps we should ask how we can help them?"

Mark blushed. He'll be a solid scientist some day, Whitt thought, especially if he continues with this work in New Houston.

"That makes more sense than mine."

"Yours is correct, too, and important. But first, since they're requesting assistance, we should consider how to provide that."

They resumed their coding input. After 15 minutes, Whitt strolled into the Oxford Room to check on the antenna array. Mark joined him shortly after, once he'd confirmed the successful upload of the transmission code.

The orbiting antennas were precisely where they needed to be for maximum power efficiency and beam coherence to Ross 128.

THE CRYING OF ROSS 128

Whitt noted the natural drift of the array, all within operating parameters, and he verified both uplink and downlink frequencies for the subspace transmitter on Mount Sutro. All appeared ready.

"It's beautiful, isn't it, sir?"

"What is, Mark?"

"I was admiring the antenna array on the screen."

"Yes, it's a dated method for ELF transmissions, especially given our travel capability within the solar system, but still highly effective."

Mark checked some notes on his tablet. "I think we're all set to transmit, Dr. Whitt."

"You *think* or you *know*, Mark? We're only going to fire off this message once."

He ran his finger down the screen. "I *know* we're ready, sir."

Marshall gave a nod, raised his eyebrows and positioned himself in front of the main screen, the one beside the monitor showing the antenna icons. "Are you prepared to make more history?"

"Yes I am."

Whitt craned his neck, looking at him with admiration. "That was a confident statement. Good for you. Be bold in your assertions and you will command respect for your ideas every time."

"Yes, sir."

"Now then, we've got the message uploaded, the array is in place, and the subspace transmitter is in standby mode." He exhaled deeply. "Shall we see who's home?"

For the second time in the history of the planet, a subspace transmission aimed at an alien ship was imminent. Whitt proceeded through the necessary protocols, the checks and double-checks, the security and access codes, and everything was ready and fully operational.

Marshall Whitt enjoyed mentally tracing the signal as it was reduced to modulated code traveling at microwave frequencies

to Mount Sutro, reconfigured to subspace frequencies, uplinked to the orbiting array, and beamed to the Ross 128 system. The entire process of accessing the satellites and the subspace transmitter took several minutes. The transmission itself was relatively short and to the point. Whitt did this on purpose. He wanted to gauge the response rate for the ship given a short transmission. It would speak to the aliens' capability to receive, record, decipher, analyze, understand and return a signal. Tonight, the transmit time was 65 seconds.
"It's almost disappointing, don't you think, Dr. Whitt?"
"What is?"
"We spend all this time developing a message, preparing to send it, accessing the array, but the transmission itself lasts a minute."
"A bit like Christmas, isn't it? Or first-time sex."
Mark laughed. "Yes it is."
Whitt followed the protocols for returning the array and the transmitter to standby modes, which took several more minutes. When he finished, he gathered up his notes. "Well, Mark, our work is done for tonight. Time to go home and get some rest. Perhaps tomorrow or the next day we'll receive a message back from the... what should we call them?"

"The aliens, you mean?"

"Yes. *Aliens* sounds too, er, broad don't you think? How about the *Rossians*?"

"Sure."

"Maybe the *Rossians* will contact us soon. Yes, I like that name."

As they left the Oxford Room, Marshall hit the light switch, then ordered the lights dimmed for the entire lab.
Walking to the elevators, Mark said, "I have a question about the message, sir."

"What is it?"

THE CRYING OF ROSS 128

"I understand why we returned *water*... that all makes sense. But this other part with binary codes and prime numbers is a bit baffling. I know we're looking for common language protocols, and that math is a good platform as long as we assume the same rules and logic apply throughout the universe, but something's bugging me about that."

Whitt stopped. "Tell me."

"Well, it's not the binaries or the primes. It's the *implied* message we're sending by using *that* math as the basis of understanding."

Whitt narrowed his eyes and scratched his beard. "Speak plainly, Mark, because it seems only logical that we'd want to establish the rules of math, chemistry, physics before inviting them over for tea."

"I agree, but I'm following this through a bit. If the aliens—the Rossians—recognize primes and understand the basics of binary code, why did they use atomic numbers in their initial signals? I mean, why not transmit in binaries, assuming any other galactic being would have to at least grasp that number system to receive signals at all? If binaries are available, then choosing atomic numbers instead is way more cumbersome and incomplete."

It was an interesting question that Marshall hadn't spent any effort considering. Short answer: Who knows? But he figured in the fullness of time, as consistent communications became established and comprehension protocols determined, these answers would be forthcoming.

"Brilliant query, Mark, and I'm impressed you worked it through the way you did. Well done. Naturally, we don't know why they chose one method over another. Perhaps by adopting atomic numbers, they accomplish the same comms goal while simultaneously telling us exactly what they're looking for. You know, more efficient." He resumed walking again toward the elevators. "I expect it'll become apparent to us the more we study their signals and the longer we're able to maintain communications."

The elevator doors *whooshed* open. Mark followed Whitt through the yawning doors and into the car.

EIGHTEEN

Monday, October 16, 2085
Late Evening

Atteberry

"It's super late, Mares, and you need to go to bed. And I want to call Kate."

"Okay, Dad, relax." Mary finally relented and closed her tablet up for the night. She gave him a hug on the way down the hall.

"Don't forget to brush those teeth!"

Mary hollered something back, but it was swept away in the kitchen noises.

"I'll be down shortly to say goodnight."

The pizza bomb had created collateral damage as he collected the plates from the pie and ice cream and wiped the table clean. Water running in the bathroom provided an odd backdrop to Mary's humming while she brushed. Then the floor shook mildly as she flopped onto her bed.

"Gonna read for a bit, Dad!"

Atteberry sat down in the kitchen and called up Kate on his indie-comm. When she answered, audio only, she spoke distantly, almost in a whisper.

"Hi Jim, how are you?"

"Good, but Christ, you sound awful. Everything okay?"

"Yeah, sure. Actually, no. I'm going through a rough patch mentally. Some days I can't tell who I am anymore."

Atteberry recalled the breakdown she had last summer although she tried to keep it a secret. The symptoms were a bit different now, but the strain of her voice rang ominously similar.

"Can I do anything? You want to come over and stay here tonight?"

She didn't answer right away. "Let me think about it."

"Sure thing. It's an open invitation, any time, no matter what else is going on."

"Thanks. So what's up? You don't often call this late."

Atteberry began pacing around the kitchen. "Listen, I've been made a job offer to study the Ross alien signals in New Houston, and I wanted to talk it over with you. Get your sense of it all."

"Wow," she croaked, "that sounds like a hell of an opportunity. New Houston, huh? What are they offering that you can't find in Frisco?"

"Well, it's with the Space Exploration Agency there, the new one operating under the Confederate military."

"Seriously?"

Atteberry chewed his bottom lip. "But the work is—"

"Shit, Jim, let me guess. Whitt has something to do with this?"

"Ah, yes, he's leading the group and I would head up the signal analysis team working specifically on Ross 128."

"Jesus," she said, "what are you doing? The asshole undermines you every chance he gets, steals your equipment, threatens you and Mary, and suddenly wants you to partner up? Did you not think this strange?"

Atteberry felt the heat rise in his gut, defensive anger poking its head up. "But think about it, Kate, it's an opportunity to influence what happens with Ross 128. Currently, I'm totally out on the sidelines with no voice. If I'm part of Whitt's team, like him or not, at least I can share my views on open access in front of other influencers. And who knows? Perhaps the military wants that balance."

Kate remained quiet other than her labored breathing and mumbled *shit* a couple of times while he expanded on it, but did not argue. An awkward, drawn out silence hovered over them as he waited for her to make the next move.

"I don't know, Jim, something's not right, and my instinct screams there's more happening in the shadows." She paused, then added, "Or maybe I'm just letting my own past and paranoia get in the way. So, backing up, congratulations. Whether you take the job or not, it's an honor to be invited, isn't it?"

"Yes, it really is, Kate."

"Speaking of which, when's the deadline for letting them know?"

"Tomorrow morning. I met with a Confederate colonel earlier today and he needs an answer before leaving."

"Hm, that leaves you no time to study the fine print, eh?"

"No, but I talked it over with Mary and she's pretty excited."

"No way."

"Yeah, surprised me, too. We just had a little pizza party to celebrate."

Kate exhaled. "So you've decided to accept it?"

"Yes I have, we have, and I'll call Colonel Piper first thing in the morning. By the way, does that name ring any bells?"

"Doesn't mean anything to me." Then she said, "I respect you a lot, Jim, and I wouldn't say this if I didn't."

"What is it?"

"Please reconsider. You already know Whitt can't be trusted, and the very fact you'd be working with him should sound the alarms."

"Kate, I—"

"On the surface, I'll bet this looks like a wonderful idea. You two guys put the past behind you, team up, study the aliens and so on. But I'm telling you, I sense nothing but danger."

"What do you mean? No question, the man's a toad, and frankly, I don't like him, but it's a fantastic opportunity to make history here."

She sniffled and was clearly struggling.

"Kate, I'm sorry. That was rude and defensive."

"Jim," she said, "please reconsider. Take the rest of the evening to study the motivation behind the offer, okay? Promise you'll do that?"

Atteberry sighed. "Of course. Your opinion is super valuable, and that's why I wanted to tell you. Still, I'll keep an open mind and go over everything, and in the morning, no matter what, you'll be the first I call, okay?"

"Yes, thank you." She continued weeping.

"Kate, please, let me help. Will you come over?"

"Yes," she said finally. "May I stay with you guys tonight?"

"Of course, get here as soon as you can. I'll tuck Mary in before you arrive."

Atteberry cut the link and sighed. Something may be strange with Whitt's offer, but something's definitely off with Kate. He hoped to talk it out.

"I'm coming down the hall, Mares!" he growled in his deepest, scariest monster voice. She squealed with delight, suddenly his five-year-old again.

Ten minutes later, he crept out of her bedroom, softly closing the door. She was exhausted from all the evening's excitement.

Atteberry had just settled down in the living room with a book when a gentle knock interrupted him. *That was fast.* He turned on the light in the hallway, unlocked the front door, and swung it open.

"Hi," she said.

His jaw dropped and tears suddenly filled his searching, confused eyes.

"You," he whispered. The world started spinning, and he felt nauseous, undone. He leaned against the wall for support.

"It's good to see you again," she smiled thinly. "May I come in?"

"I... ah, sure. Yes, yes of course."

Janet Chamberlain glanced over her shoulder and stepped inside the house.

NINETEEN

Atteberry

THIS WAS ALL WRONG. SHE WAS ALL WRONG. The once-blonde hair was dyed jet black and cut much shorter than before, and her face wore the cruel signs of premature aging: well-entrenched crows feet, hard jawline, and she had a three-centimeter scar running across her chin.

She perched upright on the edge of the sofa, leaving her overcoat on, hands folded neatly in front. Atteberry sat across her. Questions billowed through his hazy mind, and he had no idea where to begin. Over the past two years he longed to ask her so many things if the chance ever presented itself, but now he couldn't think of one.

"I can't believe this. You're here, home at last."

"Jim, there isn't much time, so I won't stay long."

He shook his head in disbelief, oscillating between smiles and concern.

"I'm not here for a reconciliation."

The words barely penetrated his thoughts as the sudden shock of seeing Janet sitting like she used to, upright and proper, struck him.

"Do you understand?"

Leaning forward, wanting to be close to her yet somehow afraid, he said, "No, no I don't understand anything at all. The last I heard from you was that cryptic note you sent about not trying to find you. So I didn't, Janet, I didn't even try. It nearly killed me." A tight lump formed, and he fought hard to keep from breaking down.

"Thank you, sweetheart." She walked over and put a hand on his cheek but he spun away. Still, she wouldn't be denied, and grabbed him by the shoulders. "Pull it together, Jim. You need to be calm and focused." Inhaling deeply a few times, he nodded.

"Are you back, Jan?"

She stared hard and said sharply, "No."

"Why not? We've missed you so much. The house is so different without you."

"Listen, let's not go down that road yet. Now pay attention and look at me!" Her voice had an unrecognizable, commanding toughness, and he glanced up wiping away the tears with a sleeve. She'd grown a lot thinner, and even though her face was hard, the soft, dark eyes remained. But that was the only thing.

"What's going on?"

"Jim, I need you to focus on what I'm telling you. There isn't much time."

She returned to the sofa, stared at the floor for a moment, then spoke. "There's no easy way to say this, so brace yourself. I've come to take Mary."

"What do you—"

"Please, listen. Her life is in danger and she needs to be protected. I can offer protection."

"For *crissakes,* Janet, what are you talking about? I'm her father. I would never let anything happen to her and I sure as hell won't let you kidnap her! Do you have any idea about our lives now?"

She raised her hand like an old-fashioned traffic cop, something she used to do since their first date.

"I completely understand what's going on, everything from Ross 128, Kate Braddock's algorithm, the break-in here last week, the job offer with Dr. Whitt. Need I continue?"

"How did..."

"Doesn't matter how, the point is Mary needs protection and as long as she's with you, her life's in danger."

"Janet, please, I don't get it. I'd never hurt her, you must know that."

She smiled warmly and briefly fought back her own tears, then quickly recovered and resumed her business-like tone. "I have no doubt how much you love her. None. And what you're capable of if she's threatened. But can't you see, Jim? The people watching this house, stealing equipment, offering you a job in Confederate territory... it's not *you* they're interested in. It's *Mary.*"

Atteberry couldn't believe what he heard. This made no sense, and his head still ached from the moment she walked through the doorway. But no one would take Mary. They'd have to kill him first.

"She's not going anywhere, Janet."

"Wrong, handsome. This sounds crazy but hear me out and then decide where she'd be the safest." Janet stood up and paced around the room, eyeing the paintings and knick knacks. "Your friend Kate was a Spacer, right? And at the end of the civil war, she was released from the program and took up a civilian career, eventually winding up here."

"Yes, yes, but so what?"

"You may not know that the Spacer Program never ended. Oh, it runs under different names now, but gifted children are still being recruited for highly complex space-related security work around the world. Not just military either, Jim."

"That's unbelievable. We would've heard something, and surely the parents wouldn't tolerate seeing their kids taken away and mutilated and—"

"Don't be so naïve, Jim. Governments are capable of doing anything, even killing their own citizens to further state goals. Too often, they simply can't help themselves. It's all part of Earth history."

"But how is Mary implicated?"

"To be blunt, they want to sterilize her, cut away her parts, train her up, and toss her into toxic space environments to do the work machines can't."

"Nonsense!"

"I wouldn't have returned except the madness is about to begin, so get your head out of your ass and listen, damn you!" She grabbed him again by the shoulders, speaking rapidly and harshly.

"Connect the dots, Jim. That high school science project she was asked to join? That was sponsored by the Confederates, and the teenagers involved in it are part of their Adolescent Operatives program. You want more? The creep spying on your home was a known Confederate agent, but it wasn't you or the alien signal he was interested in: it was Mary. And Marshall Whitt is only offering you that job so he can get her away from here. It's Mary he wants. Not you. Do you understand?"

Atteberry fought an urge to throw up, swallowing hard. His tongue was dry and foreign. "But even if all that's true, Janet, I can protect her."

"No you can't, and it's not because you don't want to. What they've been doing with child recruits lately is brainwashing them into thinking their families are evil. In many cases, the kids are forced to watch their parents being tortured and killed, or they say Mom and Dad abandoned them. Make no mistake, they'll come for her, and you won't be able to do a thing."

He tried focusing, assimilating what she said, but it was still too much to absorb and he desperately wanted time to think everything through. As well as have a no-holds-barred *other* conversation with Janet.

"But if I can't help her, what makes you think you can?"

"Because I have the resources to keep Mary safe." She pulled a sleek pistol from her overcoat pocket.

Atteberry stared, puzzled and bewildered. "Who are you? Where are you from?"

"I'm an agent with the Northern Democratic Union, trying to prevent this cold war with the Confederates from heating up any more than it already has. A spy, if you like. I have been since before the war began."

Doing the math, he realized she was probably an operative around the time of their first meeting. Another sudden urge to throw up swept over him as the room started spinning again.

"Then you and me...? I was nothing but a fool in some spy versus spy game? And Mary? Oh sweet Jesus, how could you, Janet?"

She checked an indie-comm device, the likes of which he hadn't seen before. "It began that way, yes," she said, "but when we married, it was because I loved you, and that wasn't part of the plan. For what it's worth, Mary's birth was the happiest moment of my life. That was all real, all of it. But sometimes, a greater good exists, demanding to be served, and I know you've understood this for years with your open access stance and transparency for all."

Several silent minutes passed as thoughts raced through his mind. Then Janet said, "Time's running out."

"You keep saying that, but what are you talking about 'time running out'? What's the rush?"

"Jim, you've got to trust me when I say this house is being watched, and I doubt it will take long before they figure out the strange woman at the door wasn't Kate Braddock. When they do, they'll be here before you can spit."

Atteberry remembered the link with Kate. "She's coming over this evening, so if they're watching, they'd think you're her."

"Yes."

"Wait, how do you know about her?"

Janet sighed. "We're listening in on your conversations, too."

"*Too?* What's happening here?"

"Remote sensing. Kate fixed your computer that time because one of their idiots botched the set up, but we're both listening to everything going on here with tech that Kate knows nothing about... internal bugs, satellites. In fact, if I hadn't been jamming their signal tonight, they'd hear everything we're saying right now instead of the televiewer music I gave them. That's why we're having this open conversation."

Atteberry scratched his beard, sighing, feeling trapped in his own house, under Big Brother with a microphone. "So now what? If Mary goes with you, what do I do?"

She held his gaze several seconds, then said, "It's really important that you pretend nothing has changed. Leave Mary's indie-comm in her room as if she's asleep. Keep it there during school, pretending she's sick, and move it around the house when you're home, going to the spots where Mary normally goes. That'll buy us enough time, I hope, to provide you and Mary with new identities and get you relocated."

"Can't you just arrest Whitt or whoever?"

"It wouldn't make a difference, Jim, because someone else would take his place. The Spacers are a valuable commodity, and there are hundreds of Dr. Whitts around."

"And Ross 128? What happens with all that?"

Janet raised an eyebrow and said coldly, "Nothing, Jim. Nothing. When the immediate threat is over, all evidence of the Ross aliens will be destroyed."

"They're fake?"

"Oh no, a hundred percent real as far as we can tell. But assuming they can't travel faster than light, they'll become an issue for another generation to deal with."

Atteberry ran his fingers through his hair and sighed deeply, sinking into the chair.

"So do I go about normal business?"

"Yes, and for the love of Christ don't leak that you know you're being watched. Keep using your indie-comm even though it's bugged. If you need to have confidential conversations, use public indies and meet in oddball places."

The floorboards creaked. They both turned to see Mary standing in the hallway, rubbing her eyes.

Janet knelt down. "Do you remember me, Mary?"

A puzzled look spread across her face, likely from the change in hair, then she recognized her mother and latched on to her neck. "I knew you'd come back," she said sleepily. "I just knew it."

"Mary, listen really carefully. Remember those men who came and took Dad's radio gear? They're going to return because they want to take you, too. Dad and I won't let them, but you have to do exactly as I say. Understand?"

She told her to pack a bag because she'd be staying in a secret house for a few days. Mary nodded. Then Janet shot him a glance with a moment of truth expression and he said, "Mares, please do what Mom says. There's nothing to fear as long as you're with her."

"What about you, Dad? Are you coming too?"

Atteberry fought to contain his rage and confusion. "I'm going to stay here, kiddo, and do what I can to help you both. But as soon as I'm able, I'll join you."

In a few minutes, Mary had an overnight bag packed, and she was dressed in black. A dark hovercar purred into the driveway in stealth mode. Atteberry killed the light in the hall and opened the door for them. Janet turned before stepping outside.

"Thanks, Jim. Stay safe, stick to your routines and tell Whitt you'll accept the offer. That'll buy us a few days at least. As soon as I can, I'll bring you in, too."

"Okay, but Janet?"

"Yes?"

"What does this mean for us? Are you back now? Could we be a family again?"

She put her hand up to his face and smiled. Then she slipped out the door like a shadow with Mary, ducked into the hovercar and disappeared quietly into the night leaving Atteberry completely by himself.

AT A QUARTER TO MIDNIGHT, ATTEBERRY SNAPPED AWAKE from a fitful sleep on the sofa waiting for Kate to arrive. She never did.

Panic set it and he shook his head, bolting up and checking his indie-comm for a message but there was nothing. He dared not use it after what Janet said about the thing being bugged, so he sat there collecting his thoughts, slowly waking up. After a minute, he walked to Mary's room, now empty, and looked in. This'll all work out. It must. But sitting on the sidelines of any game was not what Atteberry did, and he felt useless and ashamed for being swept up in Whitt's plans. Again.

There was a public comms booth at Neighbors pub a few blocks away. Atteberry wanted to get down there quickly and call Kate on an open line. To do so undetected, he turned off all the lights, placed his indie-comm on the bedside table, and waited several minutes before sneaking out the back door into the shadow-filled yard. From there, he crept along the sides of the dark house, through bushes, until he was almost at the intersection where the pub and a convenience store were. At that point, he nonchalantly began walking down the street.

Inside, the pub was warm and quiet. No one seemed to care who he was, and he didn't recognize a soul. He ordered a beer and sat down at the comms booth where he linked up with Kate's number. She answered cautiously.

"Jim, is that you?"

"Yeah, I'm calling from—"

"Don't speak." Clicking noises filled the line, and after a couple chimes rang, she re-joined him. "I've scrambled the call."

"Kate, Janet was by tonight right after I spoke with you, and she left with Mary."

"What?"

"It's okay, really, but what floored me was this: everything that's been happening lately wasn't about me or the alien signal at all. It's about Mary. No one was spying on me, Kate. They want Mary."

"Oh god, no."

"Janet explained that Whitt wants her for some new Spacer thing, but I thought all that was over years ago at the end of the war."

"Jesus, Jim, now it's making sense. Where are you again?"

"Neighbors pub on Smithson."

"Okay, does it look safe there? Any strange looking guys or anyone noticing you?"

Atteberry casually looked around the room. A couple of old men at the bar watched football on the televiewer. Some couples at a table were having food. Another pair in deep conversation near the window.

"It looks totally normal."

"Good, stay there, and I'll find you."

The link ended and Atteberry slouched over to a two-seater by the door where visibility was high. He pretended to watch the game and drank his beer and waited for Kate to arrive.

When she did about 20 minutes later, she motioned to the bartender for a couple more beers and sat down. A tan leather bomber jacket and a baseball cap couldn't mask the fact that she looked like hell.

"What happened to you tonight, Kate? Last we spoke you were coming over."

"Sorry about that, but after our call one of my old colleagues linked in on a secure line."

"From your program?"

"Uh huh. Said something was in play with the former Spacers, and he wanted to give me a heads up. As if I didn't have enough going on."

"Any idea what?"

"Some kind of renewed interest in our work from the war, but he didn't know any other details. All he said was to be careful and suggested hiding for a while. I can't do that, but I thought I'd better check out my apartment and tech to see if I'm being traced."

"Let me guess." Atteberry took a swig of beer. "You are."

"Yeah, that's why I didn't come over and I couldn't hit you up on the indie-comm. There was a tracer code in the operating system. It's nothing overly complex but unless you're looking for it, you'd never notice it."

She drank and gazed around the room. Then, leaning forward over the table, she said, "It's still in there but I can scramble the signal so no one can detect it." She smiled and winked. "Other than that, I'm really not well. All those toxins over the years when I was an adolescent are catching up, my brain's mushy and my emotions are buzzing around like a one-winged fly."

Atteberry studied her face. Dark circles hung from her eyes and her skin was breaking out. God knows how much weight she'd lost in the past couple of weeks, but she wouldn't talk about how sick she was. "Kate," he whispered, "we can't sit here and do nothing. It's driving me crazy, but if you're not well—"

She shook him off. "It's okay. Tell me about seeing Janet."

For the next few minutes, Atteberry recounted exactly what happened after he got off the link, right up until his family left in the hovercar.

"I dozed after that."

"I'm sorry. That must have been hard for Mary, too, seeing her mother unexpectedly like that."

"It was strange, but like nothing had changed if that makes any sense. The two of them just picked up where they were before." He paused and twirled the beer bottle on the table. "I asked her about us, you know."

"Oh?"

"Yeah, whether we could all be together again. Without actually saying the words, her answer was a big fat 'No.'"

Kate slugged back her beer. "Once part of that underworld, it would be difficult to pull away."

Suddenly, Atteberry blurted out, "How would you feel about fighting back?"

Eyes widening, Kate said, "I wouldn't. My goal is to fly under the radar and avoid making waves for the rest of my life."

"You haven't even heard what I'm going to say."

"Okay, go on."

"Listen, over the past few weeks, I've been pulled here and there by Whitt, Esther, the army guy, now Janet, and I've had enough. I want my daughter back safely and I don't want a bunch of creepy assholes messing with our lives any longer."

She watched him carefully, her eyes darting nervously around the room, and she moistened her thin, chapped lips. "What do you have in mind?"

Atteberry folded his arms and leaned on the table. "The only way to stop him is if Marshall Whitt is exposed."

Kate smirked. "Good luck with that. The pointy-head's in bed with the military, and he's the one calling the shots on Ross 128. What exactly do you hope to gain by exposing him? What does that even mean?"

"I'll tell you what it means. Getting credit for discovering an alien signal has never been my motivation, but I do care about sharing the discovery with the world, and now that he's eyeing Mary for some kind of sadistic, freak program, I—"

Kate turned away sharply as if she'd been shot.

"God, I'm sorry, I didn't mean—"

She shook her head once and pursed her lips. Then looking up, she said, "Never mind. Sometimes you can be a real prick."

They shared an awkward silence for a moment before Atteberry continued. "I want her back, Kate."

"Yes, of course, and if Whitt's interested in Mary, he's no doubt got his sights set on many others. This is likely what my colleague's warning was about."

"Exposing him to the media would be almost impossible. He's still the only one who can communicate with the ship, so if we mentioned anything, we wouldn't be able to prove it and I'd be a laughingstock all over again."

"That's true," she said. "What else have you got?"

Atteberry took a quick look around the pub and continued. "Re-establishing contact with the aliens publicly, so the whole world can see and hear, is critical. That way, whatever Whitt's doing will be redundant because once the news is out, Kate, it won't matter what he wants. He'll be sufficiently knee-capped 'cause the only leverage he has on any of us is this damn signal."

Kate's eyes narrowed. "I don't know, Jim. That lab in the TSA is impressive and impossible to access without someone knowing how. Whitt's not the kind of fellow who's simply going to invite you in. And, he's got more on me too."

"Right. If I'm his enemy, what you say is true. But what if I pretend I'm on his side? That I'm accepting the colonel's offer?"

Kate considered it, frowned, and said, "Sure, that may do it. But even so, he wouldn't let you anywhere near the transmitting console, so I gather that's where I come in?"

"Yes. Join with me, and tell Whitt you want to be part of his program too. We'll work together on the signal analysis."

"I couldn't do that," she said, her voice soft and weak.

"You wouldn't actually work for him, Kate, because if all goes well, Ross 128 will be known around the world and his power will be stripped. I'll tell him we're a package deal. I doubt he'd turn you down."

She pursed her lips and said, "Okay, assuming we do this. Then what?"

"Well, it buys us time. While he believes his own business is unfolding perfectly, we break into the remote transmitter site on Sutro and contact the alien ship from there. And we do it so the world can copy all the messages coming in and going out."

"Hm." She leaned back, watching Atteberry. "What about media?"

"Inviting them up would be too much, so no, we'll record the transmission then send it to every available outlet.

"And you know how to access this transmitter and network once we get there?"

"Esther said it's full of firewalls and other security measures, but nothing you couldn't handle, I'm sure."

Kate thought about it for several minutes wearing a grim frown. She studied him with resignation, and her eyes moistened. "Even if Whitt's power trip is out in the open, he still holds my life in his hands, remember? That won't change either way. But I will help you, Jim, for you and Mary. However, if and when the shit hits the fan, I'll go deep into hiding where no one can follow and you'll never hear from me again. You understand that?"

He stared deeply into her eyes and nodded.

THE NEXT MORNING, ATTEBERRY GRABBED HIS COMPROMISED indie-comm and contacted the number on Piper's business card, audio only. He psyched himself up to sound as normal and as excited about the offer as possible by smiling while he spoke. "Good day, Colonel. I'm calling to say that I've talked the job offer over with my daughter and we want to accept it."

"That's wonderful news, Mr. Atteberry."

"But I have two caveats."

A hint of trepidation rippled through Piper's calm voice. "Oh? What kind of caveats?"

"The first is, I want all my radio gear back before we move to New Houston. Don't care who's got it as long as I get it. Having said that, I understand the need for secrecy around Ross 128 and I'm prepared to sign whatever you want me to so I won't use it for monitoring the alien ship."

He heard Piper scratching this down in the background. "I can't promise anything, but that sounds reasonable. What's the other condition?"

"Well, it's kind of funny but when Mary—that's my daughter—and I were talking this over, she said she'd like a chance to help with my work. She's ten years old but really interested in science and I sort of promised she could join me on some projects. Could that be arranged?"

Piper responded immediately. No hesitation. "I'm confident there won't be a problem with that. We'll have to discuss exactly what it looks like with Dr. Whitt, but I see nothing wrong. He enjoys working with youngsters."

"Great! If you can provide me with a revised offer showing the changes, I'm happy to sign it."

"Perfect, expect a call from my office later today, and thanks again, Mr. Atteberry. Welcome aboard!"

He smirked at the silent indie-comm and tossed it in his brief case, then put Mary's device in the kitchen before leaving for the college.

TWENTY

Whitt

TWO DAYS LATER, MID-THURSDAY MORNING, Marshall Whitt perched on the edge of his office desk in the Space Operations Lab, growling into his indie-comm.

"Levar, let me get this straight. You're reporting her indie-comm is still active, but she hasn't left the house at all?"

"Yeah, that's pretty much it. There's been some movement within the house because we've tracked it goin' from her room to the kitchen, the basement and so on. But video surveillance confirms she hasn't been outside the home."

Whitt raised his voice ever so slightly. "Did you check if she's sick or something?"

"Sure, lots of kids gettin' colds these days with the fall weather, so that's a possibility, but we're not buyin' it."

"And why is that?"

"It's like I've been tryin' to tell you. Her device is workin', but whenever we listen in, this mornin' for example or supper time, there's no sound 'cept music, the TV, Atteberry whistlin' bad tunes. Oh, he says lots of things to her, but strangely she never answers back.

"What does this mean, then?"

"It means, Marshall, that I'm confident Mary Atteberry is no longer at the house. She's disappeared."

Whitt pounded a fist on the desk, stood up and began pacing. A couple of the techs glanced over so he smiled their way and calmed himself down. "We've been tricked, it would seem."

"Yes, that's right," Jackson sighed, "and there's more."

Whitt's frustration increased. No operation runs perfectly at the best of times, but Jackson's team was letting him down with incompetence. "Well what else is there?"

"We believe Jim Atteberry knows about the tracer on his indie-comm and the surveillance in his house."

"Really." Whitt's sarcasm oozed over the link, but Jackson ignored him.

"Yes, Marshall, he's only usin' it for his business links, all college-related. No chats with Kate Braddock and nothin' with Dr. Tyrone, although curiously, she's tried contactin' him on it."

"Maybe that relationship's over?"

"Hard to tell. Apparently, it's a busy time on campus with assignments comin' due and such, but he should have at least responded unless, of course, he knew someone was listenin' in."

"I'll follow up with Esther and see what she's up to." Then another thought struck him. "Jackson, where's Atteberry right now, this minute?"

"His indie-comm is active and in his house, so we assume he's there."

Whitt sighed. "Shouldn't he be at the college?"

"Possibly, but you know these professor types, keepin' odd hours, workin' out of coffee shops when the mood strikes."

"Yes, but I thought he had classes on Thursday mornings... am I wrong?"

Jackson briefly keyed in the background before returning to the link. "Ah, that's correct, Marshall. He should be teachin'. Strange."

Beads of cold sweat broke out on Whitt's forehead as he tried to contain his fury. Closing his eyes, he exhaled deeply. "Before jumping to any conclusions about his whereabouts, it's possible he forgot his device at home this morning, so is his car still there?"

"Just a sec..." Jackson's fingers clacked on a keyboard. "No, the car's gone."

"Damn it."

"Marshall, look, I'm sorry, I—"

"Never mind that now. Try tracking down the hovercar. He could be at the college."

"Possibly, but there's no evidence of him leavin' the house yet."

Whitt said matter-of-factly, "He's given you the slip, it would appear."

"Apparently. We'll check the school and see if he's there. I just need to contact one of my guys on campus to follow up so I'll find out shortly."

"Alright, and while you're at it, confirm that Kate Braddock is there, too. Perhaps the girl is staying with her."

"I'll get on that, Marshall."

"Good. Ping me as soon as you've found him or either of the others."

"Will do. Is there anythin' else you'd like once we get them?"

"Yes," Whitt sneered. "Haul their sorry asses into the holding cell here at the Academy under suspicion of terrorism and breaking international law."

Jackson hesitated a moment. "And the daughter?"

"Hm, the girl... when you find her, just bring her to me."

Jackson cut the link and Whitt pulled on his face to clear his head and refocus on the alien communications problem. He and Mark had made progress with binaries and were about to send images back to the ship, but now the thought of Atteberry getting the drop on him burned hard in his gut and he couldn't let it go completely. He called the autoserver over and grabbed a sandwich. *Where is that long-haired idiot, and what is he up to? Ah well, Levar will handle that.* Whitt punched the comms data up on his screen and dove into the numbers. After several minutes, he felt better and turned his thoughts to the next transmission he'd send shortly.

Atteberry

THEY'D MET TWICE IN THE COLLEGE CAFETERIA TO DISCUSS the best way to bring Ross 128 out of the dark, and it came down to this: gain direct access to the transmitter site on Mount Sutro, replace Kate's encrypted signal algorithm with one that any radio enthusiast could use, and invite the world to listen in. If successful, the alien transmissions would be received around the world and Whitt's intention to leverage first contact to further his own power would be exposed. More importantly, this would create the conditions to make Mary safe again, and all the other kids being recruited into the modern day Spacer Program. Shining a light on the activities Whitt engaged in underlined Atteberry's entire belief in openness and transparency. No shadowy secrets, no matter the consequences. The worst evil in the light was always better in the long run than the greatest actions kept in the dark.

Clouds and rain rolled in that afternoon and now camouflaged the approaching dusk. Atteberry and Kate abandoned his hovercar at the base of Tank Hill Park, climbed through the soaked green space and emerged on Belgrave Avenue. From there, it was a short hike to the Mount Sutro reserve where a series of trails led to the tower.

As they entered the woods off the street, Kate said, "I feel the weight of every one of those houses on us, like their eyes are on me. That's creeping me out."

"Oh, I imagine they all keep an eye on people entering the trailhead here as a matter of course. Feeling a bit skittish?"

"Just being cautious."

They trudged through the rainy brush. The trail was slick, covering their boots with thick dark mud and debris. Along the way, they caught glimpses of the massive tower reaching into the darkening skies.

Approaching the tower's base, they began seeing warning signs posted every 20 meters or so.
Private property.
TRESPASSERS WILL BE PROSECUTED. AREA UNDER SURVEILLANCE.
Atteberry and Kate stopped under a large cedar and she pulled out her indie-comm. On the mapping program, several blue yellow icons popped up.

"Those are the camera locations," she said, pointing to the symbols.

"And you've run simulations on all these? Angles, coverage and so on?"

"Yeah, we can reach the outer fence without being detected, but the timing must be perfect and there's no room for error even under ideal conditions." She looked up at the rain pelting through the branches and grimaced. "You know, we don't have to try this today, Jim."

Atteberry stared at her, wide-eyed. "I have to. I need to protect Mary and get her back so she doesn't have to worry about anything other than school and boys and whatever else fills her head on a normal day. Plus, I don't think Whitt'll be fooled by the indie-comm charade much longer."

"Okay," Kate said, "are you ready?"

He nodded.

"Follow me. Don't screw up."

She pointed to a small clearing several meters up an incline and gave him a silent countdown and sprinted toward it. Atteberry jumped after her, surprised at how well she moved on that fragile frame through the mud. He lost his footing once but recovered quickly and skidded to a halt when she raised an arm and ducked behind a smooth outcrop. Kate focused on her indie-comm while pointing to the next target and dashed around the clearing's perimeter. This continued repeatedly in quick succession until they crawled under the brush about ten meters from the outer security fence. Finally, a chance to catch their breath.

"There's a 32-second blackout window at this location," she said, her breathing labored. "Nothing special about the fence. The cutters you brought should slice through it easily. It's the one after, the wall of concertina, that'll slow us down." She checked her indie-comm and pointed at a camera mounted on a nearby pole. "Ready?"

Atteberry had the cutters in hand. "Yes, any time."

On her mark, they raced up to the fence, and he quickly cut through the steel mesh in a straight line. He wrenched it back and

Kate scurried through first. Then she held it for him. They dove into the shadows of a thick pine as the nearby camera swept by.

The wall of concertina proved a greater challenge, but Kate used darkness and rain-soaked ground to their advantage. Rather than focus only on cutting through the razor-sharp wire, she also scraped through the loose dirt, creating a shallow trench through which they crawled to the inside. The door to the transmitter building glowed eerily through the moist night air, illuminated by a single LED light above it.

"Cameras watch that entrance constantly," she said, "so you know what needs to be done, right?"

"Yes, race toward it, use the access card I stole to get in, then you reconfigure the signal encryption code ASAP, we fire off a transmission then run like hell, pronto."

"And if we're not caught, you contact the Astronomical Society with the subspace filter configuration so anyone anywhere can pick up what you heard that first night."

Atteberry nodded. "But if it goes horribly wrong, well, we'll deal with that if it happens."

Kate winked at him, then they rehearsed again exactly what to do when they got access. There'd be little time before guards found them, so the entire plan had to unfold perfectly.

Atteberry squatted on his haunches and peered through the brush. A 20-meter dash to the door is all that remained, then they'd be detected. How long would it take security forces to arrive? Thirty seconds? A minute? There was no way of knowing. Kate was right: an error or screw up now would land them in jail.

He glanced at Kate who'd crawled in behind him. She nodded the go ahead, and they tore out of the bushes, gunning for the transmitter building. Footing was tricky in the sloppy mud, and they both lost their balance and fell against the door. Atteberry fumbled with the card and it dropped on the muddy ground.

"Damn it, hurry up!"

He picked it up, wiped the crap off it and swiped it through the reader. Nothing. He cleaned it off and slowly pushed it through again. This time the lock mechanism clacked, and he pulled the door open. Kate raced inside and he slammed it shut.

She turned on her flashlight and headed straight to the computer. It was warm in the room. Atteberry peered at the transmitter panel underneath the operating bench and saw all the lights were green. Whitt's been using it, he thought. Kate punched codes into the computer to hack through the firewalls, but couldn't access the system without the proper protocols.

"It's going to take more time than I hoped," she said.

After what seemed like hours passed, the screen finally flashed. She'd accessed the comms logs. "Shit, Jim, look at this."

Atteberry lumbered over and watched the transmitter and receiver data scroll by until the lines stopped. A few minutes ago, it appears, the alien ship had responded to an earlier message that Whitt must have sent. That was followed by updated location coordinates and other signal parameters that Atteberry didn't recognize.

"Can you find the filter encryption program, Kate?"

"I'm trying, but I can't hack into. I'll check one final thing but if that doesn't work, we'd better scramble."

She tabbed back to the coding screen and punched numbers into the computer.   Nothing worked.

The door flung open and sudden lights flashed and blinded them.

"Freeze!"

Atteberry heard weapons being cocked, heavy boots, and the rush of rain outside the room. He glanced at Kate but she was frozen in place.

"Turn around slowly."

Two guards bore down on them, guns raised. The shadow of a third person fell from the outside light. Atteberry's jaw dropped when Esther appeared. Her face was tight and her eyes narrow, not even a hint of warmth remained.

"Esther, let me explain."

"Not now, Jim. You'll have a chance to talk later." She turned to Kate. "You must be the mysterious Ms. Braddock. I hoped we could meet under different circumstances."

Kate said nothing, but continued staring at the floor.

Esther spoke as if she was ordering a meal from a restaurant. "Arrest them both. Take them to the holding cells at the TSA."

"Esther, wait," Atteberry pleaded, "you have to know what's going on."

"Jesus, Jim, would you just. Shut. Up."

One of the guards holstered his gun and slapped mag-cuffs on Kate, then on Atteberry. "Put her in the car," Esther said coldly. "But you," she glared at him, "you're not going anywhere yet."

TWENTY-ONE

Atteberry

ESTHER DRAGGED A STOOL OVER AND TOLD HIM TO SIT. She stood in front of him, hands on hips, and ordered the remaining guard to wait outside. After he left, she said to Atteberry, "What in the hell do you think you're doing?"

He stared at the floor, dripping water and mud all around. "Esther, please, you've got to understand. This madness has to stop."

"No shit, but my sense is we define madness quite differently." She shut down the computer monitors and started inspecting the transmitter. "Do you have any idea what's going to happen to you now?" Atteberry remained silent. "You'll both be thrown into a holding cell back at the TSA until we figure out what to do with you."

Atteberry peered up at her sheepishly. "Whitt doesn't have to find out, Esther. How about just, oh I don't know, letting us off with a warning or helping us stop this guy?"

Even in the dim light of the transmitter room, Atteberry felt her face redden. "You still don't get it. Whitt's not going to throw you in the cells. *I am*. Jim, I have a duty and responsibility to the Academy to protect our assets and personnel. And right now, you and Kate are perceived as major threats."

"Esther, please."

"Listen, don't ask me to be something I'm not. Perhaps you enjoy bending the rules and playing fast and loose in the shadows, but I don't. Jesus, Jim, how dare you suggest I look the other way!"

Atteberry felt defensive rage boiling inside and thought about Mary and how her entire future was at risk. "Esther, you're the one who doesn't get it. Do you realize what Whitt's doing? What he's got planned?"

"I couldn't care less! You've broken in here to do god knows what all, and the reasons behind it don't justify your actions."

"Not even if lives are at stake? Not even if Whitt plans to recruit Mary and other kids for his new Spacer program?"

Esther processed this information. Clearly, she hadn't figured out what he was up to, and her voice softened. "I understood that he wanted you to work for him."

"It was all a ruse, a sick game to keep me quiet and onside. He's really after Mary."

"Shit."

"That's why I'm here tonight. As long as he's the only one communicating with the alien ship, he's got all the leverage with the military and with us. *'You want to sterilize some smart kids to do your dirty work? No problem.'* That's the craziness that needs to be stopped."

"So you thought by, what, sabotaging the subspace transmitter you'd stop him from transmitting?"

"Not sabotage, Esther. Opening the comms up to everyone. Kate was going to remove the encryption from her filtering algorithm he copied so any amateur radio astronomer could listen in. By opening it up, Whitt loses his power. Surely you see that."

She pushed the hair off her face, grabbed another stool and sat in front of him. "If what you say is true, where is Mary now?"

"No idea."

"What do you mean, kidnapped?"

"No, she's with, er... her mother."

Esther's jaw dropped, and for a moment the tension in her dissipated, giving way to a bewildered look.

"Janet arrived the other night and took her. As long as I'm involved in this, Mary's not safe, and Janet said the risk to her was becoming too great, and..."

"This is your wife?"

"Yes, I mean ex or... hell I don't know what she is any more, it's all muddled up. She's an NDU agent, a spy. Apparently always has been."

Esther closed her eyes. Silence filled the room for several minutes as the rain kept slashing through the trees outside and rattling off a metal box near the door.

"Please, let us finish the work here. In fact, you can help us do it faster by giving Kate access to the computer system."

"Not a chance."

"This isn't a selfish request. The entire world is at risk. Think what might happen if Whitt controls the alien links, and he's in thick with the Confederate military. Cooperative space exploration would disappear. The Martian colony and its reliance on multi-national cargo ships? Uncertain. And what about

California? The NDU? Will other nations simply allow that to happen, because as soon as they find out, they'll either want the technology for themselves, or be sure to destroy it and anything else in the process."

"Jim, it's not about what *ifs* here. It's about what *is*. Just because you perceive a threat doesn't mean there really is one. I may not like Marshall Whitt very much, but I honestly don't see him putting his own life and career at risk by selling out to any military."

"He already has, Esther."

"Well, I can't agree with you, but regardless, it still won't erase the fact that you and Kate tried to sabotage the equipment here with no authority, no evidence other than hearsay and giant unfounded leaps of logic. I'm not trying to be obtuse or stubborn, Jim. I'm trying to protect strategically important assets."

Atteberry's frustration seethed. Why she refused to understand the truth was beyond reasonable. "It seems to me you're simply more interested in keeping your precious job. Or perhaps you, too, are involved in Whitt's plan?"

"I beg your pardon?"

"Just what does he have on you, Esther, hm? Has he threatened you physically or your career?

"My obligation is not to Whitt. It's to the Academy."

"Oh, I get it," his voice rose, "you're more concerned about preserving the rep of some faceless institution than you are in protecting innocent lives. Well, the hell with you, then!"

Esther stood up and slapped him hard across his face. "You lousy piece of shit. Maybe if you weren't so self-absorbed and stuck in the past, you'd understand what was happening. But no, not you, the clever Jim Atteberry with all the answers to all the problems, so you don't even bother discussing the possibility of other reasons behind what you see."

"You know as well as I do that I'm right about Whitt."

"It doesn't matter, Jim! Christ, you still don't get it!"

"Oh, I'm there, Esther. You're so stuck up in duty and obligations that you conveniently forget to do what's morally right."

"How dare you lecture me about morals," she spat. "If you understood anything about morality or civic duty, you wouldn't be sneaking in here like a two-bit thief." She yelled out the door, "Bish! Get this piece of garbage out of here!"

"Yes ma'am."

The guard marched in, grabbed Atteberry by the arm and heaved him off the stool.

"Thanks a lot, Esther. I thought you wanted justice and peace as much as the rest of us, but apparently being liked by your colleague is more important."

"Get him out of here. Take them to the TSA holding cells."

"Yes ma'am, will do."

Atteberry resisted by dragging his feet deadweight. He stared at Esther as the burly guard hauled him past her and back out into the rain.

"You're really disappointing, but whatever, I don't need your help, anyway. I'll find a way to stop the madness without you."

She turned as the guard pushed him toward the waiting car. "Jim, I—"

"Save it, Dr. Tyrone," he growled, "I thought I could count on you to do the right thing. Obviously, I was wrong."

"Go to hell."

Bish threw him into the back of the car beside Kate and jumped in the front and the other guard pressed the thruster engines on. As the hovercar sped away into the dark, Atteberry looked over his shoulder and saw Esther, arms crossed, standing in the doorway with her head down.

Esther

THE CRYING OF ROSS 128

SHE WATCHED THE TSA SECURITY CAR DISAPPEAR down the lane, then summoned her own hovercar on her indie-comm. She looked around the transmitter room again, checking the equipment to ensure it continued to function properly. On the main computer, she reviewed Kate's attempts to access the system and confirmed she was unsuccessful. Then she flipped off the lights, heaved the door shut and locked it.

Once inside the hovercar, she pinged Marshall Whitt to explain what had just happened and that the security guards were on their way to the Academy with Jim and Kate.

"Thank goodness you were there to stop them and protect that site. Well done. I'm heading back to the lab now from home, so I'll see you shortly."

She felt miserable and distant and old. "Okay, I'm on my way, too."

"Esther, one question. What should we do with these two?"

She sighed and stared out the rain-streaked window. "I don't know, Marshall, but clearly we can't have them running around putting all of us at risk."

"I concur. Let's discuss it further in the lab."

She cut the link and leaned back into the seat.

"TSA."

"Location confirmed."

The hovercar pulled away from the muddy ground and glided down La Avanzada. Esther replayed the last scene with Jim, going over it thoroughly and wondering if there was any way she could have helped him and Kate without betraying her colleagues. What did he say about Mary and a modern Spacer program? She had no desire to be implicated in anything controversial like that, and if Marshall truly was planning a renewed child unit, then she had to come to terms with it one way or another. The original Spacer units that Kate belonged to were brutal by all accounts, and if Whitt was recruiting Mary and other kids for that kind of program, she would have to put a stop to it using whatever means were available as long as they didn't break the law or put her own morality at risk.

Refusing to help Jim his way was absolutely the proper decision. Any common moral ground between her responsibilities and his heretical actions was completely absent. *Was it really the right thing to do?* Self-doubt needled into her skin.

The car flew through the rain and fog, navigating the streets perfectly on its way to the Academy. Esther stared out the window as warm tears fell on her cheeks. It was the way the discussion ended that gnawed away at her heart. She couldn't understand why he was so stubborn about sabotaging the transmitter. Several other more reasonable options could have been considered. Besides, no proof existed of Whitt's involvement with anything underhanded other than his wanting the glory of first contact for himself.

But her whole body ached with pain, just when she finally began opening up only to be crushed by his spiteful words, Janet's re-appearance in his life, and that well-entrenched need to protect herself.

Esther, seriously, he's a jerk. Let him go and move on. Your career is more important than this asshole. But if logic instructed her to let him go, why did she hurt so much? And why all these tears? Love was an unrewarding risk, one that she refused to fully embrace in the past. This was a reminder why.

The hovercar pulled to a stop in front of the TSA main entrance, and she covered her head with her jacket and ran into the building. The lobby commissioner greeted her and they shared a comment about the self-evident weather, but she needed to get to her office in a hurry, and left abruptly.

Just before climbing the escalator, she turned to the commissioner and asked, "Has Dr. Whitt arrived yet?"

THE CRYING OF ROSS 128

He checked the screen briefly. "No, ma'am, not yet. Will I call you when he arrives?"

"Yes, please."

She stepped on to the escalator and, once in her office, closed the door and flopped on the couch. The pain rose from a deep, shadowy pit, wracking her gut and refusing to dissipate until, finally, she released it through a long, inhuman wail. Esther had come so close to love, to allowing him fully in her life, and now that had disappeared in a flash.

After several minutes she calmed down. The sadness was gone, at least for now, and she re-focused on her own actions that, in the light of sober thought, didn't appear out of line at all. So the question she posed was this: what's more important... the values, moral and ethical framework that had served her well for so long, or a risky shot at love?

Logically, there was only one answer, the reasonable answer, the safe one, the one that was always there for her. In an instant, she hardened her heart—something she'd learned years ago starting in high school. It felt comfortable, as familiar and safe as a mother's hug. In this new, old posture, Jim Atteberry was a problem, an irrational, passion-driven creature who failed to assess all the important consequences of his actions, no matter what his motivations may be. If Marshall released him tonight, perhaps because of this odd job offer or some other act of grace, what would Jim do? He'd turn around and attempt to disable the transmitter again. He was singularly focused and predictable that way.

No. If the relationship with Jim had developed into something more, she'd be setting herself up for a life of exciting, dangerous insanity. Esther could abide that if Jim played within the rules, but he didn't. Neither the Academy nor Esther wanted a maverick running around doing his own thing. It was time to truly move on and support her colleagues. Rules were rules. And even though she had grown fond of Mary and would miss her in the short term, Esther knew in her mind that the relationship with Jim was over. The heart would be forced to follow. In time.

Atteberry

THE SECURITY CAR CARRYING ATTEBERRY AND KATE arrived at the Academy and immediately circled around to the back and stopped in front of a non-descript double door. The driver stepped out and motioned for them to do the same while the other guard, Bish, kept a gun on them. The building's thick exterior doors groaned as they swung open, and their captors pushed them through a long concrete tunnel and past a myriad of darkened hallways. The guard swiped a card to gain access to a windowless bunker and shoved them into a dimly lit room.

When Atteberry's eyes had adjusted to the dark, he saw two empty holding cells at the far wall. They locked Kate in one, Atteberry in the other, keeping them separated by a barred wall. The first guard, the driver, swaggered over to a small desk and punched the computer screen.

"Yes, the suspects are here in detention."

Atteberry couldn't hear who was on the other end.

"Very well. Carson out. Hey Bish, watch 'em close, eh?"

Bish holstered his weapon, grabbed a nearby chair that looked barely capable of supporting his weight, and sat in front of the cells. He pulled out an indie-comm device and thumbed in some text.

Atteberry took inventory of the damp surroundings. There was a stained cot, a toilet and rusty sink, and a steel stool bolted to the concrete floor. Clearly, he wasn't the first prisoner kept here. Kate's was the same.

He shouted to the one called Carson, "Hey, you can't just keep us here! I've got a right to call my lawyer!"

The guard raised his head slowly and sneered.

"What you're doing here is illegal," Atteberry cried.

"Shut the fuck up, piggie!"

Bish looked over at Carson and laughed.

Kate stood motionless at the bars between them. Her clothes were still wet and covered in mud and grass. A long scratch appeared across her face, likely from the concertina. "I guess we're both a mess," she said with a slight grin. Atteberry relaxed his shoulders and nodded.

"Sorry I got you into this, Kate. I truly am," he said, reaching through the bars and picking a twig off her jacket.

"Save it. No one forced me to do anything." She looked around the cage and ran a finger along the steel rods. "But I doubt they'll ever let us out."

"Sure they will," he said. "They can't keep us locked up in here forever. Either they'll charge us with something or let us go."

"If we're lucky, we'll get nailed with trespassing and a fine."

"And if we're not?"

Kate rolled her tongue around in her mouth. "They could hang a terrorism charge on us and dump us in here to rot."

Atteberry narrowed his gaze. Surely they couldn't do that. But he remembered what Esther said about their unfettered authority to hold suspects for as long as they wanted. And she'd proven she could do that kind of nasty work, too, by refusing to release that stalker of hers.

"No way."

"Doubt all you want, but I've seen it happen during the war. Men, women, little kids rounded up, tossed in cells ten times worse than these, and left for months. No charges laid, barely enough food to stay alive. Most people have no idea."

Atteberry leaned against the bars. "But Kate, the war's over and we weren't even part of it. California isn't allied with either side politically, so as soon as we tell the authorities what's going on, they'll let us go."

She squeezed her eyes closed, then rubbed them with dirt-smudged palms. "It wasn't our fight then, sure, but it's not over. Clearly, they're still spying on each other. The goddamn Spacer Program is alive and well, and the lines between your humanist science and the military are totally blurred, thanks to creeps like Whitt. So yeah, it's our fight now, Jim."

Carson yelled across the room. "Hey! Shut up over there!"

Atteberry's blood boiled, and he was about to shout back when Kate grabbed his arm through the bars and stopped him. There was something about her eyes that made Atteberry pause and breathe deeply. He held her gaze until he calmed down again.

"I'll do anything to get out of this hole," he whispered. "I need to find Mary and make sure she's okay. Janet, too."

Kate stole a glance at the guards, then said. "From what you told me about her the other night, she can take care of herself and Mary no problem. You don't have to save the world all solo and heroic."

"I can't help it, Kate."

She brushed some of the mud off her clothes and grinned. "You have friends and people who love you, Jim. Wherever you got the idea you had to do everything yourself, it's time to reprogram that code. I'm here. Look at me."

He shifted his gaze from the guards to her.

"Do you see me?"

"Of course I do."

"Do you really see me, Jim?"

He started to speak again, then closed his mouth and studied her face, the lines, the high bony cheeks, short hair, dark eyes. But all these things meant nothing. It was only when he saw the whole picture, all of her, and peered deep into her soul that he understood what she was saying.

"Kate..."

She nodded her head and smiled.

Then he scratched some mud out of his beard and said, "Any suggestions on what we do next?"

She stroked his hand. "We cooperate fully and do whatever they want," Kate whispered. "Keep that passion of yours in check. Just be cool, go along with them, and perhaps they'll let us off with a warning."

Just then, in a massive *whoosh*, the main door swung open. Atteberry, Kate and the guards all looked up as Dr. Marshall Whitt entered the room, alone, hands behind his back, with a cold, bloodless look on his face. He stared at Kate the longest time.

TWENTY-TWO

Whitt

HE WHISPERED TO CARSON FOR A FEW MOMENTS, wrote something down on paper, then straightened up, grabbed an orange from the desk and walked over to the holding cells where Atteberry and Braddock both stood facing him. She looked sick and frightened, but Atteberry carried a guise of defiance on his face. Figures. Braddock could be useful. Atteberry, not so much anymore.

"So, what exactly did you hope to accomplish by breaking into the transmitter site, hm?" He stopped a meter away from the cells, peeling the orange.

Atteberry took a deep breath and calmly said, "We've discovered what you're up to, Whitt. In fact, a lot of people have. You won't get away with this."

"Get away with what?" he smiled.

"Whatever crazy things you hoped to do with my daughter, for starters. And other kids. Blackmailing the world for god knows what."

Marshall glanced at Kate and she averted her eyes. He took a slice of orange and bit into it. "See, Jim, you still don't understand. I'm here to discuss Ross 128, and you're all stressed out over something that hasn't happened. Your daughter Mary, for example. She's a smart girl and quite clever in science and technology."

Atteberry remained silent and narrowed his eyes, jaw muscles working.

"So, of course, I would have loved to see her helping on the alien signal analysis. We could find all kinds of side projects for her and any other young people interested in space exploration. Is that so wrong?"

This time, Kate spoke up. "That's not what you hope to gain, you lying piece of crap. Your dream for new Spacers is something you've wanted since the war."

Marshall chewed on another slice and dismissed her with a slight shrug of his shoulders.

"So you think because I recognize the skills that young people have, and could develop their talents and abilities in real-life science, that suddenly I'm one of those monsters from 20 years ago?"

"I lived it," she spat.

"Hm, well things have changed, Ms. Braddock." He stared straight into her. "Or is it Mister now? I can never tell."

"I hope you rot in hell, asshole!"

Marshall ignored the comment and focused on Atteberry, standing there, hands on bars, eyes full of hate and fear. He made sure not to get too close. A big idiot like Atteberry could easily reach out with those long arms and do some damage before the guards could stop him.

"I'll ask you again, Jim. What were you doing at the transmitter site?"

Atteberry clenched his teeth and growled. "Trying to stop you from keeping the Ross aliens your own private secret."

"Okay, now we're getting somewhere. Whoever said I planned to keep the discovery from anyone? Never mind, I'll answer that: no one. Do you really feel that I alone could keep something that important to myself? Think about it, Mr. Atteberry." He bit into the last orange slice and threw the peel into a garbage can. "Consider everyone who already knows about the aliens. The three of us, Esther, Mark... and Colonel Piper and his commanding officer. Mary, and whoever else she talked to. The list goes on and on."

A puzzled frown spread across Atteberry's face. Kate stared daggers at Marshall.

"It's logical. Even if I wanted to keep this all hush-hush, the truth would come out."

"Don't listen to him, Jim. He's full of it."

Marshall turned to Kate. "You're letting old ghosts and nightmares get the better of you, Braddock. Times have changed. We no longer live in fear of the two Americas."

"Do you not understand the notion of 'cold war,' Dr. Whitt?"

"Oh that," he said, "I don't pay any attention to such things. The world has always had its share of conflicts, overt and covert. I choose not to let fear get the better of me by focusing on research, science. Try it some time."

Atteberry spoke up. "What about those goons who barged into my home and stole my radio equipment? And the creep watching my house? How do you explain those?"

"I'm telling you, I had nothing to do with that. But let me ask you something: how well do you really know your wife, hm? Perhaps she's not who you assumed she was. Maybe she's still playing you for a fool."

Atteberry suddenly shot his arm out through the cell bars in a failed attempt to grab Whitt. "You bastard!"

Marshall flinched briefly but quickly regained his composure. Adrenaline rushed through him as he experienced the momentary fight-or-flight reaction to Atteberry's lunge. After a couple of deep breaths he said, "See, you really don't know her at all."

Kate broke in before Atteberry responded, and said, "Did you just come here to gloat, Whitt? Or is there something else on your mind?"

"Ah yes, there is another thing." He eyed Atteberry and asked, "Where are you hiding your daughter Mary?"

"I don't know," he croaked, fighting back the rage.

"Come, come, surely you do. See, I figured she was with Kate here, but clearly not. She must be with your wife."

"Mary's safe from you. Besides, I'd never tell you, anyway."

"Blah blah blah, yes, yes, you're the protective type, aren't you, full of drama and defiance and who knows what else? So let me make this really clear: tell me where Mary is, and I set you free."

Atteberry didn't hesitate. "Never!"

"Never, eh? I wonder how Kate feels about being locked away for the rest of her life."

"I'd rather die than support you, Whitt," she said.

"Oh, but that's the point, Kate. You wouldn't die. No, no, you would live a long time in solitary confinement until you go completely insane. But it won't stop there. I'll leave you to your own festering thoughts until you can't stand it any more and scratch your eyeballs out or rip off your ears." He eyed her carefully. "You've seen that before, haven't you? And you know I'd do it."

She began pleading with Atteberry. "Jim, please—"

"Kate, no!"

"See," Marshall continued, "it's really up to you, Mr. Atteberry. It's your decision. Either you tell me where Mary is or condemn Kate to complete insanity." Whitt strolled back to the desk, picked up a napkin and wiped his fingers. "Anyway, while you're considering it, I have other news for you, too."

Atteberry looked at him with a somber, stunned look.

"The Ross 128 aliens, remember? I've been communicating with them, establishing comms protocols, and for what it's worth to you now, they are indeed in a small craft looking for water. But not because they need it to drink: they need it for their own propulsion."

"Propulsion? But how—"

"Yes, delightful, isn't it? Perhaps they divide the molecule into its constituent gases, like we used to do with satellites. And you could have worked on the team if you hadn't tried to sabotage the transmitter. I can't wait to get hold of their technology."

Whitt watched Atteberry throw a cursory glance at Braddock.

"But it's too late now, Jim. I don't trust you. You're reckless and selfish and have a lot of trouble understanding the big picture." Then he turned his attention to Kate. "But you, Ms. Braddock, I can use your talents on the new team."

"Piss off," she sneered.

"Yes, of course, but remember you'll always have that option. I'm growing rather fond of your abilities."

"What do you plan to do with us now?" Atteberry asked.

Marshall checked the time on his indie-comm. "It is getting a bit late and my evening was interrupted by you two, so you'll be staying here indefinitely."

"You can't do that!"

"Wrong, Jim, I can. And I will. Unless you tell me where your daughter is hiding. Then we can all go sleep in our own beds tonight." Kate gave him a funny look, then turned away.

"All right, then. I'll be back in the morning. And when I am, the first thing I'll do is share everything I have with my colleagues in New Houston."

Atteberry

WHITT SLAMMED THE DOOR AND THE TWO GUARDS returned to their prior positions.

"He's got me, Kate."

"Hush, I've seen these intimidation tactics before."

"Thing is, I don't even know where Mary's being kept. She could be a block away or on the other side of the world by now."

Kate squeezed his arm, and tears began welling up. His eyes widened and he wished them away.

"Mary's safe. At least, we presume she is, right? So don't let him bully you around."

Atteberry wiped his tears and nodded.

"He can't do anything to me that hasn't been tried before," Kate continued. "It's all wartime and military bullshit. And if worse comes to worst, I'll work for him if necessary."

"How could you even think of doing that, Kate?"

She turned her mouth in that cute way and said, "I guess at the end of the day, my life—whatever that looks like—is more important than what I work on. And honestly, searching for intelligent life in the universe is exciting."

"Kate," he whispered, "you're all I have right now. If something happened I could've prevented... "

"That's what he's counting on, Jim. He wants you to quote 'Do the right thing' by capitulating, and probably knows you have no idea where Mary is. But that's not the point. You're under his power, just like me."

Atteberry kicked at the concrete floor.

"Besides," she said, "I'm not all you have."

"Oh sure, there's Mary of course."

"No, Jim. I'm not talking about Mary."

Confusion bubbled up within, and he struggled to stay focus.

"I'm talking about Esther Tyrone."

Right. Esther. The way they parted at the transmitter site, the stupid, cruel things he'd said made him think she'd never want anything to do with him again. But before Janet showed up, they were getting along well. He genuinely liked her even though she was too entrenched in her values. And the way she smiled and got along with Mary was wonderful.

Then Janet came along and things changed. Or at least, he thought they might change back to the way life was when they shared a home. But Atteberry was old enough to understand that you can't go back. Once words are spoken, they can't be unspoken. When you hurt someone, you cannot unhurt them. Janet's re-appearance had been beautifully shocking, and for a moment, he wanted her back. Then he realized what she must have felt too: there was nothing to go back to except a constant reminder of betrayal and secret lives, a lifetime of uncertainty, insecurity, danger to Mary.

"Are you okay, Jim?"

"Hm? Yeah, I guess. Thing is, when she showed up the other night—Janet I mean—I hoped we could be a family again once this was all over. But I can't see that happening now."

"Uh huh."

"And you're right about Esther. I said some pretty nasty things at the site, but I was desperate and didn't mean them."

"You like her, don't you?"

"Yes."

"That way, I mean."

"Yes, that way."

"Well, I'm confident she likes you that way, too." Kate smiled and held his hand through the bars. "It'll all work out, Jim. Next time you see Esther, be honest and follow where it goes."

"Kate," he said, turning to her, "I don't know what to say to her after the blow up at Sutro."

"You will when the time comes. But first, we do need to figure a way out of here."

Carson turned on a talk show from the computer and leaned back, hands behind his head. The other one, Bish, did likewise. With all this excitement, you'd think they'd be a little more revved up. Apparently not. Kate began studying the magnetic locking mechanism while Atteberry sat on the cot, mentally mapping out the room, determining its location in proximity to the Space Operations Lab.

THE DOUBLE DOORS CRASHED INWARD WITH A HORRIFIC metallic shriek as they slammed against the walls, almost tearing off their hinges. Four members of the California Congressional Republican Security Forces flew in, laser-targeting the two hapless guards before they even realized what happened. The soldiers cuffed them back to back on the floor behind the desk and gagged their mouths with thick tape before calling the all clear.

Seconds later, Esther Tyrone marched into the room. She looked at the bound guards then at Atteberry and Kate.

"Esther, thank god!" he shouted.

"Release these two immediately."

The soldier nodded, slung his rifle over his shoulder and pulled the key from the desk guard's belt. When he pressed it on the mag-lock, the latch mechanism would not engage. He showed the key to Esther. "It's bio-marked."

"Is that a problem?"

"Not at all." The soldier grabbed the pair of guards like potato sacks and hauled them over to the cells. Taking Carson's hand, he forced the key into it, then pushed the key into the slot. Kate's door buzzed open. The soldier did the same to Atteberry's cell and his door swung wide as well.

Slowly, he stepped out and looked at Esther. Her eyes were puffy and red, still moist, and in that moment of realization and openness, he took her in his arms.

"Jim, I'm so sorry. I don't know—"

"Sh, Esther, I'm the asshole. Please forgive me."

He held her in a tight embrace, felt her heart pounding and the gentle heave of her breasts. Lifting her face in his hands, he brushed her hair aside as she gazed into his eyes and opened her mouth to speak. Jim Atteberry leaned over and kissed her, and floated off the floor.

Esther

TANAKA PUT THE HOLDING CELL KEY IN HIS POCKET and checked a comms device on his wrist, then regarded Esther with cold intention. "There isn't much time, ma'am. We should move now."

THE CRYING OF ROSS 128

Esther pulled back from Jim's embrace. "Listen, I gave a lot of thought to what you said at the transmitter site about blindly following rules and protocols."

"Esther, please, don't say—"

"Let me explain. See, my whole life I've been a rule-follower, always putting ideals and institutions before any personal desires. And it's served me well for the most part with a great, safe career. Perhaps I'm loyal to a fault that way. But this is different now. At this stage of my life, I want more, much more, and that means stepping out of my comfort zone."

"How so?"

"When I tried to let you go on the drive back here, I almost convinced myself I had. Then I imagined my world of putting duty first, the Academy before truth, and I didn't like what I saw. Especially the idea that if—if anything happened to Mary because I was too afraid to stop him, I just couldn't live with that."

Her heart fluttered, and the dizziness overwhelmed her. Esther reached up, put her arms around Jim's neck and stared into his tired blue eyes. "I don't know what it's like to be a risk-taker, Jim. My DNA is much different than yours. But there's something in my gut, an intuition, that's screaming what I'm doing right here, right now, is the most important action I've taken in my life, and I'm scared as hell." Tears appeared and streamed down her cheeks. "I'll get fired for this, maybe worse. I understand that. But I'm with you now to help, Jim, if you'll have me."

Jim hugged her again and kissed her on the forehead, and she melted into his arms.

"Ah, I hate to break this up," Kate said, "but we've gotta get going. Whitt must be stopped."

"Esther, do you know where he is?"

She wiped her eyes and replied, "No, but we might be able to shut down the satellite array from the Space Ops Lab." Looking at Kate, she said, "I'll need help with access codes on this one."

"You got it!"

"Wait," Jim said, "Can't we just find Whitt and hold him? I mean, we don't want to wreck the equipment. We still have to contact the ship."

Esther shook her head. "It's not that simple, Jim. Since that colonel was in town, we've detected all kinds of odd activity around here. Kieran thinks agents from the Confederate Union have infiltrated the Academy. We stop Whitt, someone else will take his place. This is bigger than him now."

"Besides," Kate added, "You heard what he said about sharing his work with New Houston. He means the military scientists there. He's about to give it all to them, Jim."

The soldier cleared his throat. "Let's talk on the way, ma'am. Now, where's this lab?" Tanaka sounded nervous.

Jim scanned the area and said, "This place have camera surveillance?"

"The external cams are out of commission, sir, but not inside." The soldier nodded to the corner above the desk and another over the cells. "TSA security will show up any second, and no one wants a fire fight. Time to move!"

Atteberry

TWO OF THE SOLDIERS TOOK UP POSITIONS AT THE BROKEN DOORS. One rushed through, followed by the second.

"Clear!"

The other soldiers motioned for Esther, Atteberry and Kate to follow them through to the tunnel. Esther pointed to a hallway about 20 meters up on the left and whispered something to the soldier beside her, the one she called Tanaka. The first two crept to the hallway, then signaled for the others.

THE CRYING OF ROSS 128

Esther slashed her bio-card through the access port and the doors unbolted. They filed through quickly and half-jogged down the dark corridor until they came to a stairwell near the bank of elevators.

"The lab's another four flights of stairs down," she said. She pushed her card through another reader to the stairwell, and they flew down single file.

The hallway outside the main doors to the Space Ops Lab was in shadows with only a couple of emergency lights on. One of the soldiers glanced inside the lab through the glass window on the door and nodded to Esther to swipe it open. She crouched down below the access panel, reached up and slid her card through.

Nothing happened. No latches released.

She looked at Atteberry and Kate nervously, then swiped the card again. Still nothing.

"My card's not working!" she whispered.

Atteberry looked at Tanaka. "Can you blast your way in?"

"Doubt it. Not without taking down half this section. That'll impact the structural integrity of the building itself."

"Esther, is there another entrance?"

Panic began setting in as she slumped against the wall, her eyes darting around. "There's a heavy equipment delivery port on the other side running to the surface. We use it for all kinds of equipment. But if they're on to us, my card likely won't work." Esther looked at the soldiers. One of them said, "Less dangerous using explosive up there than down here. Let's do it."

She swiped her card at the stairwell doors, but they wouldn't open. The access key at the elevator bank had the same result.

"They'll know we're down here," she cried. "They'll see the access attempts."

"Is there another way out?"

279

"No... wait, there's a service stairwell at the end of this corridor. It needs a card too, but your men could probably smash through the door. It's not heavy."

"Let's go!"

They ran down the tunnel, three soldiers in front and one at the back, weapons at the ready and helmet lights leading the way. When the group arrived at the service stairwell, Tanaka barked an order at two others. One carried a portable ram and prepared it for action. Esther tried her card again, but the locking mechanism held fast.

The soldiers swung the ram and the entire door crumbled under the force. They stepped carefully over the crushed metal and broken glass and raced up the stairs to the surface.

The door leading outside was solid. Although there was no access card reader on the inside, Esther knew it would be locked with the same mechanism as the other doors. One of the soldiers took a device and scanned the door and its edges.

"What is that?" Atteberry asked.

"Sir, it's a portable GPR unit. Shallow field microwave radar."

The soldier finished the scan and pointed to an area above the latch. "Here," he said. Checking the screen on the device, he touched a second point at the lower hinge. "And here."

Another soldier pulled grey putty out of his pack and molded it on at those two points. He rigged up the explosive and motioned for everyone to take cover down the stairs. A quick toggle of the triggering device and he blew the door off, sending it flipping and flying outside.

Cold air hit them as they ran into the rain. Esther pointed to the right. "Around that corner. You'll see the docking bay." Moments before they reached the side of the building, bullets whistled by and exploded into the concrete above them.

"Get down!"

The soldiers laid down fire in the direction the bullets came from, shooting high.

"Move! Now!"

Atteberry pulled Esther up from the ground and took Kate's hand. He pushed them around the corner then dove behind it himself.

A soldier took a position behind a tree 30 meters away. Another was somewhere on the other side, and the remaining two fell in with Atteberry and the others.

Tanaka said, "This is bad, ma'am! They'll be calling in reinforcements and we can't afford an all-out fire fight with these guys."

"What are you saying?" she asked.

"I recommend we abort the mission and retreat. My men can keep them at bay while you leave through the woods. We'll call in reinforcements and shut this thing down from a safer viewpoint." He pointed to a line of trees by the hovercar recharging station. "I'll have a team pick you up on the service road on the other side there. We'll follow shortly."

Atteberry looked at the two women. "We can't give up now!"

Esther caught her breath and said, "We don't have to." Turning to the soldier, she shouted, "Can you give us time to get to my hovercar? We'll head up to the transmitter site and dismantle it there."

"Roger, ma'am, but that's risky."

"We'll leave here in blackout. By the time they realize we're not with you, it'll be too late for them."

"Okay, but I'm coming with you." Tanaka signaled the one under tree cover, who motioned the soldier beyond their line of sight. In an instant, the misty night sky lit up with fire, smoke and artillery simulators. Esther pulled on Kate's arm and the three of them dashed through the shadows to her hovercar, followed closely by Tanaka. They crept inside the vehicle and ducked low.

It wasn't built for four, and Atteberry wondered if the thrusters could handle the extra weight.

"Mount Sutro transmitter site, stealth mode."

"Acknowledged."

"Override speed limits and get us there as fast as possible."

"Acknowledged. Please be advised that—"

"Understood."

The thrusters strained under the load but finally lifted the vehicle off the ground and it flew out of the TSA compound, heading over side roads toward Mount Sutro. Esther looked back at the shallow glow in the sky over the Academy and closed her eyes. Atteberry put his arm around her and breathed deeply.

TWENTY-THREE

Atteberry

THE HOVERCAR VEERED OFF PARNASSUS AVENUE onto Medical Center Way and dimmed its lights again. Esther felt that coming in this way, through the Open Space Reserve, would be safer. They floated along at low speed, the car silently climbing through the hills. When they arrived at Adolph Sutro Court, Esther commanded the vehicle to stop. They tumbled out and gathered in the shadows of the woods.

The rain had eased by this time, but Esther, Atteberry, Kate and the soldier Tanaka were quickly soaked from the trees and bushes as they moved carefully through the reserve towards the transmitter site. Tanaka stopped them as soon as he spotted the guardhouse and security arm on La Avanzada Street.

"I'm not used to... all this... climbing," Esther said, panting to catch her breath. But Kate looked the worst, crouching, hands on knees, gulping in air in quiet spasms.

Atteberry put a hand on her back and she winced.

"I'll be okay. Let me rest for a second." She managed to throw him a quick smile.

Tanaka pulled an odd-looking pistol from his holster and loaded it, facing the others. "There's a solitary guard there at the house and I'll take him out with a tranquilizer. No bloodshed."

"How do we get inside the transmitter room?" Atteberry asked.

"My access card probably won't work here if it didn't at the Academy," Esther whispered.

Kate grunted. "What about the card you used before, Jim? They may not have thought of disabling that one."

Atteberry looked at Esther and she shrugged her shoulders.

"Okay," Tanaka said, "Move quickly. Once they see us on their surveillance cameras, this place'll be crawling with guards."

"Hang on a second," Atteberry whispered. "Sh." He listened for a moment, thinking a twig snapped in the surrounding woods, but there was nothing, only the sound of wind through the trees and water dripping off the leaves onto ground and brush. "Thought I heard something."

Tanaka made them wait another few minutes in silence, but no more strange sounds appeared. Finally, Atteberry said, "What do you need to destroy this thing?"

"The timer's set for 30 seconds. We don't want to destroy the entire building, only the transmitter, right?"

"Right," Esther said.

"And if my access card doesn't work anymore?" Atteberry asked.

THE CRYING OF ROSS 128

"Then I'll blow the crap out of that whole damn barn. Either way, that transmitter will no longer be functional."

Tanaka peered into the dimly lit guardhouse in the clearing. Atteberry had trouble seeing through the windows from his position, but caught the odd glimpse of movement in the shadows. Perhaps his eyes were playing tricks.

"I'll move ahead and try to draw him outside," Tanaka whispered. "When he drops, head for the building double time, but stick close to the woods. Dr. Tyrone? Ms. Braddock? Stay here if you like. The fewer people, the better."

"Not a chance," Kate said.

Esther looked at her, then over at Atteberry. "I'm coming too."

Tanaka crept through the brush and in seconds, he disappeared into the night. Atteberry and the others watched the guardhouse from the bushes. In a few minutes, a snapping noise in the woods brought a trim man out from the building, one hand on his holster, the other shining a flashlight around the tall grasses by the road.

"Get down!" Atteberry whispered. They fell prostrate on the ground behind thick shrubs. The light beamed over them without stopping. Then there was a sharp *crack!* and the light disappeared. Atteberry crawled to his knees and peaked through the brush at the guardhouse. The man was down, lying beside the security arm, his flashlight pointing back toward the house, carving odd shapes out of the debris on the ground.

"Come on! Let's go!"

Atteberry was the first to dash out and run along the side of the road to the security arm, followed by Esther and then Kate. They wriggled around the heavy mechanism and were joined by Tanaka. He tapped Atteberry on the wrist, signaled he had eyes on the transmitter building entrance, raised his semi-automatic weapon, and nodded at Atteberry to go.

Atteberry bolted for the entrance. At the door, he pulled the access card from his jacket pocket and swiped the reader. Surprisingly, the latches clicked, and he heaved the door open. Tanaka, Esther and Kate ran toward him and ducked inside the dark room.

Esther hauled the door shut behind her. The computer screen glowed blue over the transmitter bench in the darkness. Data scrolled across it in white lettering. Atteberry recognized spatial coordinates being updated every few seconds, but he didn't understand them all.

"Esther, what do you make of this?"

She hit the light switch, then she and Kate stood beside Atteberry looking at the screen while Tanaka busied himself with his kit, pulling plastic explosives out and speaking into his radio.

"Something's being tracked," she said. "These are coordinate readings in space, but they seem really strange, like the satellites are faulty."

"Any guess what it might be?"

"Hard to tell. I'd have to study it for a few minutes to get a better sense of it."

Tanaka placed the explosive on the transmitter unit. "I'm afraid we won't have time for that. The captain says the TSA is on full alert. They'll find us soon enough."

Kate, looking gaunt and shivering, pointed at a static line of data near the top of the monitor. "Jim, check this out."

The screen flashed, spitting lines of numbers and symbols, and he studied the streams of code, slowly realizing what it meant.

"Oh shit."

Suddenly, the light went out and the door latches clacked open. Before Tanaka could reach for a weapon, two armed security guards overwhelmed him. One of them crushed Tanaka's hand with the heel of his thick boot, the crunching sound of minute bones breaking made Esther gag. A deep, lonesome howl crawled out of his mouth as he held the bloody pulp of what moments ago were his fingers.

Atteberry lunged at a guard but was easily tossed against the wall. They cocked weapons and trained them on Atteberry and the women. A large man in a leather coat entered, followed by someone else in the shadows. The large one shone a flashlight in their eyes, disorienting the group. Kate leaned gently on Esther's shoulder.

"Restore the power," the familiar voice in the gloom said, and the light in the crowded transmitter room blinked on. Dr. Whitt emerged from behind the large man, hands in his coat pocket.

"Levar, please shut off that flashlight."

"My pleasure, Marshall."

The one called Levar put the flashlight on a shelf near the door and crossed the room to frisk Tanaka, Atteberry, Kate and Esther. He found a small knife on Tanaka's leg and pocketed it.

"Hail, hail," Whitt said, "the gang's all here!" He looked closely at Esther and spoke in a low voice, "I'm actually not surprised to see you here. Just terribly disappointed. I expected more from you, Doctor."

She glanced down at the floor. Whitt crouched on his haunches and studied Tanaka whose grey face appeared distant and ghostly. Tanaka threw him a cold stare, clenching his teeth and breathing hard.

Atteberry sat against the wall, flexing his jaw muscles and rubbing the side of his face where he fell. "You can't keep the Ross 128 ship a secret forever, you know. Too many people have been exposed to it and they won't all stay quiet."

"You have no idea what's really going on."

"Doesn't matter. You'll never get away with this."

Whitt shrugged his shoulders. "On the contrary, Mr. Atteberry, I already have."

"What do you mean?"

"I mean, you won't be leaving here alive." He nodded at the large man. Levar returned a smile, drew a handgun from his belt and pressed the barrel up against Atteberry's forehead.

It felt cold and hard as it ground into his temple and the hammer cocked. He closed his eyes and thought about Mary.

TWENTY-FOUR

Atteberry

"NOT HERE, JACKSON," WHITT SAID. "Take one of your men and head to that clearing we passed."

"Will do."

"Ping me when it's finished, and we'll rendezvous back at the Academy."

Levar Jackson motioned to the first guard, and they hauled Atteberry and Tanaka up from the floor. Then they mag-cuffed their hands, did the same to Kate and Esther, and shoved them out into the damp night air.

"This way, and don't try any funny stuff, or I'll make sure you all die slowly."

The guard took the lead, followed by the two women, Atteberry, Tanaka and Jackson. He fired up a powerful flashlight, and they hiked single file along the wooded path leading away from the transmitter site. Tanaka was clearly in a lot of pain, grunting and breathing erratically. What remained of his left hand had begun swelling to double its normal size.

So this is it, Atteberry thought, trudging through the mud and brush. *I'll never see Mary again, I've sentenced Esther and Kate to death, and I caused this poor soldier the use of his hand and his life. Well done, Jim, well done.*

"Kate," he said in a hoarse voice. "I'm so sorry you got dragged into this."

"Don't apologize, Jim. I wouldn't be here unless I wanted to be here. You're stuck with me if you haven't already noticed." She whispered something to Esther that Atteberry didn't catch, but he saw her nod in the shadows.

"Still, if I could go back a few weeks and change things, I would. That damn signal... I should have alerted the media right away, then none of this crap would've happened." Tanaka struggled behind him, probably in shock. "You okay, Tanaka?"

"Been... better, sir," he replied, his voice strained and broken. "But honestly, you can't be sure... none of this would've happened. All actions have consequences, even the ones we think are harmless."

"Hey, shut up!" Levar Jackson spat out the order, then barked ahead, "How much further?"

The leading guard called back. "Another five, six hundred meters, sir. Not far now."

THE CRYING OF ROSS 128

Kate slipped on the greasy path, couldn't break her fall with her hands cuffed behind her, and crashed down hard on her shoulder. She yelled out in pain. Esther turned quickly but could offer no help. The guard scrambled back, lifted Kate up by the armpit and grinned in her face. In the glow of the flashlight, Atteberry caught Esther's gaze, eyes wide and full of fear. Still, she smiled weakly, and he tried to appear confident. The ensuing darkness wiped their hope away.

"Come on, keep moving." The guard brushed his way past Esther and continued climbing the path toward the clearing, picking up the pace.

Atteberry felt completely helpless. The dull ache in his gut that first appeared back at the transmitter site kept growing and gnawing away, and it had to do with Marshall Whitt. His obvious involvement with the Confederate States and the increasing tensions between the two Americas had brought Janet to San Francisco in a supremely ironical twist. So this initial discovery of his—the alien signal from Ross 128—carried far more implications for global and personal upheaval than he had ever considered.

This wasn't just about bragging rights, either. It also had nothing to do with the tired debate over first contact protocols. Atteberry realized that Whitt had positioned himself as the sole point of contact with the alien ship and, in so doing, had created some kind of pact with the Confederate military that gave him the power he coveted. The discovery provided access to kids for that Spacer Program, or whatever they called it now—the program that stole Kate's identity and scrambled her emotions, leaving her sick and broken. What would have happened to Mary, no doubt, unless Janet had intervened.

The group emerged from the woods into a small patchy clearing where the bigger trees had been removed. Atteberry caught glimpses of bushes and stunted pines peppered over the area in the brief sweeps of the guard's flashlight. The sky radiated an odd, ethereal greyish-blue color, reflecting the glow of the city, and fog continued to roll in over the hills.

Levar Jackson stood in front of them and raised his gun. "Remove their cuffs."

The guard circled behind them and, beginning with Esther, waved the demagnetizing key at their wrists and gathered the cuffs on his belt. Esther immediately held Kate in her arm. They were separated from Atteberry and Tanaka by several meters, and Atteberry couldn't see them well in the gloom.

Jackson spoke. "It's a shame the evenin' has to end in death, but Dr. Whitt's work is too important to be undermined by you all. So, please understand, this is nothin' personal. Everyone dies at some point, and this is your time."

Atteberry shouted, "Wait! Do you realize what Whitt is doing here? Do you know what he's planning to do with the new Spacer children?"

"I got no interest in that."

He lowered his voice, trying to reason with him. "Do you have any kids, Jackson?"

"Two, yes, and they're grown up."

"Remember when they were young? Ten, eleven? Whitt wants to take kids just like yours and throw them into these toxic environments, the same as what happened during the war. You remember the horror stories, don't you?"

Jackson considered this momentarily, then said, "Still not my concern. Robots can't do everything in space, and kids are cheaper, as crass as that sounds." He shifted his weight in the dark. "That's the way life works, Atteberry. The greater good dictates it, like that socialist *'Needs of the many trumping the needs of the few'* bullshit." He motioned for the guard to join him and the two faced the group, execution-style.

Atteberry thought of something he hadn't considered before. It was his one last chance to save the others.

"Jackson, look. I'm the threat here, not them. Take my life, but please, for the love of god, let the others go." He took a step forward and stopped.

"Sorry, I can't do that."

"You can, Jackson! Let them go. If you won't then at least spare their lives. Whitt needs me out of the way, not the others. Please, Jackson."

Jackson spat on the ground. "No can do, amigo." He nodded to the guard, and they both cocked their guns. "For the sake of your families, I hope your bodies are found before the feral dogs and coyotes get 'em."

Atteberry turned to face the others. Tanaka held his broken hand and stood proud, tall, facing his executioners. Kate whimpered and coughed while Esther held her. She looked at Atteberry stoically and nodded her head, tears filling her eyes.

"I'm so sorry," he said, fighting back his own tears. "I truly am." He turned to Jackson and pleaded. "I'll do anything you want me to do if you can spare their lives. Please, Jackson, I'm begging you."

"Not goin' to happen, Atteberry, but for what it's worth, I admire your courage. You coulda been an effective mercenary with the right training." Jackson ordered, "Let's waste no more time." The guard raised his gun at the others as Jackson sauntered over to Kate. "You're the runt of this litter, so I'll put you out of your misery first." He raised the weapon and pressed it against her forehead.

Kate pulled her shoulders back and eyed Jackson with a ferocity Atteberry hadn't seen before.

"Damn you, Jackson, not her! Take me instead and let them go," Atteberry pleaded.

The executioner rolled his eyes, then turned to say something to Atteberry. In that instant, Kate spat in his face and Tanaka jumped forward and ran his heavy combat boot into the back of Jackson's knee. The man collapsed in a heap.

"Son of a bitch!" he scowled, rolling onto his side.

Tanaka glanced at the guard who stood frozen in front of him, uncertain about what to do, then, still cradling his injured hand, he moved toward Jackson for another kick before the man could recover.

He was too late. Jackson's good leg swung around, clipping Tanaka low and sending him down to the ground. In a blink, Jackson was up and on him. His knee dug into his chest and his arm crushed Tanaka's windpipe.

"I hope you roast in hell," Jackson growled, sounding out each word slowly.

He pushed the muzzle of his gun into Tanaka's mouth and squeezed off a round. Bits of brain and shards of his skull flew across the clearing, the sound reminding Atteberry of heavy raindrops falling off leaves in the wind. Esther gasped and turned away. Tanaka's body convulsed briefly, making eerie gurgling noises.

"Now where were we?"

Atteberry cried out, "You don't have to do this! Let them go. I'll do anything you want, just let them go."

Jackson pulled himself up and stood awkwardly in front of him, favoring his bad leg. The residual smell of the fired gun permeated the damp air.

"Please, Jackson, do the right thing and show mercy."

Jackson smiled and opened his mouth and started to say something when a loud *crack!* echoed through the night, followed by random pops of gunfire. Instinctively, the two men both turned their heads in the direction of the trail they'd walked up.

THE CRYING OF ROSS 128

"The hell?" The guard stepped gingerly down the path and stopped.

"See anything?" Jackson shouted.

Another series of shots rang out accompanied by shouts and panic in the night.

"It's coming from the transmitter," the guard yelled. "What do you want to do?"

Jackson backed up a few steps to keep an eye on all his prisoners. "Take a look and tell me what's happening! Use your indie-comm!"

"Copy that."

The guard trod carefully down the darkened path. He hadn't gone a few meters when a weapon fired at close range and he grunted as if he'd been punched in the stomach. Silence followed.

Atteberry watched Jackson. He was clearly nervous and uncertain now, scratching his head with the side of his gun and pacing back and forth in front of them. Esther held Kate and looked like she was in a state of shock. Kate shivered uncontrollably and vomited.

"Let them go, Jackson," Atteberry pleaded. "I'll stay here with you."

"Shut up, asshole!"

Jackson took a few paces along the path, maintaining a close eye on them and waving his gun wildly. Then he suddenly hobbled toward the transmitter. Atteberry heard him slide and tumble down the slick trail until the night swallowed him up.

Esther cried out loud and gasped for breath. Kate fell on all fours, retching; Atteberry knelt beside her and peered into the surrounding darkness.

Kate said, "I'd love to get that asshole alone. Just me, him, and a box of my needles."

"We need to get you to a hospital."

She pushed him away. "No, I'll be okay, but let's get the hell out of here."

He led them away from the clearing and back into the woods, creeping through the thick brush and avoiding the trail that Jackson took. Then there was a sudden sharp flash of light in the sky followed by an ear-splitting, grinding noise. The whole Earth shook.

"Over here," he said, leading them to a large granite outcrop. They crawled around it and from the other side, they could all make out the transmitter site below. The building itself was engulfed in flames and several bodies lay strewn on the ground.

Esther pointed up to the tower. "Jim, look!"

He followed her arm. One of the four massive legs had buckled. More grinding and snapping sounds came from the tower top, but the fog and mist were so thick he couldn't see anything.

Another explosion ripped up from the base and they fell to the cold, wet ground behind the outcrop as the world shook anew. The moan of twisting metal and rivets popping cracked the air. *The damn thing's coming down!* They peered over the rock again and this time, two more tower legs had collapsed. The weight of the entire structure now stood on the one remaining leg. It teetered and caved in under the strain.

In a slow motion scene, the Mount Sutro Tower collapsed on itself, section by section. Men shouting and groans of grinding metal filled the air, and the ground shook as violently as any earthquake Atteberry had felt before. Massive blue electrical sparks flew overhead and ozone singed his nostrils. Finally, in a strangely quiet and thorough movement, the remaining tower collapsed and tipped over, smashing into a wooded area behind the destroyed transmission site. An eerie silence followed.

"Everyone okay?" he asked.

Esther held his hand. "I—I'm okay Jim, but I'm not sure about Kate."

"I'll be fine," Kate said. "Bit shaken up and cold, but I'm good."

Esther said, "Jim, what the hell just happened here? Who did this?"

"I wonder." He crept around the outcrop again and peered into the reddish gloom and embers of the rubble. The fire below hissed and spat in the moist air surrounding the wreckage of the once massive, powerful tower, now reduced to scrap metal.

Below him, the smoke and mist hung in the air. He didn't know if he should investigate or wait and see if something else happened. As he considered his next move, a shadow played against the wreckage, a shadow all too familiar.

Janet crawled purposefully into the light from the dull tower wreckage. She was dressed in black, carried a gun in one hand and hauled a body out behind her in the other. Then she dumped the body like a bag of garbage in the middle of the clearing. Even in that gloom and flickering light, Atteberry recognized the silver beard and short stature. There was no mistaking the identity of the corpse splayed on the cold ground.

Marshall Whitt would never threaten anyone again.

TWENTY-FIVE

Atteberry

"MR. ATTEBERRY, WILL YOU COME WITH US?"

Atteberry turned around sharply from his position near the outcrop and saw three soldiers, their weapons lowered, a few meters away.

"Who are you? You're not Republican forces," he asked suspiciously.

"NDU agents, sir. Janet Chamberlain is our squad leader. Come on, follow us down. She'll want to speak with you, but you've got to hurry."

THE CRYING OF ROSS 128

One of them produced an emergency blanket and wrapped it around Kate. Esther was offered another, but she declined it. The three agents, two men and a woman, moved deftly along the trail, hardly making any sound at all. Atteberry and the others couldn't keep that pace, so the taller commando stayed back and helped them over the rough parts of the path.

In a few minutes, they emerged from the woods into the clearing at the remains of the transmitter site. The bodies Atteberry had seen earlier were gone. Janet approached them quickly, confidently. Her hair was tucked up under a knit cap and she was also dressed in black.

"Jim, I'm glad you're well," she nodded, then looked at Esther and Kate. "The danger's over now. Whitt's been taken out along with his goon, Jackson, and as you can see, the subspace transmitter is no longer functional. I'm sorry we couldn't help you in time to save that soldier with you."

"What's going on?"

"There's no time to explain, Jim, and in the end, it's probably best that you don't know what happens in the shadows. But I can tell you we've been watching Marshall Whitt for some time—didn't pay too much attention to him until the Ross 128 signal came around and he played his military card, but we couldn't let that continue."

Janet walked over to Esther and said, "Glad to finally meet you, Dr. Tyrone." They shook hands and passed a knowing look. "Kate, I hope you'll be okay after all this."

Atteberry looked at Kate huddled there under the blanket, covered in mud and puke, soaked through, but she still managed a thin smile.

Then Janet checked her indie-comm and spoke quickly. "You've only got a couple minutes before the firefighters and cops show up. There's a rendezvous point you can—"

"Janet," Atteberry interrupted her, "please tell me. Where's Mary?"

"Safe, Jim."

His body shook from a combination of adrenaline, fear and fatigue. "Where's my little girl?"

Janet waved over to an agent near the guardhouse and a hovercar silently pulled forward. Before it had completely stopped and nestled on the ground, the door opened and Mary tumbled out, carrying her backpack and running toward her dad in new rain boots.

"Mares!" Atteberry lifted her up and hugged her like never before. "Are you all right?"

"Yes, Dad, I'm good, but I'm glad to be with you again."

Janet shouted, "Gotta move now, Jim. You, Mary and Kate follow Agent Chen here to the rendezvous up by the old school house. A car will meet you there and take you to safety. Dr. Tyrone, you'd better get your ass back to the TSA right away. There's a hell of a mess to clean up. I'll drive you."

Esther stared at Atteberry, uncertainty on her face. In the distance, the approaching sirens grew louder.

"Esther, you want to come with us?" he asked.

"Yes."

Turning to Janet, he said, "We'll all go to my place." She studied him, then the others. "Chen, get them out of here now."

They fell in line behind Agent Chen. Esther took Mary's backpack and held her hand, then they all hurried towards another trail. Atteberry stopped abruptly and returned to Janet. She was about to step into the waiting car when he called out and she turned.

"Thank you, Janet. I wish I knew more about what you're doing, but I understand now that won't happen."

"For what it's worth, I have missed you terribly, Jim. But you know we can't return to the past. My life belongs to the shadows now. And yours is, well, chasing aliens." She smiled. "You'd better go."

Panic suddenly seized him. "And if I ever need you again?"

"I've got your back, Jim—and Mary's—I always will."

She slipped into the car and it sped away into the night. Atteberry quickly joined the others along the trail just as the lights from fire trucks pierced the fog and shone around the guardhouse.

They trudged about a kilometer through the woods and eventually emerged at an old school house. Chen had them wait on the porch under a large eave, then checked his indie-comm.

"A car will be here shortly. Best to stay close and quiet."

They sat down on the steps, Mary hopping up on Atteberry's lap and wrapping her arms around his neck. Esther joined them and put her hand on his arm. Kate wandered out on the stone walkway, the blanket still wrapped around her shoulders, and stared up at the gloomy sky. The fog and clouds had lifted in a few places, and they caught glimpses of stars.

Esther said, "I guess we'll never know about that alien ship, at least, not until we find a way to get another transmitter online. But after what's happened here, I doubt anyone will pursue first contact for some time."

Kate stopped looking up and stared intently at Atteberry.

"What is it?" Esther asked.

He shifted Mary's weight so he could see Esther better. "Remember in the transmitter room tonight, before Whitt and his men showed up?"

"Sure."

"The data scrolling across the screen was familiar but parts of it were muddled with error messages."

Kate spoke up. "We didn't understand the information being dumped at first because it was moving so quickly and didn't make sense, but you know that alien ship drifting along up there?"

"Yes?"

"It's on the move."

"What are you talking about?" Esther's voice trembled slightly. Atteberry put Mary down beside him.

"That ship's in motion, Esther. She's not adrift."

"Is it possible Marshall helped them somehow?"

"Doubt it. From what I could tell, he'd barely figured out rudimentary comms protocols. If there was something wrong with their propulsion system, it's unlikely he'd be able to understand it, run diagnostics, and figure out repairs. Remember too, the Ross aliens are at least as technically savvy as us, if not more."

Esther remained quiet for a few moments. Kate strolled back up to the porch and sat down, and Mary, watching her, smiled sleepily.

"So it's on the move, eh?" Esther said. "Do you know where they're going?"

"Yes," Atteberry replied, "on an intercept course with us."

Esther shook her head.

"They're coming here, Esther."

She glanced across at Kate.

"But there's more. The reason why the coordinates were updating so quickly, and why we didn't understand the error messages at first, is because this ship is traveling at a speed faster than light."

"That's not possible."

"Apparently it is."

Kate said, "I didn't have time to confirm, so I can't tell how long it will take to reach us. Eleven years max, of course, but I'm thinking we're talking months, maybe weeks. Or less."

Chen interrupted them. "A couple more minutes, folks. Stand by."

"Sure, thanks," Atteberry said. Mary tried to stay awake beside him, and he smiled, stroking her hair.

"Jim," Esther asked, "did we make a mistake? Fall into a trap?"

Atteberry shrugged and reflected on the question. The last month or so had been wild, and now his adherence to open access above all else seemed like the entirely wrong approach to take.

"What have we done?"

He squeezed Esther's hand, gazing up into the black sky, imagining who or what screamed toward them through compressed space-time, and how they were doing it. This was bound to happen one day; either humankind would find other sentient creatures in the universe, or they would find us. Perhaps, like the old poem he'd read years ago, the universe was unfolding exactly, perfectly, and precisely the way it should.

A full-size black hovercar whirred out of the shadows, stealth mode, startling Kate. Chen threw the doors open and signaled for the others to come.

"Are we ready?"

ABOUT THE AUTHOR

David Allan Hamilton is a writer, teacher, and publisher living in Ottawa, Ontario. He has edited and published numerous collections of stories from writers attending the Ottawa Writing Workshops since 2017, through DeeBee Books.

David has enjoyed a career with the Federal Public Service and has been a contract instructor at Carleton University. He holds a B.Sc. (Honours) degree in Applied Physics from Laurentian University and a M.Sc. in Geophysics from the University of Western Ontario and has undertaken literary studies at the University of Sheffield. His own stories often combine his love of the natural world and the possibilities of science fiction.

You may wish to contact or follow David at the following:

Davidallanhamilton00@gmail.com
davidallanhamilton.com

Twitter: @DAHamilton
Facebook.com/davidallanhamilton

Acknowledgments

I would like to thank the following who helped create this story: the wonderful writers in the Ottawa Writing Workshops who provided feedback on early drafts, in particular Heather Gray, Debbie Bhangoo, Frank Kitching, Mike Marshall, Glen Packman, and Nick Forster. Your early feedback and suggestions helped me immensely. I also want to thank the beta readers including Dorothy, Margaret, Sandy and Jen; Rick Saikaley at Bulldog Photography, and my family for their continuing support.

Thanks for reading! Please add a short review on Amazon and Goodreads and let me know what you thought!

Be sure to read the next exciting instalments of the Ross 128 First Contact Trilogy!

Available on Amazon

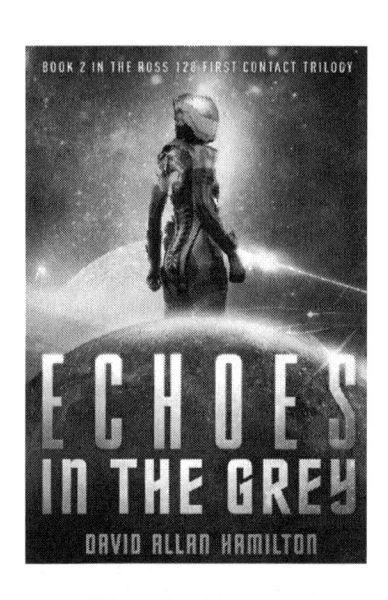

Made in the USA
Middletown, DE
30 April 2021